DESTINED

WAR OF THE COVENS

S. YOUNG

DESTINED

War of the Covens
Book Two

By S. Young
Copyright © 2021 Samantha Young
Previously titled 'River Cast (Tale of Lunarmorte #2)'
Copyright © 2011 Samantha Young

Edited by Jennifer Sommersby Young
Cover Design by Samantha Young
Cover Stock Image by Inara Prusakova

OTHER TITLES BY S. YOUNG

For Robert

PROLOGUE

The State of Things

Existing in the shadows of our world are supernatural races, children blessed by the ancient Greek gods with unimaginable gifts. At present, they are fighting a two-thousand-year-old war with one another. The Midnight Coven, an alliance of dark magiks, faeries, and daemons born of black magik, believe that the vampyres and lykans are lesser supernaturals and a threat to mankind. They are at war with the Daylight Coven, a confederate of light magiks, faeries, vampyres, and lykans who believe in the equality of the races.

Into this war nineteen-year-old Caia Ribeiro is born ... a lykan with a heritage unlike any other. A consequence of the manipulation of the gods and fate, Caia is unique—half lykan, half water magik. And to make it even more compli-cated, her mother was the daughter of the Head of the Midnight Coven: Caia is half Daylight, half Midnight.

1

No one is sure of the extent of Caia's abilities, not even her mentor Marion, the sister to Marita, the Head of the Daylight Coven. All they know is that after her explosive killing of her uncle Ethan, Caia is the heir apparent, and with it has trace magik—the ability to sense the emotions and whereabouts of every member of the Midnight Coven. The pack, Marita, and all their allies believe Caia is the key to bringing down the Midnights. But Caia is not so sure.

Not only is she an nineteen-year-old girl trying to come to grips with adulthood but she's also reeling from the death of her friend, Sebastian, confused by her feelings for the pack's Alpha, Lucien, excited but terrified by her magikal powers, and frightened by the contradiction of the trace magik.

Caia is beginning to realize that the war isn't black and white. There are members of the Midnight Coven who are good people, magiks who have long forgotten why the war began, magiks who don't view other supernaturals as a threat, Midnights who would happily see the war end. Is the trace wrong? Is she going insane or falling to the other side? Because everyone closest to her would believe her to be a traitor if she shared her concerns ... wouldn't they?

And if all that weren't enough, her best friend Jaeden is still missing from the pack, having run off after being rescued from the malevolent clutches of Caia's uncle Ethan. Caia had seen through Ethan's eyes the atrocities he committed against Jaeden's young body and mind; only she understands Jaeden's need to be separate from the pack for a while.

However ... perhaps it's best Caia isn't fully aware of Jaeden's true situation. It would be just one more major worry to add to her never-ending pile of responsibilities. For not only is Jae out hunting rogue vampyres—a crime against the coven, as the law constitutes that only a vampyre can hunt a rogue vampyre, and only a lykan can hunt a rogue lykan—she has even bigger problems.

When Ethan had Jae locked in a cage, messing with her body and mind, using an enormous amount of fire magik to torture her, something … happened. It had to have had, right?

What else could explain Jae's sudden telekinetic abilities?

CHAPTER 1

Lone Ranger

"Son of a—" Jaeden launched into a somersault to avoid the bullet whizzing toward her head. She whipped around from her position on the muddy grass in time to propel a blade at the vampyre's wrist. The vamp girl screamed as it hit, the gun falling to the ground as she clutched her bleeding artery.

"You bitch!" Blondie screeched, glaring at her as Jaeden stood and sauntered toward her with an intimidating lack of fear. The wound caused the vampyre's eyes to glow with deadly intent.

"Ouch." Jaeden winced wryly. "Your oh-so-original comeback is like a veritable stake to the heart." She paused as her fingers brushed the line of steel blades she had strapped to her belt.

Blondie hissed, her incisors lengthening. "My boyfriend is not going to like me coming home wounded."

"Oh, honey, you've been such a bad little girl, chewing on humans and breaking the coven laws ... your boyfriend is going to be a little more concerned with the fact that you won't be coming home *at all*."

The husky laugh that comment provoked was eerie. "*I'm* breaking coven laws? What about you, wolf girl?"

That didn't even deserve a response. She was breaking coven laws for the common good. Blondie here got off on killing human boys after she had sex with them. Yeah, she wondered how the BF felt about that.

Jaeden opened her leather jacket and pulled out the small ax she kept hidden there. The vampyre's eyes widened and then shuttered when she realized Jaeden was watching for her reaction.

"So, vampyra"—Jae grimaced, hitting the blunt edge of the ax on the heel of her palm—"you ready to meet your ma—"

The vampyre launched at the gun on the ground, cutting off Jaeden's unoriginal parting quip. With a flick of her wrist, Jaeden pushed with her mind and the gun jumped from the grass, inches from the vamp's fingers, flying into Jae's outstretched and waiting hand. She then tucked the gun into the other side of her belt and smirked at the amazed look on the girl's face.

"I thought you were just a lykan." Panic swirled in her eyes.

Jae shrugged. "I am."

"Was that magik?"

Her question received another shrug. Truthfully, Jaeden didn't know what her telekinetic abilities were. Her greatest fear, in fact, were those abilities ... and whether it meant, as she suspected, that some of Ethan's malevolent energy had transferred to her during her captivity and torture.

"Hey ..." The vamp giggled a little hysterically. "Why

don't we just forget about this? I'll go home, you go home, and I'll never come back to your turf again, okay?"

No. Not okay.

"See that guy?" Jae pointed to the dead teenager who lay slumped against a gravestone. His neck had been ripped open so horrifically, it was a wonder his head was still attached to his body. She concealed a shudder, turning away from the gruesome and tragic sight. "Did he suggest the same thing to you when he first felt the bite of your teeth? Did you listen? Apparently not."

Blondie spluttered, "He's just a human!"

She snorted in response. "Yeah, well, weren't we all once?"

"I have money." The vamp backed up as Jaeden drew closer with the ax. "Whatever you want."

Jeez, when were these chicks ever going to learn?

"This isn't a negotiation. You kill humans … you pay the price."

The ax was spinning through the air before she finished her sentence. It sliced through wind and then straight into the vampyre's jugular. Her eyes popped wide, and she made an awful choking, gurgling sound. Her legs gave out, and the choking worsened as blood poured from her mouth.

Jae didn't even flinch.

She strode toward the vamp, knelt beside her, and put pressure on both ends of the ax until it cut right through, crunching and squishing until it hit the muddy ground beneath, her head completely detached from her undead body.

Silence.

Jae pulled at her ax and then wiped the blade clean on the girl's cashmere sweater, using her own scarf to wipe the blood splatter off her face.

A quick glance at her watch. 5:20 a.m.

The sun would rise in fifteen minutes, burning the body

to nothing. No one would ever know she had been there. That was funny, she mused, standing up and turning away from the consequences of her soldiering—a vampyre could walk around in the day no problem. But once their undead bodies were really ... well ... dead ... the sun did a cleanup job.

Legend had it this began after Apollo, the Greek god of the sun, had a child, Asclepius, who pissed off Hades by bringing the dead back to life with his healing powers. Since the dead were Hades' charge, he went to his brother, Zeus, who had Apollo's kid killed. In revenge, Apollo killed the Cyclops, enraging Zeus, who caught up with him and threatened to send him to Tartarus. With a little sweet-talking from Leto, Apollo's mama, Zeus lessened his punishment, with the proviso that Apollo help him keep the deadly creatures a secret from humankind by cleaning up their bodies when they died. Apollo gave the job to the sun, and the rest is ancient history.

Jaeden's attention settled back on the boy. She hated to leave him like that, but she couldn't be involved. He would just have to be found by a human in the morning. It was a large, central cemetery. It wouldn't be long. Not that that made her feel any less like a monster for walking away.

Before she had walked into this new life with Reuben, she hadn't known much about other supernaturals. Pack Errante, being so small, was protective of their kids, and only a few of them really knew much about the world outside the pack. Learning that for the past few centuries vampyre bodies had evolved because of the goddess Demeter's fertility curse, and had begun to die by the time they reached three or four hundred years old, made Jaeden feel somewhat better that they weren't overpopulating the world, thus making the job of tracking down rogues even harder.

But there were still a few out there whose bodies hadn't

evolved, and if the legends were true, a rare number who were second-generation vampyres: the first to be born, after Hades stole Persephone (Demeter's daughter) and made her Queen of the Underworld, thus enraging Demeter enough to curse Hades' vampyres with fertility. The ability to have children gradually changed their natures over time. They became less aggressive, more human. Well ... in general. Jaeden shuddered at the thought. If there was still a vamp out there from that time, it was probably a feral killer with the survival skills of a god.

She pushed the folklore meant to scare small vamps around the campfire out of her mind and wandered back to her basement suite. With her head lowered, she bumped into some late-night revellers. The closer she got to the apartment, however, the quieter the streets became. The sun had risen, and soon those quiet streets would buzz with city slickers who had no idea they shared their world, their jobs, and sometimes even their homes with supernatural beasties such as her.

More importantly, they had no idea a war was raging, and that if a certain young woman didn't live up to her prophecy, that war might spill over into their lives.

There would be nothing left of them.

She walked through the building's dark entrance and quietly jumped down the stone stairwell at the back. Jae could hear voices from the end of the hallway and smiled as she approached the sliding steel door. Lily and Adam were fighting over the Xbox again. She rapped on the door and it slid back within seconds. With an annoying crease of concern between his eyebrows, Reuben stepped back to allow her entry.

"Where have you been? You missed all the action."

Jae shrugged and nodded at the two vampyres playing video games. Josh and Styx were sleeping in one of the back rooms. She wandered through the apartment, dropping her leather jacket here and her blades there. She placed the ax in safekeeping on a wall mount in the bedroom she used to share with Lily. She could feel Reuben prowling behind her.

"Jae, what's up?" His cool hands slid up her arms and massaged her shoulders.

She shrugged him off and sat on the bed, pulling off her boots as he glared at her from the doorway.

"Well?"

"I hunted a rogue by myself."

He nodded, biting on his lip ring, a tic he had when thinking hard about something. "You've been doing that a lot lately."

She knew where he was going with this, and she was just too damn tired. Ignoring him, Jae pulled off her T-shirt and rifled through her drawers for a clean one.

Reuben hissed, bringing her gaze snapping up to him. His eyes narrowed on her as he looked her over. "Some people would call that teasing."

Inwardly, she flinched; outwardly, it pissed her off. "Is that a warning, Reuben?" she sneered, pulling on a clean shirt.

"Maybe."

She blanched at the anger in his voice. "I'm sorry, okat? I just forget. Lykans are used to undressing in front of each other."

"I know. Just try to remember. I'm not made of stone."

She flushed, an awkward silence falling between them as they both remembered the night he kissed her—and was thoroughly rebuffed.

He cleared his throat, and she sensed a now-familiar discussion on the horizon. "Why the solo hunting?"

She was right. "I'm tired."

"I want to talk about this. Hunting by yourself? You've been doing it since that night in here with Lily."

Jae winced just thinking about it. "She could've been killed."

"But she wasn't," Reuben replied, approaching her. He sat down beside her on the bed, seeming afraid she would snap at him like a wounded animal if he got too close. "You've been controlling your telekinesis."

Not that night. Not when she had nightmares. When she was awake and in control, she was able to harness whatever energy it was that gave her the ability to move things with her mind. But as soon as her emotions went into overload, there was no stopping the chaos. She had been fine around Reuben and his gang—killing vampyres who preyed on humans, pouring her hate into pounding the living daylight out of them and feeling nothing more than a tangible connection to these good vamps she worked with. They were colleagues, nothing more. She wouldn't let them be.

But two weeks ago, she'd started having nightmares about her time in the cage. She didn't know why or how … but they were vivid and horrifying and kicked her telekinesis into high gear. She'd been awoken by Lily's screams. Six blades were stabbed into the walls around them, her precious ax embedded above Lily's head as she cowered in the corner. Books, furniture, and clothes were strewn everywhere, and Lily's nose was bleeding, a black bruise blossoming on her porcelain face. Jaeden had refused to let her sleep in the same room with her since, refused to go hunting with any of them in case she got them killed.

"Only when my emotions are stable. I can't take chances."

For her, that was the end of the discussion.

"Do you want to talk about these nightmares?"

"Uh, no."

"What about *that*?"

Jae frowned and looked up. He was pointing to her ax mounted on the wall. "What about it?"

He tried to appear calm, but his jaw clenched. "If you're saying you can't control it, why do you have a weapon in here that could kill you in your sleep?"

Because it doesn't matter.

She didn't say that. Reuben would kill her himself if she said that. He wanted her to be so happy here with him and the gang, taking out bad guys, living off Lily's inheritance. But she was miserable. She ached for the pack with every part of her body. She wanted her mother and father and her little niece Jaela. She wanted to run free with them through the woods behind Lucien's house and play and tussle with Sebastian. Her dresser began to shake at the thought of Seb, and she quickly threw him out of her mind.

He was gone. She wasn't ever getting him back.

She *could* have the pack back if she wanted.

But she didn't. She wouldn't.

She wouldn't live with the people who reminded her of when she was whole and pure and good. She was something else now, something broken and corrupted, and she couldn't face that kind of disappointment from the people she loved after everything that had happened to her.

"Well?" Reuben pressed.

"I'll take it down." It would be easier than explaining to him about how messed up she was. She guessed he knew already, though.

"Jae … " He placed his large, cool hand over hers.

Crap, she winced, looking up into his face. She shouldn't make eye contact with him. His black eyes asked for way more than she could give.

"Don't." She snatched her hand back.

He snapped up off the bed. "If you would just let me in, I could help you. Tell me what happened to you."

No way. No one could ever know how bad it got.

At her silence, he heaved a heavy sigh. "Fine. I'll let you sleep."

"Okay."

He turned to leave and then looked back at her. "Just so you know, we may have to leave the city. The rogues have cottoned on to the fact this is no longer an easy target for breaking coven law."

She nodded, not caring where they went.

"I'm going out."

Again she nodded. Reuben had a tendency to disappear now and then to goddess knows where. Jae didn't ask about his mysterious loner ventures. That would imply she cared.

CHAPTER 2

Midnight Rebel

*A*s Caia finished the last sentence on her report for Marion, she eased back in her desk chair. The fading light outside brought memories she couldn't dispel. It had been months now since she'd killed her uncle Ethan after his kidnapping and torture of Jaeden—since Sebastian had been murdered in the crossfire.

Months since the pack had seen any semblance of normalcy.

She turned and, like many nights, let her gaze drift outside her window and into the darkening woods. Jaeden had been gone for months, and only Caia, and perhaps Lucien, knew why. The torture she'd endured at Ethan's hands was unimaginable, and Caia hadn't been able to tell her family how bad it must've been for Jae to leave the pack.

Jaeden's father, Dimitri, was distraught and constantly

demanding Lucien do something about it, but one look at Caia's face and Lucien knew it was best to leave Jaeden to come to terms with things by herself.

She was strong enough to make it through the cage, so she was strong enough to be alone.

But it wasn't forever. Caia was giving her another month, and if she wasn't back by then, she'd fulfill Dimitri's wishes and bring her back to the pack herself.

Caia sighed, her eyes drifting down and across her bed, and with it, heated memories flooded her. *Dear goddess*, she scoffed. She was lucky she hadn't fallen pregnant! Since lykans couldn't carry disease, nor become pregnant unless mated, protection during sex was usually only necessary for mated couples who weren't ready for children. Since she and Lucien had no idea having sex would cement their betrothal, they hadn't used any protection.

Yeesh.

She was sooo lucky she hadn't gotten pregnant.

The close call, however, didn't stop her from yearning ... remembering. She could no longer look at her bed without a reminder of the night she gave herself to him, the night when, for once, they'd been in total agreement about something, safe together, passionate, happy. The moment hadn't lasted, and ever since there'd been a constant tension between them despite their "united front."

She missed him.

"Caia."

The familiar voice sent a wave a longing through her and she turned to stare up into his silver eyes. "Yeah?"

Lucien threw her a sympathetic look, acknowledging how tired she was. "Marion's here."

She smiled wearily and stood, gathering her papers. They walked in silence down the stairs and into the sitting room where Marion sat having tea, and Saffron, her faerie, stood studying her cuticles in utter boredom.

"Ah, Caia." Marion smiled warmly in greeting.

For the past few months, Marion's weekly visits had been the pack's only constant. Pack runs had dwindled—there had been two rather shabbily put-together ventures, and even then, the mood had been melancholy. School was out for the summer for Mal and the others, and Caia, lucky to have finished her finals, couldn't enjoy graduation since Jaeden had missed it and she had only Alexa to share it with. And any plan Caia had had for the future was gone: no college, no apprenticeships, no job. Her job was here, training with Marion, writing reports on the activities of the Midnight Coven.

As the weeks passed and her reports proved more and more helpful, the more Marion had hinted at Marita's growing curiosity. The day was coming when Marita would ask to meet Caia, ask for her to come to the Center, maybe even take a physical part in the war.

The Center was the main training ground for Daylight soldiers, and because a magik's power didn't reach its full potential until their eighteenth birthday, a magik had to be eighteen to join the Center. The same was true for any supernatural being—it was like joining the army. A supernatural had to be a legal adult to make that choice.

From what Marion had told Caia, it not only involved physical training and strategizing but provided classes on how to use magik and elements. The majority of magiks taught their children all they needed to know, but the most powerful magiks tended to be those who were taught at the Center. It sounded like an interesting place, and Caia would go if only to get it over with so she could return to the pack.

"Marion." She sat across from her on the sofa. "Saffron."

The faerie smirked, which was more of a response than

anyone else got out of her. She was beginning to think the shapeshifter liked her.

"So." The magik smiled brightly, but Caia detected the strain in her expression. "What news from the Dark Coven?"

Caia obediently handed over her written report. "You asked me to look specifically for any mention of the New York Króls. I learned that Nikolai has asked to abandon the attack. Too risky in light of the instability of the Midnights."

Nikolai Petrovsky was the new Regent of the Midnight Coven and had been appointed by their Council since Ethan had gone "missing." The fact that Gaia would not imbue Nikolai with trace magik when the Council put him forward as the new Head led the Midnights to believe that Ethan was still alive somewhere. For now, the Council voted in Nikolai's rule as regent. Of course, they were blithely unaware of Caia's existence.

Caia looked between Marion and Lucien, unsure of their reaction to her next piece of news. "In fact ... Nikolai has asked that all attacks against us be abandoned until there is definitive news of Ethan's whereabouts."

Lucien quirked an eyebrow as he glanced at Marion, interested more in her reaction than anything else. Marion, for her part, had stiffened in surprise. Even Saffron looked up from her nails in interest. After a few minutes of silence, Marion cleared her throat.

"Well ... that's unexpected."

Yeah.

"But what does it mean?" Caia asked.

The witch shrugged. "You should know better than anyone what it means."

"I don't. Nikolai is strong, and his emotions are not as easy to read through the trace as it is with the others."

She nodded. "The Petrovskys are an influential family, have been for many generations."

Caia knew this; she'd felt the respect he garnered from other Midnights and the reasons why. His decision to stop attacks against the Daylight Coven confused Caia, not only because she couldn't feel the reason from *him*—only what he told the others—but because lately, her connection to the Midnights had raised questions. She was feeling emotions from some of them that suggested the war was not exactly what she thought it was—or had been led to think it was.

She snapped out of her musings to find Marion frowning at her. "Caia, it doesn't mean anything significant. Nikolai is obviously rallying the troops until he feels the coven is secure enough to return to their tried-and-true style of warfare." She curled her lip distastefully. "Neanderthals that they are."

Lucien turned to Caia. He seemed to read her confusion and smiled reassuringly. "Marion's right. The Dark Coven is just a little shook up right now. They're taking precautions, but it doesn't *mean* anything."

If that was true, then why didn't she feel so sure?

Caia nodded reluctantly because what she was about to impart was going to further their belief that Midnights were not to be trusted to play the game with a cool head. She took a deep breath. "Despite Nikolai's orders, he has a rebel in his midst. A guy called Pierre du Bois?"

A wrinkle of concentration appeared between Marion's eyebrows. "Du Bois? Du Bois? I know that name, but it's not one belonging to the old families. What is he up to?"

"This warlock has gone behind Nikolai's back and raised a small group of dissenters against Nikolai's decision. It seems he has a problem with one of the city packs from *here*. The MacLachlans?"

Lucien grunted in surprise. "The MacLachlans live, what, three hundred miles north of here? But ... they're not a huge pack." His eyes swung to Marion. "What are the Midnights doing going after a relatively small pack?"

"The MacLachlans are an old Scottish pack," Saffron spoke up, moving gracefully closer to them. "They sprung up around the end of the thirteenth century in Renfrewshire, Scotland, and have gifted the Daylight Coven with great Rogue Hunters throughout the centuries. I've worked with …" She perched beside Marion, studying her mistress as if she would find the answer in her face. "Hmm … eight, nine generations of Rogue Hunters from that pack."

Marion nodded, turning back to Caia and Lucien. "Saffron's right. They may be small, but to older members of either coven, they are a well-known warrior pack."

Well, that explained that.

"Pierre is arrogant and young." Caia stood to stretch her legs. She hadn't been on a run in weeks, and it was telling on her body. "Which is why you don't recognize him as an old warlock. I thought because of his ability to arouse such devotion that you may have heard of him, but I'm thinking he's just very charismatic. His trace is malevolent, his prejudice against the Daylights extraordinary considering how young he is. And … I think he might be quite powerful. Some of the others seem afraid of him.

"From what you've told me, and from my understanding of Pierre's character, wiping out a respected and feared pack of lykans would cement his reputation. Although I can't feel it in his designs, he might use a victory like taking down the MacLachlans as a reason to take to the Council and ask them to make him regent instead."

"When is this attack going to take place?" Lucien narrowed his eyes, folding his arms across his chest defensively; the muscles in his biceps rippled. His body language had become so familiar to Caia—Lucien was preparing for war. The butterflies in her stomach, dormant for the majority of the conversation, fluttered into a riot. She knew this news was going to be the beginning of something. Something big. Something irreversible.

"Four weeks."

Marion pursed her lips. "I'll be back in five minutes. I have to speak to Marita. Come, Saffron."

And the witch was gone, along with the faerie. Not for the first time, Caia envied their flawless use of the communication spell that allowed them to travel to an intended destination instantly.

I knew it.

This is big.

"You okay?" Lucien's eyes had softened with concern.

"I'm fine. Just preparing myself."

"For what?"

She snorted. "The apocalypse."

Lucien grinned. "Let's just make sure it's them and not us that end up in the Underworld, huh?"

"Wow, talk about pressure."

"I'm kidding."

"I'm not."

He sighed heavily and strode toward her. Her every nerve ending came to life the closer he got and then sizzled when he cupped her chin in his large hand, his eyes shining with faith and strength. "You can only do what you're doing, Caia. Yes, you're important to this war, but are you going to end it?" He shook his head, stroking her cheek. "One person can't stop a war, especially when you're not the one running the show."

She nodded gratefully, trying not to melt into his embrace. Goddess, these last few months had been hard pretending not to want more from their relationship. *Or friendship, as it were,* she thought grumpily. She inwardly sighed as his hand dropped away, and he pulled back from her.

"What do you think Marion's saying to Marita?" he asked, voice gruff, almost as if he'd been as affected by their momentary intimacy.

"Well—"

"I was relating the situation as it stands." The magik suddenly appeared before them, minus Saffron.

Caia smiled at her. Like she had with the pack, Caia had come to know Marion well over the last few months, and despite her businesslike approach to everything, she had a penchant for mischief that was funny, depending on if you were her target.

"And?" she asked expectantly.

Marion's smile faltered, and she drew her small shoulders back as if bracing for battle. "Marita would like you to play a part in the defense of Pack MacLachlan."

Lucien growled. "Isn't it a bit soon?"

"I want to." Caia placed a placating hand on his arm, her eyes hard with determination. "I knew this was coming."

"I'm afraid Marita is quite adamant about it. Anyway"— Marion turned to Lucien with a sarcastic smirk—"not to worry. She would like to meet you as well, Lucien."

Caia frowned. "Wait. Are we going to the Center?"

Marion nodded. "As soon as possible."

"And how are we getting there? I thought it was in Europe."

The magik chuckled as if Caia had said the funniest thing in the world. "Really, Caia, you should know better than that by now." At their continued silence, she seemed to sense that neither Caia nor Lucien had the patience for ambiguity. "Okay. We want you, you and Lucien only, to travel to the MacLachlans. Not to them, exactly. There is a gymnasium on Bryant Street called Magic Fitness—"

Caia snickered. "You're kidding?"

Marion ignored her. "Go in as inconspicuously as you can." She threw a pointed look at Lucien. "To the left of the front entrance is a doorway that takes you down a corridor. In this corridor is a studio room, studio number three. Go in and stand in front of the first pane of floor-to-ceiling mirror on the back wall. Caia, if you place your hand on the first pane, the mirror will recognize you as a magik. Take Lucien's hand and walk into the pane."

"What?"

She smiled almost arrogantly. "It's a portal. To the Center."

"And when do we leave?" Lucien asked quietly.

"I'll give you a week to arrange a suitable situation for the pack."

He nodded and looked ready to ask another question when Marion cleared her throat, appearing uncomfortable. "There is something else."

The hair on the back of Caia's neck rose in warning. "Yes?"

But Marion was looking at Lucien.

"My sister has become aware that Jaeden Rodriguez is breaking coven laws."

A snarl erupted from Lucien's throat, his entire body tense with shock and anger. "I doubt that very much."

The witch looked saddened. "Jaeden has been killing rogue vampyres." She pulled a piece of paper out of her pocket and handed it to Lucien. He snatched it from her. "She's been living with a group of vampyres and hunting with them."

Caia felt herself shaking. "What does this mean?"

"Usually imprisonment. But considering the circumstances, Marita has agreed to let Ryder retrieve her and bring her back to the pack."

"She's getting off on a warning?" Relief moved through Caia.

Marion nodded, and Caia felt the tension drain out of Lucien. He grunted and tucked the paper in the back pocket of his jeans.

"I'll call Ryder immediately."

CHAPTER 3

Find and Retrieve

Ryder cuffed the hands-free around his ear and pressed speed dial one.

Three rings rang out before ... "Lucien."

"You and Caia ready to hit the road?" he asked without preamble.

Lucien exhaled down the line. "Bored already, Ryder?"

Ryder grinned, his eyes darting to the rearview mirror at the sound of sirens. The flash of light could be seen weaving between cars in the distance, and he pulled over to get out of the way. "Hey, do not get me started."

"I thought—[*ne naw ne naw ne naw*]—already."

"You'll have to repeat that, man. Police sirens just drowned out what I'm guessing is an irritating observation on my progress in this 'rescue Jaeden from herself' project you got me heading up."

Lucien snorted. "I was just wondering what was taking so long."

"I left three days ago."

"And?"

"It's a three-day drive, not including rest br—you know what, never mind, I'm nearly there."

"Yeah, well, Magnus has agreed to oversee the pack, so Caia and I are nearly ready to hit the road as well."

Ryder smirked. "Nice."

"Shut up."

"I didn't say anything."

"You were thinking it."

"Thinking what?" He laughed.

"Shut up."

"Does this journey include a motel break, because in the interest of romance, don't. Last night I slept in a motel room where the carpet literally moved beneath my feet, there were so many fleas in it."

"Beautiful."

"I might have to make a pit stop on the way back so Jae can enjoy the delights of the place."

"Go easy on her."

Ryder grunted as he glided into the next lane. "Yeah, yeah."

"I gotta go."

"I'll let you know when I retrieve our wayward pup."

"Do that. Take care, man."

"You too."

Ryder was making pretty good time, so he should hit the city by nightfall. He wondered whether she would be an adult about this and come in peace, or if he was going to have to haul her ass into the truck. He grumbled under his breath as he rubbed the tension out of his forehead.

* * *

"IT'S PRETTY cool that you've started hunting with us again." Styx smiled sweetly as she stood up from the ground, her machete bloodied by the dead vampyre's neck juice. Jaeden felt a twinge of guilt at the mixture of hurt and hope in the young vamp's eyes. Out of all of her newfound comrades, Styx was the most sensitive and had clung to Jaeden from the get-go. She was a baby for a vampyre, only sixteen, and Jae had felt sort of protective toward her.

Styx was built like a child, fragile and small at a tiny five foot nothing. Her size was deceptive, and the reason the big vampyre on the ground was dead. None of the "bad teeth" (as Reuben's gang of misfits liked to refer to the rogue vamps) expected the sly strength of Styx.

Jaeden looked away from the dead guy. "Yeah, well, it gets Reuben off my back." She winced as Styx's face fell in disappointment. "And of course, I missed hanging out with you guys," she added quickly. The young girl smiled, but Jae could tell it was too late.

"Aren't you happy with us, Jaeden?"

Oh boy, how to answer that question?

She gestured to Styx to walk with her out of the alleyway. They were supposed to have been back at the loft half an hour ago. Lily, Adam, and Josh would already be there hitting the Xbox. She doubted Reuben would be there. He'd gone on one of his disappearing acts yesterday and probably wouldn't be back for a few days.

"I guess I'm just ready to move on from here." She indicated their surroundings. "It's quiet now that the bad teeth know we're hunting them. That vamp you killed back there is the first one in days."

Her answer seemed to cheer Styx up, now grinning from cheek to cheek, her little fangs visible. "Well, that's okay.

We'll just move. Reuben will be totally cool with that. Ooh, yay!" She bounced from one foot to the other, clapping her hands like a perky cheerleader. "Maybe we can convince Reuben to buy an actual loft apartment ... you know, one with windows!"

Jae laughed and shook her head. "I don't know. I sometimes think Reuben forgets you guys can actually stand the sunlight. Too many episodes of *The Vampire Diaries*, I think."

"He does think that Elena girl is hot."

Jae smirked. "So does Lily."

Styx sighed longingly. "Ian Somerhalder all the way."

"Uh-uh." Jae scrunched up her face. "Too pretty. I prefer my men a little rough around the edges."

"Like Reuben?" The vamp giggled.

Jaeden laughed and punched her arm playfully. Despite Styx's matchmaking attempts, Jae enjoyed the young vamp's prattle as they wandered back to the apartment. Her chatter about anything and nothing was soothing, allowing her thoughts to settle nowhere and be at peace for the moment.

"Ah, home sweet home." Styx chuckled as she pulled the building's main door open. "But not for long." Her blue-yellow eyes twinkled happily at the exciting thought of moving up and on.

Jaeden snorted. "One can only hope."

"You know, I'm thinking we should go abroad. Like Rome or Egypt or something. I'm betting there are a lot of bad teeth over there," she said as they headed down the hallway to the loft. Her small hand clasped the door handle. "I mean, all that culture and beauty. The bad teeth would want to rip that sh—"

Styx stopped as the door slid open, her doll eyes wide, rosebud mouth parted in shock. Jaeden's heart thumped loudly as she dared to step around the vamp and look inside the basement. The blood rushing in her ears drowned out any sound.

How had he found her?

* * *

RYDER FELT like smirking at the shocked look on Jaeden's face. All along, he hadn't wanted to believe the information on the little paper Marion had handed to Lucien and then Lucien to him. He knew the girl had been through a lot. But she knew the rules.

You did not hunt other supernatural races.

If he hadn't witnessed the horrific situation Jae had been in with Ethan, he would've been yelling at her by now. But he had seen only a fragment of the damage inflicted upon a girl who'd once been the spunkiest, most vivacious kid in the pack. He wasn't going to condemn her for this recent stupidity. He was going to put her in the truck and leave this mess in the past where it belonged. That was if she ever made a move into the apartment toward him.

He frowned as her blue eyes flickered toward the vamp kids who sat terrified on a dilapidated old sofa.

"They're fine. No harm done." He smiled, holding up his hands in surrender. And he wasn't lying. After they had come home to find him there, they had attacked, but quickly saw reason after he blocked and outmaneuvered all three of them. And that tall chick had game; he inwardly winced, recalling her near blow to his groin.

He waited patiently. Jaeden didn't respond.

Finally, she took a tentative step inside, her slender hands gripping the tiny female vampyre behind her, pulling her in before she slid the door closed. Ryder waited as she turned toward him, her face expressionless.

She was different, he realized.

It wasn't just that her manner had changed. She used to be a bundle of energy, always in motion, her sentences forever flowing into one another. Now she was cool and aloof, a reserve in her gorgeous blue eyes that had never been there before.

Ryder shrugged off an uncomfortable, unwelcome feeling as his eyes drank her in. Jaeden had grown up ... and the effect was, well ...

She was hot.

Crap.

"What are you doing here?" she asked warily.

Ryder decided now wasn't the time to mess around. "I've been sent to return you to the pack."

Her eyes narrowed; her body shifted into defense mode. "I don't want to go back."

For the hundredth time, Ryder wondered why Jaeden couldn't stand to be around her pack. When anything got to him that badly, all he wanted was to *be* with the pack. The bubble of irritation under his skin threatened to vocalize itself, but he checked it at the last minute.

"I'm afraid you don't have a choice," he replied evenly. "It's either the pack or imprisonment."

Her mouth fell open.

Finally. A response.

"What?" She growled, her lykan distorting her voice.

Ryder chuckled, crossing his arms over his chest. "What, you thought you could break a major coven law and not have to deal with it?"

Panic shot through her eyes, but only briefly. Ryder watched in amazement as she hid the emotion with ease as she walked toward him, her shoulders drawn back defiantly. The girl really had become something; he enjoyed the panther-like way she moved.

"Why am I not arrested, then?"

"Because of Caia."

"Ah." Jae nodded, smirking at the irony. "They need her, and they know that throwing away the key on me would piss her off."

Ryder gave a brief nod.

She harrumphed.

What the Hades did that mean? he wondered in annoyance.

"I guess I have no choice."

"None whatsoever."

* * *

IT WAS weird seeing Ryder again.

His presence filled the truck cab as he drove them out of the city and toward the pack. The fact that he was singing "Sweet Home Alabama" didn't help matters.

Jaeden groaned and burrowed deeper into the passenger seat. She couldn't believe it. How had she gone from being a Rogue Hunter one minute to being … what … Ryder's babysitting job?

"'Sweet home Alabama! Yeah! Where the skiiiieees are sooo blue! Sweet home …'"

Oh goddess, help me, she whimpered. He was so out of tune.

"'Alabama! Woo! Swe—'"

"RYDER!" she exploded. "If I am to survive a road trip back to the pack, I'm going to need you *not* to do that."

"Lynyrd Skynyrd?"

"Nope."

"'Sweet Home Alabama'?"

"Nope."

He looked at her in confusion, his warm hazel eyes round, his usually sexy grin missing and replaced by a near-childish pout. "Then what?"

"Singing. Ryder. The singing."

"Excuse me?"

"Please tell me you are not delusional enough to think you can actually sing."

He looked genuinely affronted. "I will have you know that my voice has been praised by many lovely ladies."

"Wow, you really must be good in bed, 'cause they've been feeding you a crock of crap."

"What?" Ryder huffed, glancing from her back to the road. "Well … what? You know, I have been dropkicked by a lykan on steroids, had an actual samurai sword sliced through my shoulder, and been shot in the chest with buckshot … but that shit there *really* hurt."

A silence descended upon the cab.

And then Jaeden erupted. She was laughing so hard she could barely breathe, and the longer she laughed, the wider Ryder's grin got. When at last her giggles dissipated, she felt exhausted and mildly uncomfortable for having really laughed for the first time since Ethan.

"That was nice to hear," Ryder said. "Even though I was being completely serious."

The smile he threw her was soft and coaxing, and she suddenly remembered why he had been her school-girl crush. The wolf was gorgeous, no question. She looked away, trying to make out the passing landscape in the dark.

Reuben was going to be pissed off when he returned and found her gone. As it was, the goodbye had been harder than she'd ever wanted it to be. All this time she thought she had truly cut herself off from people, but no. The sight of Styx crying had done her in, leaving her with painful regret at not being able to put a comforting arm around the girl and tell her she was sorry, that it would all be okay. She'd left Lily to do that, who glared at her the entire time she packed, refusing to speak to her. Josh and Adam said their goodbyes, their eyes nervously returning to Ryder. She wondered what the lykan had done to them before she got there.

So she had left them. Styx was sad. Lily was pissed. What did they expect her to do? Fight the coven? Were they crazy?

No. She was going home. Where she belonged.

What?

A languorous, melting sensation spread through her body, and a tension she'd gotten so accustomed to slipped from her mind. She felt like she'd been sleeping for the last few months and now found herself awake. A rush of feelings, so in contradiction to what only minutes before she'd been so sure of, washed over her.

She wanted to go to the pack. She wanted to see her parents.

Wow. She was so sure she hadn't wanted that at all.

Here's hoping the telekinesis doesn't kick in then, huh? she thought wryly, confused by her sudden desire to return to the pack.

"Hey, Jaeden?"

"What?" she asked without looking at him, trying to hide her sudden disorientation.

"Earlier when you said Caia would be angry at the coven if they locked you up, what did that sarcastic noise you made mean?"

"What did you think it meant? It meant, why the Hades would Caia care if they locked me up? We knew each other for all of five seconds."

The growl that rumbled from Ryder's chest alerted her. Perhaps she'd made a mistake.

"You ungrateful pup."

Yup. Definite mistake.

"Caia risked her ass to save you from Ethan, and don't give me any crap about it being her fault you were there in the first place, because it wasn't. It was mine and it was

Lucien's, and it was your father's. It was the pack's fault we didn't protect you. But Caia"—Ryder shook his head in anger —"that girl did everything she could. She risked everything to find you. And don't you forget it."

She wanted to scream at him, wanted to rail and rage that he had no idea what she'd been through, so how dare he? But in the end, she knew he was right. No matter how much she wanted to blame Caia for Ethan taking her, deep down she knew if there was one person in this world she might count on, she was guessing it was Caia Ribeiro. Ryder obviously thought so, too, and clearly had a lot of respect and admiration for her.

A sneaking feeling swept over Jaeden. His defense of Caia was quite vehement. Did he … did Ryder have a thing for Caia? For some reason, the thought irritated her more than his condescending lecture.

"Point well received," she sniped. "And just so you know, I thanked Caia for saving me. I thanked Sebastian, too, before you bring that up."

Another tense silence fell between them until finally Ryder replied, "I'm sorry. I didn't mean to—"

"Why don't we just be quiet for a while, hmm?"

He nodded and relaxed into his seat.

And just as Jaeden felt herself drifting to sleep, Ryder chuckled. "I heard this really funny joke on the radio the other night. You want to hear it?"

She shrugged.

"I'll assume that's angry teenage girl gesture for yes." He smirked. "Okay. So there's this koala up in his tree, smoking a joint, and this little lizard walking past looks up and notices. 'Hey,' the little lizard calls, 'what's up?'

"'Nothing. Just smoking a joint, getting stoned. Wanna join?'

"'Sure,' says the little lizard, and he slithers up the tree and starts getting stoned with the koala.

"A little while later, the little lizard says his mouth is dry and he needs a drink, but on the way down the tree, he leans over too far and falls into the river. A big crocodile sees it happen and swims over. 'What's up?' he asks the little lizard. 'You okay?'

"'Sure.' The little lizard nods. 'I'm just too stoned from smoking some joints with the koala.'

"'Joints?' The big crocodile's eyes light up. 'I gotta check that out, man.' So the big crocodile swims out of the river and takes a wander into the trees until he reaches the one the koala's in. 'Hey!' he shouts up.

"The koala looks back down at him and shouts, 'Fuuuck, duuude! How much water did you drink?'"

Ryder slapped the wheel of the truck, laughing as he finished the joke. "Ah, man, that's funny." He shook his head, wiping at a tear in the corner of his eye. "It kills me."

Jaeden hadn't said anything. She'd managed to hide her answering grin by looking out the passenger window.

"What?" Ryder huffed. "Come on, that was funny! That was comedy gold right there."

She shrugged, enjoying teasing him. "It was okay. Kind of elementary."

"Elementary? It's an effing joke."

"Whatever."

"Aw, this is going to be a looong drive home."

Jaeden hid her grin with her hand. Teasing and arguing with Ryder was the most normal she'd felt in a long time. She sneaked a glance at him again, and a rush of old feelings hit her like a battering ram. She remembered how just the thought of him had sent butterflies into chaos in the pit of her stomach, back when she'd been naively carefree; how daydreaming about him had gotten her through her boring history class; how she'd promised herself that when she turned eighteen, she would finally let Ryder know that his mate had been under his nose the whole time.

A golden peace briefly whispered through her with the memories.

Goddess, she had made a mistake leaving the pack. Instead of running from them, she should've let them fix her. And maybe she would've felt infrequent bursts of that golden peace until one day she didn't feel so broken.

A hollow regret formed in her chest. Running from the pack was probably the biggest mistake of her life. She'd been so afraid of her family not understanding who she was now. But that wasn't an excuse, was it? Why had she done it?

She held in the gasp of pain her confusion and regret created and kept her face turned from Ryder. A single tear escaped, trickling slowly down her smooth cheek, feeling like a heavy stone scoring her skin.

It was the first tear she'd shed since leaving the pack.

This time she did gasp. She was cracking, the steel armor she'd put up around herself rusting off, and all because she was with one of her pack. Coins on Ryder's dash shuddered, and Jaeden flinched, willing her telekinesis into control.

"Are you all right?" Ryder asked, deep concern in his words.

"Yeah," she managed. She turned to him, wide-eyed. "Yeah, I think I'm going to be."

He smiled gently, seeming to understand.

CHAPTER 4

Wants and Fears

The smell of coffee, eggs, and crackling bacon taunted her senses and made her stomach roil. She followed Lucien, who followed a waitress, to a booth at the back of the roadside diner.

"Here you go, hon," the young woman purred, handing a grease-covered menu to Lucien, the look in her eyes indicating that if he wanted, he could order her off the menu. Caia slid into the booth, ripped edges of maroon leather catching on her jeans. Of course, the waitress didn't even glance her way, let alone give her a menu. Good thing she wasn't hungry.

"What are you having?" Lucien asked as he managed to fold his huge frame into the too-small booth.

"I'm okay."

"Caia, you have to eat."

"I'm not hungry."

"At least have some coffee and a sandwich."

"I don't think I could keep it down."

"I'm ordering you a sandwich."

"Fair enough. Hope you can afford new upholstery in the truck."

He grimaced. "Maybe just the coffee, then."

As his eyes wandered the menu, his expression changed, a big wolfy grin spreading across his face. "I, on the other hand, am going to have a burger. A huge, juicy, meaty burger with a hunk of melting cheese, maybe some thick mayo, and—"

Caia felt herself turn green. "Stop, I beg of you."

The portal to the Center was just over a five-hour drive away. They'd left at sunrise and would be there in a few hours' time. The thought of meeting Marita and Vanne, of taking part in the war, was causing not only sickening nerves but trembling, cold shakes. The hairs on her arms stood on end and her teeth chittered.

The drive so far had been fraught with tension. The cab in Lucien's truck seemed smaller somehow. She could hear and feel his every move, her eyes wandering to his strong hands and sinewy forearms every time he reached for something. Tingles shot through her whenever she caught a glimpse of his profile, or when he turned to smile at her, his hard silver eyes softening to smoke the way they only seemed to do around the people he really cared about. Momentarily, her nerves over the Center were forgotten, instead replaced with new nerves, sad, achy nerves over Lucien, over the stupid mistakes she'd made when she learned he'd been keeping things from her.

In the end, it'd turned out there were more important things in life than petty grievances. And her grievances had been petty in comparison to what had happened to Jaeden and Sebastian.

Hindsight sucked.

In fact, hindsight should be assassinated.

Lucien frowned over having been stopped in his meat salivation. "You sure you're okay?"

She nodded mutely.

His eyes narrowed. "Last time I'm asking. I'm a guy, after all."

Caia laughed. Olympus forbid anyone consider him sensitive or considerate. "Some coffee will be fine. I'm just a little nervous, that's all."

The waitress returned and Lucien gave her their order. When he was done, she offered him a huge come-get-me smile and then turned unexpectedly to Caia. "He your boyfriend?" she asked.

Her mouth fell open at the woman's brazenness, and she looked over at Lucien to see him grinning, enjoying the interlude, waiting for Caia's answer. He quirked an eyebrow at her as if to say, "See ... I'm hot."

She glared at him and turned back to the waitress. Caia smiled sweetly, checking her name tag. "Oh no. He's all yours ... Melissa, is it?"

Melissa grinned. "You're not dating?"

"No. Never. Not gonna happen." She turned that sweet smile back on Lucien whose smirk had been replaced with a glower. "I would have to be paid—"

"Okay, she gets the picture," he snapped and turned to Melissa. "Can we just get our order, please?"

Melissa nodded. "What are you doing later?"

"Going to France."

She giggled. "Yeah, right. Seriously, you want to, like, do something?"

"I'll be in France."

The waitress lost the grin, straightened up from the table,

and gave him a dirty look. "If you don't want to go out with me, just say so."

As the girl flounced off, Caia chuckled. "You're so getting a loogie in your coffee."

"I don't get it, I was telling the truth." He looked adorably confused and irritated.

"She's human. She doesn't understand that there are portals to Europe in gym. I didn't realize there were portals to anywhere, let alone Europe, in gyms until last week, and I'm a half-lykan, half-magik."

"Not a label that trips off the tongue, huh?"

"Still working on a name for what I am."

"How about a mykan?"

"Or a lykik?"

Lucien screwed up his face. "Stick with half-lykan, half-magik for now."

She smiled, and for that moment, they were comfortable in each other's company. She bit her lip, remembering the first time they'd taken a walk together in the woods behind their house, when Lucien told her about Pack Errante's origins. It had been comfortable then too. If only it could be like that always.

Abruptly, the moment between them changed as Lucien's eyes fell to her mouth. It was the same look he'd given her when he kissed her for the first time and when he had initiated the night they slept together.

Oh boy.

Her cheeks flushed.

And then Lucien seemed to come back to himself and coughed, shifting in his seat. "Where is that coffee?" he grumbled, his eyes not meeting hers.

Caia tried to hide her smile. Maybe Lucien wasn't quite as unaffected by her as she'd thought. Maybe there was hope after all. Maybe—

What is that?

An icy tingle shot through her, and she stiffened in response. She was fully in control of her trace magik now. She tapped into it whenever *she* wanted, but if a Midnight magik was nearby, the trace alerted her to it. Glancing around, Caia tried not to show her panic. It didn't mean the Midnight was here in the diner. The magik could be a few miles away.

She allowed herself to relax and let the magik's essence pour through her. A man. A young man. He was happy about something. It felt like love—he felt like he was in love. She stiffened again.

"Caia, what's wrong?" Lucien reached across for her hand.

"Nothing," she whispered.

And that was the problem. The young Midnight's essence was untainted. There was no malice or hate in his soul. No bloodlust for war. And his wasn't the first Midnight's trace she'd felt this from. Why were there Midnights who didn't seem to care about the war? There was no evidence of that black, syrupy pool of hate Ethan had reveled in, that Pierre du Bois and his followers swam in.

She wasn't stupid. Caia knew there was no black and white in war, or in most situations, for that matter, but the centuries of beliefs and warfare had taken on its own soul, its own being. Daylights were supposed to want equality and peace; Midnights wanted the extinction of "lesser" supernatural beings they considered a threat to mankind. So why the Hades were there Midnights who cared more about the kind of puppy their fiancée might like than whether their Head of Coven had gone missing?

"Caia?" Lucien reiterated.

She shook away the trace at the sound of Lucien's panic.

"I'm okay," she reassured him.

"You look upset."

Should she tell Lucien what she suspected?

Her eyes drank in his concern, her whole body warming over his distress for her. Lucien was a big believer in "Midnights bad, Daylights good." He would think she was crazy or reading the trace incorrectly. No. For now, she'd keep quiet, and Lucien would keep smiling at her.

"Just nerves again."

He snorted and shook his head. "I don't know what you're nervous about. You're like a god to these people. I, on the other hand, am the Alpha whose pack you chose over the Center."

Caia laughed. "Yeah, I forgot about that. Hey, maybe *you* should be nervous."

"Nice. Thanks."

"Ooh, look, your loogie coffee is coming."

"You're cute, you know that? I think if you continue to be this cute, I'm going to leave you here to go out on a date with Melissa yourself tonight. I'll send a postcard from the Center."

"You can't go through the portal without me."

His answering look would have frozen water. "How much do muzzles cost these days?"

* * *

HE COULDN'T HAVE BEEN MORE relieved than when they finally pulled into the lot of Magic Fitness. The day spent in close quarters with Caia had been harder than he'd imagined. Lucien glanced at her as he parked. She was smiling nervously back at him, her long, pale hair pulled away from her face making her catlike green eyes seem larger and more vulnerable.

She should have been his.

41

He shook off the aggravating thought that settled a heavy rock on top of his heart. He was acting like a whipped pup.

"Ready?" he managed.

"Sure." Caia nodded and climbed out of his truck.

They walked in silence into the gym, and he had to stop himself from taking her hand. Her anxiety was oozing out of her pores, and he had a feeling there was more to it than just the Center. Sometimes he thought it might be because of him, but she had gotten good at hiding her feelings. As far as he was aware, she didn't see him as anything more than a friend and her Pack Leader.

So what in Hades was up with her? He was the one who should be nervous, as Caia led them through the gym to studio number three. No one approached them, despite how inconspicuous a huge, dark-haired guy and his tiny gorgeous blond companion were.

This was it. This was where he might lose whatever hold he had on Caia.

"We're here," she said, reaching to grab the gold door handle under the sign that said *Out of Order*.

"Yeah." He took a deep breath, running his hand through his hair, readying himself. Her green eyes met his. *Should I?* she seemed to ask. His answer was a brief, stoic nod.

This was about more than them. That had been their problem from the start.

The door swung open and he followed as Caia tentatively entered the barren space. The mirrors were attached to the back wall just as Marion had said they would be. Lucien shut the door behind them and walked as quietly as he could to where Caia now stood facing the first pane of mirror.

She blew air out between her lips. "This is it."

"Yeah."

"Take my hand."

He reached for her and they clasped hands, and slowly,

as if moving in slow motion, she reached a slender arm out toward the pane. He saw her hand tremble, and he squeezed the one enfolded in his own. That seemed to spur her into action, and she laid her open palm against the mirror.

The atmosphere in the room charged and the air pressure changed; it felt like they had climbed too high. The floor-boards creaked and shifted, and Lucien grabbed tighter on to Caia. And then his eyes widened in amazement as the mirror turned to liquid under Caia's touch, her entire hand sinking through the mercury mass. She looked back up at him, smiling in astonishment and excitement, her nerves seeming to have disappeared.

"Are you ready?" She grinned, the dimple in her cheek flashing invitingly.

How could he say no?

He smiled back at her. "After you."

It felt like cold gel sliding and clinging to his skin as he walked through the pane. He could no longer see Caia. There was only darkness, but he could feel her hand still clasped warmly in his. The gel-like feeling disappeared, and as he kept walking, the darkness dissipated to white light. He stopped, blinking as the light glared brighter, bringing his arm up to shield his eyes from the intrusion.

"Lucien," he heard Caia whisper.

Cautiously he brought his arm back down and blinked open his eyes.

Whoa.

They stood in an enormous space. In front of them were a couple of security gates and three guards. It wasn't hard to guess they were warlocks trained in defensive magik. Beyond the gates was a huge reception area—there was even a cute receptionist behind the circular desk. And behind the desk to the right of the foyer were floor-to-ceiling windows that curved along the right side of the building instead of steel and brick.

"Oh my ...," Caia said, and Lucien echoed the sentiment as he realized they were looking out on to water, and beyond that a beautiful cityscape. And towering behind the bridges and stunning architecture was the top of the Eiffel Tower.

"You made it."

They both turned to see Marion, grinning like a child as she sidestepped the security gates.

"Paris?" Caia shook her head in amazement.

Lucien watched as her mentor smiled smugly. "The River Seine, to be exact."

"Wait." His stunned gaze flew to the windows. "We're *on* the River Seine?"

Marion chuckled. "Compliments of two of our finest magiks. An earth and air magik worked together to create the Center in another plane that exists within Paris. We can see them." She pointed to the outside world. "But they can't see us."

"Wow."

Lucien nodded. "You said it."

"I'm so glad you made it." Marion grabbed hold of Caia's elbow and escorted her through the reception. "First things first, introduce you to Marita and Vanne, and then show you to your rooms. And then in the morning, I'm going to introduce you to another water magik I picked out for you, Mordecai. He shows amazing promise. Mordecai will show you around the classes I want you to take part in while you're here. Communication spells, martial arts, water element lectures, glamour class, natural materialization ... Oh, and we have altars to all the individual gods here. I'm sure you would like to see Artemis's and Gaia's. Oooh, maybe ..."

Lucien trailed at the back, drinking in their modern yet rich surroundings, taking in all the excitement Marion had planned for Caia. He smiled as Caia glanced back at him, her eyes wide with the exhilaration of being somewhere she could really try out her magik. With that quick glance, she turned back to listen to Marion, leaving Lucien behind.

And that was exactly what he was afraid of.

plunged her Caia. She smiled as Caia glanced back at him, her eyes wide with the realization of being somewhere she could really ... [illegible] With that quick glance, she turned back to listen to Marion, leaving Lucien behind. And that was exactly what Lucien intended to ...

CHAPTER 5

Sizing Up

$\mathcal{T}$he witch and warlock that stood before her were not exactly what she'd been expecting.

Throughout Marion's chatter, Caia had been completely aware of her and Lucien's surroundings as they entered a large elevator near the rear of the massive reception area. The back wall held three elevators, and Marion led them to the middle one that needed a security code to open it.

As soon as the doors glided smoothly apart, Caia could see why. She was guessing this was the "presidential elevator," clad in mahogany and gold, sparkling-clean mirrors reflecting three of each of them. Marion explained that this was the only elevator to the Head of the Coven's suite.

When the elevator stopped and the doors opened, Caia's eyes widened. Before them stretched a long, wide corridor, decorated richly in butter creams and gold. The carpet felt like clouds beneath their feet, and here and there sat pieces of Louis XIV furniture and rich, dark oil paintings favoring the Italian Renaissance. More surprising, however, was the lack of doors, except for the large double doors at the very end of the long corridor. Furthermore, ten magiks stood vigilant guard, five against either wall, dotted along the hallway in exact formation.

Those colossal double doors, which would not have looked out of place at the Palace of Versailles, had swung open to reveal a breathtaking room furnished with eclectic taste. But it was neither the furniture nor the decoration that caught Caia's eyes this time. It was the magiks in front of her.

"Caia Ribeiro." Marita gave a tight smile, nodded at her before shifting her attention to Lucien. "Lucien Líder."

Caia gulped and looked up at her Alpha whose eyes were narrowed on the couple. Was she supposed to curtsey? Lucien was doing his usual, calculating their characters, judging how to respond. The brief nod he gave revealed that whether he liked them or not, Lucien would respect the Head of the Coven and her "mate."

Marita was very like her sister. She was as small and fragile looking as Marion, as elegant, her hair as fiery red. But where there was gentle warmth in Marion's features, Marita seemed sculpted in ice. Her eyes were tight and sharp, her jaw tense, her hands clasped rigidly in front of her. Vanne, on the other hand, was almost as tall as Lucien, except leaner and wiry. Seeming far more relaxed than his wife, Vanne stood, smiling widely at Caia. He didn't leer at her, she was sure of that—but he did seem to find her extraordinarily fascinating, as if he was waiting for her to do something unexpected.

"I'm glad we have this opportunity to meet," Marita said, walking gracefully toward them. She took Caia's hand in her own and shook it quickly and soberly. "Please, have a seat."

"Thank you," Caia managed. With a subtle nod from

Lucien, she followed Marita and Vanne farther into the room. She and Lucien sat on a Louis XIV sofa facing the Head of the Coven who perched primly across from them in a matching chair. Vanne lazed back in a leather La-Z-Boy that was so out of place and stared, entirely relaxed, at the fire blazing brightly in the massive, ornate fireplace to their right.

Caia knew she must look like the biggest dolt, her eyes wide as she took in the rich surroundings. Her gaze fell on Marion, who took a seat away from the small gathering at the fireplace. She smiled at Caia in reassurance.

"Well," Marita began, her ocean-blue gaze fixed like granite on Caia, "Marion has filled me in on your reports about the Midnights. However, I would like you to reiterate for me this Pierre du Bois's plans for the MacLachlans."

Caia nodded, feeling the butterflies dissipate a little now that she had some control in the situation. "In three weeks' time, Sunday the fourth to be exact, Pierre and a few of his agents intend to ambush the MacLachlans during one of their pack runs. He was investigating best possible attack strategies, and then he learned that, like us, the MacLachlans have organized pack runs every month. They drive out to Remnant Forest, the woodlands that border the city to the east. According to Pierre's agents, the MacLachlans have employed a magik to mask their activities on public property?" she queried, having never realized such business went on.

Vanne grinned at her. "Some of us are extremely enterprising. We like to think on the whole that the Daylights are a tight group. We work well with each other regardless of race. And yes ... we are aware that one of our magiks is employed by the MacLachlans. Seems only fair, considering the MacLachlans have been providing the coven with excellent Rogue Hunters for many generations. One of the finest currently, in fact, Phoebe MacLachlan."

"A female hunter?" It was Caia's turn to grin excitedly.

He chuckled. "There are a few. We're not as backward as you may think, Caia."

"Having lived among humans for so long without any supernatural influence other than one measly lykan"— Marita smirked and Caia bristled at the condescension she sensed in her tone—"it's only natural that you would think human females have more rights than supernatural females—"

"Lykans in particular," Vanne teased, grinning at Lucien. Caia felt him tense beside her.

"Hmm, well, no matter the race, we are aware your opinions may be unduly influenced by your upbringing, but I assure you, the Daylight Coven has much to offer. Why, I'm a woman. One could surely say I'm one of the most powerful supernaturals today. A very bright future awaits you here."

Okay, so how did her detailing the MacLachlans' plans suddenly detour into a sales pitch? She wanted to laugh. They had jumped on her surprise and delight at there being a female Rogue Hunter because they thought she was being oppressed by Lucien? And suddenly their sales pitch turned into some feminist bull?

She managed to keep the smirk off her face as she leaned closer to Lucien to reassure him.

"As I was saying," she managed diplomatically, "Pierre will ambush the pack in Remnant Forest with ten magiks, guard the place with four, and he'll have five spies watching the MacLachlans. Together they live on five streets in town. So we're looking at nineteen magiks."

Marita frowned. "That's an impressive arsenal."

"I'd say overkill." Caia nodded.

"It also means Pierre has the beginnings of quite a rebellion," Lucien added, his voice husky from concealed anger.

Marita nodded in agreement and then snapped her fingers so abruptly, Caia flinched. A magik appeared almost instantly beside the Head, a tall, hulking figure of a man whose face held no expression.

"Noble, I assume Ms. Ribeiro's and Mr. Líder's rooms are in order?"

"Yes, madam."

She turned back to them. "Noble will show you to your rooms. Get some sleep. Tomorrow, after Mordecai and Marion have shown Caia around the Center's facilities, I want the two of you to reconvene here at five o'clock to discuss our plan of action. Lucien, I thought you might be interested in our Second Unit."

His brows creased in confusion, as did Caia's. What on earth was their Second Unit?

"Lykans." Vanne grinned.

"Yes, quite. Our Second Unit are our infantry of lykans. I'll have a representative sent around to your room tomorrow morning."

Lucien nodded politely.

"One more thing before you retire for the evening, Caia."

It was said pleasantly, yet an unexpected chill shot through her.

"Yes?"

Marita's frozen smile melted into a grimace. "You should be aware that despite my sister's championing of you, and her utmost belief in your sincerity and trustworthiness, not all of Daylight is inclined to believe her."

"What does that mean?" Lucien's tone had bite.

She cast him a withering look. "It means, Mr. Líder, that some of my people are uneasy around someone of Midnight blood."

"Daylight blood as well," he reminded her through

clenched teeth.

Caia felt those nervous butterflies returning as Marita shrugged. "Perhaps if she had come to the Center as a permanent resident, everyone would have been able to look past the fact that her mother was a treacherous Midnight whore who killed many Daylights, including your father and her own."

"Marita ..." Marion stood, her expression pained.

Her sister merely raised her hand, the polite mask falling back into place upon her marble face. "I don't mean to be cruel." Her eyes turned to Caia whose own were bleak with uncertainty. She felt Lucien's tension beside her and was reminded once again of all the differences that stood between them, of how much he had been there for her despite that.

"If I can get past it, so can they." Lucien's voice rumbled around the room. He moved closer to Caia, his arm brushing against hers. The butterflies abated, and she turned to look at him in gratitude.

"One can only hope they will." Marita drew her attention back to her. "However, I would encourage you, Caia, to think about staying longer than this business with the MacLachlans. It would go a long way in securing you the right allies."

She plastered on an equally polite smile. "I thank you for the advice, Marita, but I hope my very *temporary* visit to the Center will be enough to show the people here whose side I'm on. I'd have hoped killing my own uncle would have incurred some kind of faith, but ultimately rescuing a pack of strangers will just have to do the trick."

Lucien didn't disguise his amusement, and neither did Vanne. Marion was the only one who tried to hold on to a straight face as Marita narrowed her eyes first at her husband and then Caia.

"You might do well here after all."

Caia raised an eyebrow in surprise at the grudging respect she found in the magik's eyes.

"We'll see, though."

"These people who might take issue with me being here, does that include the Council?" Caia asked.

Marita smiled. "The Council does not reside here on a permanent basis. They only convene on their schedule, or for emergencies."

It wasn't exactly an answer. Marion had taught her a lot over the last few months, including some pretty in-depth history lessons. Like the Midnights, the Daylights had an appointed council, which included members of the more influential families within the coven. Their existence was a precaution—an acting body of control that disavowed the idea of an autocracy, even though Marita had complete autonomy as long as her methods were morally correct, as well as providing the coven with adequate protection and defense.

Caia had learned from Marion that three hundred years ago, Marion and Marita's great-grandmother had taken a stand against the Head, a tyrannical warlock whom she discovered was plotting to overthrow the Council and take complete power for himself. She went to the Council with this information—a difficult task, considering she'd had to hide her intentions from him in her trace—and asked to be put forward as a candidate for Head of the Coven.

Usually, this would've led to a political campaign wherein the Daylights would be allowed to vote for whomever they wanted to lead. The loser was killed so they could ask Gaia to imbue the winner with trace power. In Marion's great-grandmother's case, the Council had been so horrified by her discoveries, they'd had the Head killed immediately, and placed her in power. Their family had been ruling ever since.

So far, the Council was very happy with Marita.

"But do they take issue with Caia?" Lucien persisted.

Reluctantly, Marita shook her head. "They are impressed by your service to the coven and interested to see what you are capable of in the future."

Satisfaction washed through Caia, and she shared a relieved look with Lucien.

Marita harrumphed again, and with that, they were ushered out of the room behind an impassive Noble. They followed him back to the elevator, which then led them down to floor five where they were deposited on another elevator that took them back up to floor twenty-three.

It was like something out of a sci-fi movie. Everything was white. White tiled floors, white walls, white doors, and florescent lighting that made all the white blinding.

"Have we been abducted by the Third Kind?" Lucien cracked. Caia chuckled and then choked on her laughter at Noble's severe glare.

"These are the candidate floors. We prefer to keep everything clean, simple, and equal amongst the candidates."

Caia frowned in confusion. "I'm sorry, what are the candidates?"

Noble sighed as if he were speaking to a dumbass and growing rapidly impatient with it. "The candidates are those Daylights in training."

Lucien twisted his mouth sarcastically. "Recruits."

"No." Noble looked as if he'd eaten something rotten. "We prefer the term *candidate*. *Recruit* sounds so aggressive."

Caia smirked at Lucien. "Let me guess—that was Marita's idea?"

"Yes."

They grinned at each other behind the pompous facto-tum's back as he led them past door after door. Finally, he stopped at one with the number 48 on it and handed a swipe card to Lucien.

"Your room, sir. Marita has taken the liberty of securing a spell within the key cards of non-magiks, so that their fellow magik students can't invade their privacy with a spell of their own."

Lucien took the tiny piece of card in his hand, puzzling over it. "Gee, thanks."

"Am I next door?" Caia was curious as to what the rooms looked like on the other side.

"No. We will be taking *that* elevator." He pointed to a white elevator a few meters down the hallway.

"Another elevator?"

"Why?" Lucien frowned again, tensing, and he straightened to his optimum height.

"I've been instructed to put the young lady in one of the guest suites."

"But Lucien's a guest."

"Caia, don't—"

"No! You're not a candidate." She turned to glare at Noble. "By the way, sounds like he's entering into an asylum for the disturbed."

Noble sneered. "I'll be sure to pass along your compliments to Madam."

No. Caia's heart thumped angrily. They were not going to treat Lucien like some C-list recruit while they pandered to her, just because they wanted something from her. And she needed Lucien close by. This was all so weird, so fast; she needed his strength beside her.

"Yeah, well, while you're at it, ask *Madam* to arrange a guest suite for Lucien in close location to mine."

He frowned. "Together, you mean?"

Caia flushed. "No, not together. Next to one another."

Lucien was beginning to look seriously pissed off. "Caia, you don't—"

"It's not for you, it's for me, so swallow it or choke on it."

His eyes twinkled back at her as he gave a stoic nod in obeisance.

"One moment." Noble turned from them, pressing something behind his earlobe. "Get me Marita," he grumbled at someone, and it was then she realized he was wearing a small, flesh-colored earpiece and a security headset of some ultra-mod-tech kind.

Expensive.

Her eyes flashed to Lucien and he seemed to understand; his own eyebrows rose in speculation. It was certainly some operation they had running here.

"Madam, our honored guest requests a redress of the accommodation situation for her Alpha."

He was nodding to whatever reply he was receiving. "Hmm, yes, well, she would like him situated in a guest suite near her own."

Silence.

"Yes, madam. Of course."

Noble pressed behind his lobe again and turned to them with a false smile. "The key card, sir?"

Lucien handed it back, and Caia smiled smugly. "To our rooms, Jeeves."

* * *

HER GUEST ROOM WAS UNBELIEVABLE. It was decked out in the plush Louis XIV décor that Marita seemed to favor. Huge canopied bed in the Center of the room, large roaring fire at the opposite end, a massive, marble-tiled en suite, and an insane walk-in closet. And to top it off, the east-facing side of the room was part of the curved glass window that looked out over the river and Paris.

Its beauty was enough to make this trip worthwhile.

And right next door was Lucien. The object of her near-constant thoughts. She'd been excited when Marion had explained about the classes she could inspect while here. But Marita's warning that not everyone would welcome her had really brought home how much Lucien had done for her.

And of the one thing she hadn't done for him.

"Hey." He looked surprised to see her on the other side of his door. "You okay?"

"I need to talk to you."

Lucien nodded and stepped aside to let her into a room that was much more masculine. It looked like Vanne had gotten his way here with the style.

"If it's about the room ... thanks," he said, shutting the door behind her and following her in, watching as she took a seat at the fireplace. "I have no doubt that this is far more comfortable than a candidate's room."

Caia laughed at the mocking look he gave her. "Do you think it was a test to see if I understood my position here?"

"What ... you're pulling power?" He smirked, sitting across from her, relaxing his big body into the leather sofa. "I have no doubt *Madam* has been testing your intelligence and mettle since you arrived."

Caia looked nervously at her hands. Coming to the Center was a mistake. Marion may have some kind of mother-figure faith in her, but Marita was going to expose her for the fraud she was afraid she was. Feeling traces of *good* Midnights? Was she crazy?

"Hey, you're gonna blow her away," he reassured gently, his voice sending a soothing hand down her back. "You're more than a match for her."

She smiled, hoping her feelings weren't so obvious in her eyes. "Thank you. But believe it or not, I didn't interrupt your rest for a confidence boost. I'm not quite that selfish ... yet." She chuckled nervously, sucking in some dust and then spluttering and coughing.

Oh goddess, she was the queen of un-cool.

"Caia." Lucien sounded like he was choking on laughter as he moved beside her, patting her on the back more roughly than necessary.

"I'm okay." She held up a hand, eyes watering more from his help than the coughing.

"Can I get you some water?"

"No," she croaked. Then she looked up at him and realized how close he was, the heat from his body stroking her skin, his silver eyes curious and concerned, inches away from her. "I came to apologize."

A wrinkle appeared between his brows. "Apologize?"

She took in a shuddering breath, her eyes falling to her hands again. "I never apologized for what … for what my mother did to you … to your father … to your family …"

"Cy—"

"No, let me say this. She did all those horrible things, and when I found out the truth, the first thing you said was that you were sorry. You didn't have to do that. She deserved what she got. But *I* never apologized properly. More than that, I never thanked you for supporting me without question. I *am* part Midnight and you refused to judge me for that. Thank you."

"Caia!" Lucien grabbed her chin, jerking her eyes up to meet his own. He looked angry and sad … and frustrated. "You have nothing to apologize for. You. Are. Not. Your mother."

A tear slid down her cheek, and he caught it with his thumb, rubbing the salty liquid into her skin.

"Do you really believe that?"

His eyes widened in disbelief. "Of course. Caia …"

"I'm scared, Lucien," she whispered.

He gruffly pulled her into his arms and she sighed, inhaling him, clinging to him like a liferaft.

"You're not her. They will see that. You have to know that."

Thoughts of those Midnight traces she'd been feeling trickled toward her tongue. She needed to tell someone. Maybe Lucien *would* understand. Maybe it was a mistake. Maybe ...

"There's something I—"

Tap tap tap.

Lucien groaned. "Sorry, that'll be room service."

Caia pulled back, grinning tremulously. "You ordered food already?"

He grinned wolfishly back. "Of course. We haven't eaten in—"

"Three hours."

He laughed and got up to open the door. "Bring it on in, thank you." He stood aside as a guy in a waiter's uniform pushed a trolley of food into the room. The guy nodded and left quickly.

"You're unbelievable." Caia chuckled, watching him lift dish after dish to inhale the aromas. Her own stomach ached in protest.

"Hey." He grinned again, almost licking his lips. "Thought I'd cash in on your powerful pull with these people and get me a proper meal before prep work tomorrow. I'll need all the sustenance I can get if we're gonna kick some evil Midnight ass."

Caia's face fell. Well, there went that window.

"You wanna join?"

"Uh, no." She shook her head and made for the door. "I'm tired."

"Okay. Hey." He frowned. "Didn't you have something to tell me?"

She locked on to his concerned gaze and wished she'd told him. But her previous instinct had been right. Hating

Midnights was too ingrained in a Daylight to make what she had to say understandable.

And Marita was right. She needed all the allies she could get.

"No, not really. Night."

"Night."

* * *

"You're late," he reproached, watching beneath his lidded eyes as the large man walked sedately into the room.

"I had a few issues to deal with before coming here," the distinguished magik said in his heavy accent before brushing off a chair and easing into it. He straightened the lapels on his long wool coat before crossing one leg over the other in a gesture that was at once elegant and masculine.

"I have people to get back to. I don't have the luxury of your abilities, remember."

"Be quick with your news, then, by all means."

"My contact tells me you have a problem, Nikolai."

Nikolai chuckled, lifting his hands in a gesture of disbelief. "I would really like to know how you ... have contacts within my coven."

"I'm very old, Nikolai. I have had many years to garner enough knowledge with which to blackmail people."

"Of course."

"My contact told me your problem goes by the name Pierre du Bois."

Nikolai stiffened. "What is du Bois up to now?"

"You know him?"

"Da. He is a thorn to say the least. What is he up to?"

"My contact doesn't know the details."

"You believe your contact?"

"Yes. Let's just say he has no pain threshold."

"You must watch your methods. If we want our plan to work, we must project a certain image."

He nodded. "Believe me, I know. Don't worry about me. You better find out what du Bois is up to, Nikolai."

"I have every intention of doing so. If it's what I think he is up to, it will provide me the perfect opportunity to have him … misplaced."

A silence settled upon the room. Then …

"And the document—is it finished?"

Nikolai nodded gravely and stood. His large hand delved inside the wool coat and reappeared with an envelope. He pushed it across the desk separating them, the small diamond in the onyx pinkie ring winking in the dim light.

He opened the envelope, his hands almost shaking in anticipation. The paper inside was the beginning of the end. He was sure of it. He pulled it out and unfolded it slowly, his eyes widening at the information printed in Nikolai's scrawling penmanship.

"The Septum," he exhaled the words.

"Da."

"And we're sure this is correct?"

"Positive. We've been searching a long time. I would not have brought it merely based on assumption."

He nodded impatiently. "I know, I know. I just can't believe we're this close."

His heart thudded loudly in his chest. All they needed now was the girl. He needed to get back. His plans so far were not going as smoothly as he'd hoped, but it was time to take matters in hand. He needed the girl, and at present, he only had one avenue to her.

"Will we get her, you think?"

"Have no fear, Nikolai. Caia Ribeiro will be in our hands before the year is out."

CHAPTER 6

Why?

"*W*ell, ain't you a picture," Ryder boomed as Jaeden threw open her motel door, face pale, eyes squinting against the sun.

She sighed heavily, slipping a pair of dark sunglasses over her eyes. "You know, I've never noticed how annoyingly chipper you are. Have you always been so, or is this a recent development?"

He laughed as she pushed past him, heading across the lot to the motel bar and grill. "Not a morning person, huh?"

"Please be quiet."

He grinned behind her, enjoying her obvious irritation, and noticed by the stiffness in her body the likely effects of sleeping in the worst bed in the state.

Doing as requested, Ryder didn't direct any conversation at her until they were seated and had ordered. He waited until she finally took off the sunglasses before deciding to hit her with the question that had been bugging him for a while.

"Tell me ... why did you leave the pack in the first place?"

Her dark blue eyes narrowed, and her full lips thinned in discomfort at his directness. She glared.

"Hey, I'm just asking what everyone will be asking when we get home."

More glaring. Wait, was she snarling?

Ryder snorted and leaned across the table toward her. "Jae, you are going to have to talk about this at some point. Dimitri was going nuts while you were gone. He probably would have had a search party out scouring the country if Lucien hadn't given him a direct order to leave you alone."

He watched the surprise flit across her face, her mouth open in astonishment. It was fascinating, watching the way she wiped the expression clean and replaced her cool facade. And just when he thought he wasn't going to get a reaction ...

"Why would Lucien do that?"

Ryder smirked, smug (and a little relieved) that he still knew her enough to know she couldn't resist that bit of information. "Caia asked him to."

Jae frowned. "Wait ... why?"

Suddenly, the memory of her broken, of her young skin lashed and burned, her bright eyes blank and numb with torture, flooded his thoughts and sobered him. "Because after what happened to you, she thought you deserved the time you needed to yourself."

She looked down, shielding her eyes and thoughts from him. "That was ... kind."

"The girl you met for those, what, two weeks—you liked her, right?"

Still not looking at him, Jae nodded. "She was cool."

"Caia cares about you a great deal."

She frowned again, and he was caught in her curious gaze. "You respect her, don't you?"

Ryder chuckled. "Yeah. She's my friend ... actually, she's more like a sister."

"So you don't ..."

What was she trying to ask?

Laughter bubbled inside him as realization dawned, but he managed to contain it as he replied in a strangled voice, "Nah, I'll leave that particular privilege to her mate."

Sitting back in her seat, seeming more relaxed, Jaeden smiled at him. Ryder tried to ignore the sudden speed in his pulse.

"Yeah, what's up with that? Lucien doing what Caia tells him to do?"

The whole Lucien-and-Caia thing was mind-boggling to him. It was obvious they were crazy about each other, but neither one could see it, and neither one wanted to talk about it. He'd had his head bitten off enough times to shut up on the matter. Hopefully, they'd work it out before it really was too late, and someone did something they would regret.

"Cy's got Lucien wrapped around her little pinkie and vice versa."

"Before I left, I got the impression they were going to ignore their mating."

"Nothing's changed. They're still idiots."

Jaeden chuckled and sipped at her Coke. "I've missed the pack and all the drama."

"I would've thought breaking coven laws and hunting vampyres would have been enough drama."

"That was bad drama. The pack is good drama."

"So why did you leave?"

She went back to glaring at him. He enjoyed annoying her further by grinning at her.

Jae sighed. "You never give up, do you?"

"I'm tenacious. Persistent. Determined. Dogged—"

"You're like a rash that won't go away."

His smile widened, but he didn't have a chance to retort because their food arrived. The first few minutes of silence descended on their table while they dug in. Ryder decided to choose his moment carefully, waiting until a moan of pleasure escaped from Jaeden. Now that she had eaten, she might be more amenable to answering the damn question.

"Why did you leave?"

This time she watched him as she chewed carefully, swallowed, and sipped her drink. She was deliberately tormenting him, fully aware of his lack of patience.

"You really want to know?"

Finally.

He nodded, afraid he would say the wrong thing and lose the moment.

At first as she spoke, Jae held his stare, strong and steady. "After what happened, I was in too much pain to be comforted, and I knew my coldness would only hurt my family." She stopped and her gaze dropped. "I didn't know how to tell them all that had happened to me. I didn't want to hurt them any more with that knowledge. And I was just … a mess … I didn't want them to see me like that."

She refused to meet his eyes.

You're lying.

Oh, he was sure what she'd just revealed was partly the truth, but there was more. He could feel it. What was she hiding from him, from them all?

Ryder concealed his interest. She ate the rest of her food, seeming more relaxed, believing he had bought it.

Well, let her relax, he mused, *while I find out what the Hades she's been up to.*

* * *

Jae was feeling lighter. She didn't have any nightmares last night, no telekinesis kicking in. Ryder seemed to have bought her story and was no longer asking annoying and prying questions. In fact, the rest of breakfast had been fun. They talked and laughed, and he filled her in on what had been happening with the pack while she was gone. If the rest of the pack was this easy, perhaps her return would go smoother that she'd thought.

Ah, she couldn't wait to go on a run. Her body was screaming for the change.

"We'll be home soon enough and you can run as much as you like." Ryder smiled, walking closely by her side as they crossed the lot back to her motel room.

Goddess, she hadn't realized she'd said that out loud.

"My stuff's already in the truck. You got your bag together?"

"It's already packed." She unlocked the door and wrinkled her nose as she stepped inside the rank room. "I can't believe you made me sleep here."

Stepping farther in, a slight coppery smell tickled her nostrils, and she abruptly stopped.

"Oof." Ryder banged into her back, sending her stumbling forward.

She whirled to face him, her eyes narrowed in concentration. "Do you smell that?"

He puckered his brow, twirling his keys impatiently. "Don't smell a thing except urine, beer, and sex. Can we please go?"

She shook her head, unconvinced, eyes searching the room. "I smell … I dunno … something familiar."

"What's not familiar about urine, beer, and—"

She smirked at him as he flushed. "And?" she prompted, enjoying his discomfort.

"Just get your bag," Ryder muttered, turning away from her.

Jaeden laughed and turned toward her things, only to stop again. "Hey!"

"What?" Suddenly he was right at her back in defense mode.

Her T-shirt and jeans lay strewn across the ancient chair in the corner of the room, crumpled beside her now-open backpack.

"I could've sworn I packed this before we went for breakfast."

"Is that all?" he whined. "Goddess, Jae, I thought there was an *actual* problem, not some hormonal imbalance causing female memory loss."

"Hey!" She snapped around at him, glaring while she stuffed her things back into her bag. "I know you're more of a gentleman than that to talk chauvinistic crap to a lady, so stop trying to irritate the life out of me, Ryder, before I go crazy and end yours!"

He grinned, his golden-brown eyes glittering with humor. "Why would I stop when it's this much fun? Truly ..." He placed a hand on his chest. "You bring such joy to my life."

She was not going to laugh at him.

Or think about how lighthearted he made her feel.

How good.

No. *Down that road, there be complications.*

Instead she threw her backpack at him and strode past his laughing face. "You're funny," she said sarcastically. "The fact that you've been designated the pack golden retriever really doesn't seem to have dampened your spirits at all."

"Uh, hello," he called to her back, and she heard his pounding steps catching up to her as she neared the truck. "Retrieving you, and saving you from imprisonment, was a very important job."

She turned back to him, smiling sweetly. "But hardly the job of a Rogue Hunter."

"I'm not a golden retriever."

"No? What's that bell around your neck?" She pointed innocently to his throat.

He grimaced glancing down, which sent her into hysterics.

"You looked! You actually looked! I can't believe that—"

"Get in the truck," he growled and stomped around to the driver's side.

She chuckled happily, jumping into the cab and twisting to face him as she buckled herself in. "What's the matter, Ryder? Can't take a little teasing?"

He snorted and glanced up at her from under his enviously long lashes. "Oh baby, I can take a little teasing. But you just made this a war."

She chuckled. This *was* going to be a looong drive home.

But at least he would be too distracted to ask any uncomfortable questions along the way.

* * *

WELL, *well*, *well*, Marcus thought, watching as the lykan climbed into the truck with her mate. This was turning out better than he'd thought. Marcus had tailed the tall female wolf from the city, following the scent he'd found at his dead girlfriend's body before the sun destroyed any evidence of Cora's existence.

He'd thought to capture the lykan, torture her—perhaps even show her how a man of his species showed a female a good time.

But this was better.

Much better.

The lykan took his female ...

Before Marcus killed her, he'd just have to kill her mate and make her watch while he did it.

And there was no doubt in his mind that the brawny male lykan escorting her out of the motel room was her mate.

He waited five minutes before jumping into his car and following their exit. He'd refreshed himself with the female's scent by breaking into their room and sniffing her clothes. He'd be able to tail them until their next stop ...

And then he'd make his move.

CHAPTER 7

New Friends, Old Acquaintances

Caia was in awe. The fact that some of the students in the huge hall were clearly uncomfortable with her presence didn't dispel how excited she was to be watching young magiks and faeries learn communication training from their elders. She could feel Marion beaming beside her, Caia's apparent enthusiasm rubbing off on the older magik.

"Have you watched enough, Caia?" Mordecai smiled. "You want to try?"

That morning, she'd opened her guest room door to Marion, a perkier Marion than Caia had ever encountered—eager, Caia was beginning to realize, to show off her protégé. Apparently Lucien had already gone with his escort to check out the Second Unit. At first she felt a little anxious about being separated from him, but now she was too caught up in the activities of the Center.

Their first stop was to pick up their "tour guide," Mordecai. A stocky, bookish magik in his late twenties, he had kind eyes and an easy smile. From his warm reception, Caia was guessing Marion had not only picked him as her escort because he was a powerful water magik but because he obviously didn't care that Caia's mother had been a Midnight.

She beamed like a little girl. "Can I? I mean, I wouldn't know where to start."

He chuckled, enjoying her keenness as much as Marion was. "Well, we'll keep it simple. You haven't seen much of the Center, so the farthest we can allow you to travel is from here to your guest suite."

Butterflies awoke in her stomach, churning her breakfast. "Wow. I want to, you know, but ... those guys make it look easy. I'm guessing dematerializing and rematerializing isn't exactly popcorn?" She drank in the bright room, watching as magiks and faeries popped in and out at the quiet instructions of their teachers. As if sensing she was about to attempt the spell, some of them stopped what they were doing, along with their instructors, to stare at her. She could make out what the closer ones were whispering to one another.

"She doesn't look like much. What is everyone afraid of?"

"I can't believe they let her in here. What if she's a spy?"

"I heard she eviscerated her uncle without any remorse. Apparently she was smiling while she did it. Ugh."

"I think we should give her a chance. If Marion says she's trustworthy, then she's trustworthy."

Caia drew in a shuddering breath, finding solace in Marion's face.

"I don't know what you're hearing with those ears of yours, but block them out, Caia." Marion smiled gently. "Mordecai will talk you through this."

"But they're all watching."

"Yes. So? Just forget them. And remember, it can take many, many attempts to pull off your first travel. No one here"—she sneered around the room, as if sensing their disapproval of her for bringing Caia—"has ever done it their first time."

Exhaling, Caia turned to Mordecai who smiled reassuringly. "Let's give it a go."

He brushed his thick locks off his forehead and pushed his glasses farther up his nose. "Now, Marion has explained that you can differentiate with ease the two energies that make up your lykan and your magik. Is that correct?"

"Yes."

"Okay. The tricky thing for you in a communication spell is the other energy bobbing in the background. For any other use of your magik, you tap into the energy and expel it from whichever part of your body you want ... usually your hands. But to travel, you need to grab hold of that energy and wrap it around your body's system—cells, muscles, bones, everything, everywhere. You'll know when you've done it, believe me. It's hard to explain, but you will.

"Thing is, though, it takes a lot of concentration, and at first a lot of time to go through the process. *You* have the added complication of having your lykanthrope energy. What we need you to do is wrap your magik around that energy without merging the two energies together."

Caia blinked, her pulse picking up speed. "What happens if they merge?"

Mordecai glanced briefly at Marion and then back to her. "We don't know. We just don't want to take that chance. We need you to treat that energy as carefully as you would an artery. Wrap around it, but don't rupture it."

"You don't have to do this, Caia," Marion assured quietly.

She felt the stares of the trainees burning her cheeks and willed her heart to slow down. There was no way she was going to fail in front of these people. That was exactly what they wanted. And if she was going to make a difference in this war, she was going to need to prove herself to the Daylights firsthand.

"No. I'm doing this."

Mordecai grinned. "Good. Now close your eyes ... and do as I ask."

Quickly and easily, Caia grabbed hold of the steely vapor that was her magik energy and completely disengaged from the heat that allowed her to change into a wolf. Now for the hard part: she was to wrap the energy around every molecule of her being ...

Ohhhkkaaaay.

She started with her toes, and Mordecai was right. She knew when a part of her body was complete in the process. She followed it through until her very hair tingled with energy.

"Done," she said and was surprised to hear a flurry of whispering.

"Uh ..." Mordecai seemed to hesitate. Her eyes flew open, and he stared at her, incredulous. Marion smiled, almost smugly. "Caia, are you sure?"

She nodded, holding on tight to her transformation. "Yeah, you said I would know, you were right. It's a weird kind of certainty."

"But you did that in seconds?" He gaped like a fish.

She frowned. "Is that wrong?"

Marion chuckled. "It usually takes a lot longer the first few times. You've done it like you've been doing it for years."

Oh. Well, that was good, right?

Mordecai gulped. "I see what you've been talking about, Marion."

"What?" Caia asked, looking between the two.

"Uh, Caia, now for the next part." Mordecai seemed even more excited to move along. "I want you to visualize your guest suite. Think of a suitable spot you can materialize, and go there. But … you have to have an extremely clear vision in mind."

She closed her eyes and imagined a spot on the thick beige carpet that felt like clouds beneath her bare feet, a spot in front of the chaise longue placed at the end of the opulent bed. Yeah, there was plenty of room to crash-land there.

"Okay."

"You're sure?"

"Pretty much."

"Now tighten your hold on your energy and picture yourself in that spot. Move yourself into that spot with your mind."

She did as he asked.

"Okay. Now what?"

She was met by silence.

"Guys?"

Wait. The floor had gotten squishy beneath her feet. And was that lavender air freshener?

Her eyes flew open, and she stumbled back, gasping. Holy moly, she was in her suite. She did it! She did it!

"Aaaahhh!" She laughed, jumping up and down like a little kid. She had freakin' done it on her first go! She grinned at the city. "Take that, Daylight snobs!"

Her face was about to crack under the pressure of that grin, her adrenaline shooting through her whole body, sending her into shaky excitement. She had to calm down … it was time for the finale.

Following Mordecai's instructions, she visualized her place back in the hall, and suddenly a flurry of excitement hit her ears.

"Caia!"

Her eyes opened to Mordecai staring in stunned amazement. Marion rushed forward to grip her arms, laughing.

Caia looked around. All the trainees babbled excitedly, their eyes on her, their bodies moving closer.

"You did it! I knew you could do it!" Marion squealed like a little girl, her usual cool abandoned.

"I've never ..." Mordecai took off his glasses to rub off a nonexistent smudge. "Wow." His eyes flitted between her and Marion before a huge grin broke out on his face. "This is going to be fun. I want to see what she can do with natural materialization."

* * *

LUCIEN WAS HAVING A BLAST.

That morning he'd awoken early to a banging on his door by a lykan around his age with an attitude and bad hair. Julian was a pain in the ass, and Lucien had a feeling he'd been given to him specifically because he was a pain in the ass. He made deliberately malicious comments about the pack, about Caia, anything to try to make Lucien lose his temper. If only he knew that the transparency of his attempts merely irritated rather than angered. He was like a puppy, nipping in frustration because you won't play back.

However, the Second Unit? Now *that* was fun.

The Center had set up a simulator of a large woodland arena where the lykans could work out strategies in human form but execute them as wolves. The arena was amazing—the smells, the mud, the trees, the air, all of it as real as could be. And Lucien was getting to stretch his legs, battling sandbag dummies and holograms of Midnights. The sweat was thick in his fur, his muscles screamed, and his jaws ached from ripping apart so many faux Midnights. But Hades, it was a buzz. What a way to work out the frustration.

A piercing buzzer went off, signaling them to return to base point and change. He laughed at his disappointment and set off with the others. Unabashedly they changed, men and women alike, and pulled on their clothing.

A hand slapped down on Lucien's shoulder. "Gaia, you're quick!" Julian was grinning at him now, all contempt wiped from his face.

"Yeah, dude," one of the largest lykans in the unit said gruffly, his dark eyes glittering in respect. "I've never seen someone your size move so fluidly."

"What do you say, Lucien?" Anders, the unit's Alpha grinned at him. "Sure we can't convince you to become a permanent fixture around here?"

Lucien laughed, enjoying the camaraderie, and truthfully, he snorted, the boost to his ego.

"I'm too old to start now," he joked.

"No way." One of the female members, Lyla, ran her tongue across her bottom teeth flirtatiously. "You look in shape to me."

"I have a pack to run."

Julian sneered again. "You like being king of the mountain, huh?"

Lucien slapped *him* on the back. "Yeah, I do."

Anders and the others laughed. "Well, we've been pushing hard today. We really should get you a meal before your meeting tonight."

He nodded and followed them out of the simulator. Thoughts of their five o'clock with Marita and Vanne got him wondering how Caia's day had gone so far. It bugged him to be apart from her, especially not knowing how she'd been received by the others. Had they been cruel? Kind? Indifferent?

He stretched his neck, unfurling his fists from the tight balls he'd pulled them into. If she was harmed when he got her back tonight, he was going to crack some heads, regardless of being under the supervision of the Head of the Coven.

* * *

IT LOOKED like he had nothing to worry about. Caia greeted him outside his room with Marion, brimming over with excitement. Apparently his little Cy had awed everyone by picking up the communication spell on the first try.

Great.

Not only could she now slam a door in his face from a great distance, but she could actually disappear from his very arms within seconds. That certainly didn't even things out in a fight.

Ah, he knew he was being belligerent. And she looked so damn pleased with herself.

"Did you know that some magiks use words?"

"Ethan," he replied grimly.

He watched her blanch as she remembered the fight with her uncle, the spell Ethan cast under his breath to get out from the shield Caia had put around him to stop him from hurting Lucien and Jaeden.

"Right," she said hoarsely.

"Caia—"

"No, right, I forgot." She pretended to be unaffected and then grinned, though it was a little hollow. "Anyway, they use words to focus their magik. I haven't been doing it because I've been taught by Marion and she doesn't do it, but Mordecai has all these funny little words he uses when he's transforming something or materializing an object out of his element. It's very cool, very 'Warlock Weekly.'"

Lucien pasted on a smile to try to ease the unpleasant tension he'd caused and went on to tell them what he had been up to, once they finally let him get a word in.

"They have a simulator here?" Caia's eyes were bright with anticipation as they stepped out of the presidential elevator that took them to Marita and Vanne's suite.

"Yup. It's like the real thing."

"Do you think they'd let me use it? You know, to take a run in ... my bones are desperate to crack."

Marion laughed. "Ask, and I'm sure it's yours."

Yeah, Lucien mused, as they walked down the corridor, Caia certainly was getting the royal treatment here. He knew she was an important weapon for them, but this seemed above and beyond what they had expected.

It made him suspicious.

"Glad you're punctual." Marita's cold tones blew past him as they sauntered inside. He watched as her shrewd eyes nailed Caia to the wall. "I've been hearing interesting reports from today."

"Yes, very interesting." Vanne winked at Caia.

"Yes," Marita continued, "apparently, our guest is a natural at natural materialization. She produced a bird, an apple, and for her finale, a grand oak that nearly broke the windows. Oh, and let's not forget that she completed a communication spell on her first try."

"Impressive." Her husband nodded his head deferentially, and Lucien watched as Caia blushed.

Marita nodded, her eyes glittering strangely. "Of course, we all know that it really *is* impressive, but already gossip has reached me. Some of our occupants think Marion had already trained you on how to do a communication spell."

He felt a growl rumbling from his chest.

"It's okay," Caia whispered beside him, and as usual her perfect understanding of him settled that strange peace over him.

"Well, they're idiots," Marion snapped. "Mordecai was most impressed, and the others tend to fall in line with him."

Vanne smirked. "Yes, very well done in choosing Mordecai. Powerful, influential, and apparently has a thing for petite blonds who can blow his socks off."

Lucien's attention snapped to Caia. Had this Mordecai been flirting with her? The guy sounded a little awe-inspiring ... should he be worried?

Marion smiled. "I'm not stupid, Vanne. I knew this whole process was going to liken to a political campaign. I rallied the best."

Marita strode forward, gesturing to a dining table at the far end of the room that had been set up as battle plan central. "Yes, well, you are *my* sister. Take a seat, people."

"We also heard that Lucien performed well today," Vanne murmured as they congregated around. "Anders was very impressed."

His wife sniffed, eyeing Lucien narrowly. "Anders forgets that Lucien has taken down a few rogues in his time, as well as Adriana Vang, the heir to the Midnight Coven. If we are to go by how very shocked he was by your performance today, I would say he wasn't listening when I told him not to under-estimate you."

"That sounded like a begrudged compliment."

Marita huffed in amusement. "Oh, you are so very suspicious, aren't you, Lucien?"

She knew he wasn't sure of her, which meant he was giving far too much away. He had to rein in his natural compulsion to observe stonily and try harder to shield his feelings through her trace magik. He didn't want to seem calculating; if she really was up to something—and he was sure she was—then she would be too on edge to let the smallest thing slip.

"Vang?" Caia mumbled.

Marion placed a comforting hand on her shoulder. "Your family name."

Lucien watched worriedly as an emotion he couldn't identify flittered across her face. And then she was shaking herself, tensing under Marion's hand. "My family name is Ribeiro."

He ached for her then. She never allowed herself a moment to feel her mother's betrayal. Lucien smiled kindly. "And don't you forget it."

She turned and smiled up at him. "Did you know it means river—Ribeiro, I mean?"

"Of course."

"It's kind of ironic, don't you think?"

He chuckled. "I guess it is."

"Excuse me," Marita said imperiously. "Can we return to the matter at hand? We have a strategy to sort out."

"Let's get started, then."

"First, I'd like to introduce you to the operatives who will be helping us coordinate." She turned and gestured to Noble who in turn pulled open the door with a flourish. "First, Anders Rosencrantz, Alpha of our Second Unit, with whom Lucien is already acquainted."

Lucien nodded in acknowledgment to the older lykan who strode purposefully into the room, taking time to shake hands with Caia.

"And Mordecai Cherstvennikov, head of the First Unit, and the water magik who has been instructing Caia."

Lucien pulled in a breath and then quickly let it go as the stocky young man who looked to be about the same age as him walked stiffly into the room toward them. He shoved at the black glasses that slid down his nose and smiled tensely at Lucien, shaking his hand, and then grinned at Caia and Marion.

Well … that guy certainly didn't look how he sounded. But he and Caia looked awful chummy awful fast. Lucien resisted the urge to growl possessively.

"And Michael Brown, head of our Third Unit of vampyres." A tall, slender man who looked to be in his forties

—but was probably closer to a hundred years old—glided into the room and over to them. His sharp face remained stony as he shook everyone's hands.

Marita looked over them all. "I decided not to take any precautions in the defense of the MacLachlans, which is why I am enlisting the aid of every unit. The bonus is that Lucien and Caia will have an understanding of how all of you work individually, and as a team. However, we have two more operatives I would like to involve. I feel it is only right that the MacLachlans have a representative, and so I have asked Phoebe MacLachlan to join us."

They all turned and watched the gorgeous female sashay into the room. Lucien had heard reports of Phoebe from Ryder who said the Rogue Hunter looked like an angel, fought dirty like Hades, and had a heart of stone. It looked like he was right. She was tall and curvy with heaps of golden hair cascading over her shoulders, but her ice-blue eyes were hard and calculating as they drank in the team, her mouth twisted in what looked like scorn.

She shook hands with no one, just braced herself against the nearest wall, her gaze straight ahead at Marita.

"And Phoebe has requested we involve another lykan whom she trusts. Rose Bronson."

Lucien felt like he'd been sucker punched.

Rose. Rose was here?

Yup. There she was.

The statuesque redhead almost galloped into the room, and as soon as her brown eyes spotted him, she broke into a wide smile and launched herself at him. He instinctively caught her, although his mind was still in shock.

"Rose," he murmured, and she pulled back, her citrusy scent bringing with it a rush of memories.

He met Rose two years after he'd left the pack. She was a Rogue Hunter, and he stayed with her pack for three months.

Three months in which they'd engaged in a passionate affair before he had to break her heart by telling her he couldn't mate with her. He'd never been able to explain the reason, and she told him she would never forgive him. Her hatred over his betrayal had made it easier to walk away ... but it had taken him a long time to get over her.

"Lucien." She tenderly held his face between her hands. "I understand now," she whispered.

She knew about Caia, then.

Caia!

Lucien glanced down beside him to see how she was reacting, but her gaze was on the floor, her long hair hiding her expression.

He managed to put Rose at a physical distance without hurting her feelings; she just kept smiling at him and holding on to his arm.

"You two are acquainted?" Marita asked.

His head snapped up at her tone, and he knew ... he knew just looking at her eyes, slightly round with innocence, that she had done this on purpose.

Phoebe MacLachlan didn't know Rose Bronson; their packs were on different sides of the country. Marita had brought Rose here as a distraction.

He stilled the growl in his chest.

Whatever was going on here, he was going to get to the bottom of it.

CHAPTER 8

Consequences

*H*e couldn't remember when he'd had this much fun.

The daytime drive hadn't seemed so long with her beside him, cracking jokes, teasing him. Sparring with Jaeden had him strung out ... but in a good way.

Almost like foreplay.

He clenched his hand around the steering wheel at the thought, but there was no getting around the fact that he was extremely attracted to the now-senior Jae, with her gorgeous smile and caustic wit. The truth was, he wasn't known for sticking with one female, and he had a pretty colorful past as a player. Thoughts of having a respectable young female like Jaeden in his bed were enough to have her father kill him if he ever found out.

But the scary truth was ... he'd never been this comfortable—and this attracted—to a female in his life.

Could Jae be his mate?

His heart stopped.

Yeah, Dimitri was *so* going to kill him.

Ryder sighed heavily.

"You okay?" she asked. He could feel her curiosity. That much hadn't changed about her anyway—as curious as a cat.

He nodded, throwing her a weak smile. Yeah, he was cool. Just getting a little ahead of himself, that was all. For Gaia's sake, they hadn't even kissed yet. Not to mention the fact that he still didn't know what the Hades she was hiding, which brought him back to another dilemma. They were having such a good time together, and he didn't want to spoil it, but if he was going to consider "courting" Jaeden, then he needed to know everything there was to know about her.

He cleared his throat. "*So* ... question."

Not unexpectedly, Jaeden groaned. "Why, Ryder, why? We were having such a pleasant journey."

He chuckled and glanced at her, enjoying the cute way her nose wrinkled in distaste. "I'm curious, that's all."

"And you know what they say about curiosity."

"Good thing I'm a wolf and not a cat then, huh?"

She blew out a dramatic breath, asking in a beleaguered tone, "What's the question?"

"How on Gaia's green earth did you end up with a bunch of vampyres?"

"Oh."

Ryder grunted, turning his head from the road to see her expression. She looked caught off guard and ... embarrassed?

"Well, there's definitely a story to tell."

She frowned. "Watch the road."

"Are you going to answer the question?"

"Yeah, but dying won't get it out of me any faster."

"Okay, I'm watching the road!" he exclaimed, staring straight ahead.

Silence.

"Jaeden ..."

"Okay, okay. I ended up with vampyres because I met one on the bus who told me he ran with a group of hunters, and it would be a good way to work out my aggression."

"He?" Ryder did not like the sound of that.

"Reuben. He was cute and funny, and I think he's older than he lets on because he's very intuitive. He seemed to know there was something wrong with me before I even opened my mouth. He told me that maybe doing something as worthwhile as hunting down killers, and saving a few people, would help."

"This random guy approaches you and you just, what ... move in with him? I'm confused—I thought schools taught 'stranger danger' from kindergarten?"

"Reuben is a good guy," she replied defensively. "I didn't tell him all that much until we knew each other better, and even then, I didn't really explain the full scope of my *issues*." Her voice lowered. "He was a good friend to me. I feel bad about leaving without saying goodbye."

"Was that all he was? A friend?"

Oh Artemis, that's all he better have been.

"Yeah. He wanted more but ... to be honest, I wasn't even a very good friend to him, never mind anything else. It's weird."

"What?"

When she didn't say anything, he pinned an unrelenting narrow-eyed stare on her.

"The road!" She pointed at the windshield, unimpressed.

"Say what you were going to say."

"You know, Lucien and my dad are going to be so interested to hear that you threatened my life on this little retrieval of yours."

Ryder shrugged, even though he knew Dimitri would tear

him a new one if he learned of Ryder's interrogation of his only daughter.

"Fine," she snapped, and he reluctantly pulled his attention away from her and back to the road. "When I was staying with the gang, I didn't feel anything. I mean, I didn't allow myself to feel close to them, just as much as I didn't allow myself to feel anything about the pack. But ..."

"Yeah?"

"As soon as we left the city, give or take a few hours of your incessant, terrible singing, I had all these ... emotions. Guilt for not being a better friend to Styx, Reuben, all of them. And relief. To be going home."

He could tease about how that meant he'd somehow opened her up again, melted some of that ice she'd been building as a defense around herself, but he knew this was an important moment for her. She would hate him for teasing, belittling something that, in fact, made him more convinced they might be mates.

He was the truth she couldn't hide from.

It was kind of overwhelming ... but kind of nice.

"That sounds stupid, doesn't it?" She sounded so young and unsure.

Reaching out, he clasped her small hand in one of his own and watched with pleasure as she blushed at the intimate contact. "Not at all. It sounds just right."

She smiled shyly at him and got caught in his heated gaze. Abruptly, her eyes dropped, and she pulled away. "Watch the road."

Ryder laughed and indicated left, pulling into the motel he'd been driving toward. It was dark, he was hungry, and she was probably tired of being cooped up in the truck all day.

"We're stopping?"

"Yeah, let's get a couple of rooms and some food out of the vending machines."

"Oh goody, Ho-Hos and chips. You certainly know how to show a wolf a good time."

"Shut it, and get out."

They walked across the barely lit lot to the motel reception, and all the while, he surreptitiously watched her. He couldn't keep his eyes off her. How had this happened?

"Evening, folks," the young guy at the counter said without even looking up. "How can I help?"

"Two singles," Jaeden replied.

At the sound of her throaty voice, the guy looked up. His eyes widened along with his smile as he drank her in. "Uh ..."

"Two singles," Ryder echoed and watched with satisfaction as the kid took in his size and determinedly kept his eyes off Jae.

"Uh ... we have a slight plumbing issue at the moment. I have one room with two twins."

"That'll do."

"But—" Jaeden's mouth dropped open in protest.

Ryder sneered, "I'll try not to give you cooties."

She huffed at his side while he paid and grabbed the keys. He had to usher her across the lot to their room. It wasn't so bad. Yeah, it would suck being stuck in the same room with the object of his misguided desire, but he was a Rogue Hunter, for goddess' sake. He had taken down a pack of three rogues by himself. One little slip of a female couldn't be that bad.

She threw her bag on the bed nearest the bathroom. "This place is disgusting. You would think with the amount of money the pack has they could've financed the journey home."

"They did."

"And this was all it paid for?"

"What part of 'you broke a major coven law' translates into five-star hotels and room service?"

"So, this is punishment? This room ... with you?"

He grabbed his chest. "Baby, you gotta stop with the love, it's embarrassing."

"Funny."

"I try. Now, move your ass back out here ... the vending machines are across the lot."

She grumbled, but he had her back to laughing while they collected a small picnic from the machines and walked to the room. Later, he was going to blame his newfound infatuation for why he didn't pick up the disturbance in the air, the thick coppery smell that clung to the door of their motel.

Instead he stalked inside, looking back at Jaeden, laughing. The door crashed, closing them in, and he felt the cold press of metal against his temple. Jaeden gasped, seeing the presence he felt beside him in the dark with her wolf eyes.

"The light, please," a nasal voice rumbled in his ear.

Jaeden reached to the wall, and with a click, the room flooded with bad lighting.

He couldn't believe this. He couldn't effin' believe this! And he couldn't move ... there was no coming back from a close-range bullet to the head, even if he was a lykan.

Jaeden stood stock-still as her eyes drifted from Ryder to his captor.

"Vampyre," she said quietly for his benefit so he would know who had a hold of him.

"Yes," the voice sneered. "You stinking, lykan bitch."

Ryder bristled and immediately felt the gun press deeper into his temple. "What do you want?"

"To kill you. While she watches. And then kill her."

"How succinct." Jae's mouth twisted in distaste. "Can I inquire as to a motive?"

"Cora."

"I'm sorry, a what now?"

Ryder muffled his laughter. Goddess, she was something, wasn't she? Cool as a cucumber, even though she was probably petrified inside. He glanced around the room, looking for a suitable weapon against the vamp. There was the television set ... it could cause a distraction. If only he could communicate this to Jae with his eyes.

"Cora!" the vampyre yelled. "My girlfriend! My girlfriend for thirty years, until you came along and cut off her head!"

Jaeden shrugged casually. "I'm sorry, but I've cut the heads off quite a few bad teeth who slaughtered humans."

"Cora. She was blond. Beautiful. You left her to die in a cemetery a few days ago."

Ryder watched as recognition dawned in Jaeden's eyes. She remembered whoever it was the guy was spewing about.

"She murdered a human boy."

The gun pressed even harder to Ryder's head now. "Well, you took care of her for that, didn't you. Now I'm going to take care of what's important to you."

The gun cocked.

"No!" Jaeden shouted and threw up her hand.

Suddenly the cold metal disappeared from his temple, and the gun, with its sinister silencer attached, flew past his face and into Jaeden's waiting hand.

What the ...

She took aim and shot behind Ryder as he ducked for cover. Ryder whirled to see a tall, abnormally thin male in slacks and a striped sweater stumbling back against the wall. This ... this was the would-be assassin? Holy Artemis.

The vampyre regained his footing. A bullet wasn't going to do much. He saw Jae make a move toward the guy out of the corner of his eye and hissed in disbelief. He threw out his arm, pushing her behind him more roughly than he intended, and then turned on their attacker. The guy threw a punch that would have sent him through the wall had he made contact, but he missed, having thrown too much weight behind it. Ryder jerked to his side, grabbing hold of his arm, and twisted it hard enough to break it. The vamp howled. This gave him the leverage to whip the supernatural around and grab his head. As quick as lightning, Ryder wrenched it clean off his neck.

"Yuck." He dropped the dismembered head on the body and turned around to glare at Jaeden. "Don't you have some explaining to do?"

* * *

WHY DID he have to go and ruin the moment? Here she was, trembling with shock at the violence, and yet overwhelmed with admiration at the swiftness of Ryder's actions as he'd dispatched the vampyre. She could tell by the way he hadn't lingered over the kill that he was a Hunter not because he enjoyed it but because he was strong and good at it. Fast, efficient.

But could he allow her to ogle him in admiration for just a few minutes? Nope. He had to jump right to the fact that she'd used telekinesis. And whatever friendship they'd formed in the last thirty-six hours was going to die a sudden death when he realized she was polluted.

Maybe she could feign ignorance.

"I think we should get rid of the body just before dawn. We'll put it out back and it'll be gone within seconds. Nice job, by the way. I've not quite managed the art of decapitation by bare hands, but I'll work on that. Yes, siree. Is there a technique—"

"Jaeden," he warned quietly and took a few intimidating steps toward her. Automatically, she backed up against the wall. "Jae, is this what you're hiding?" He pointed to the gun she'd forgotten was still in her hand. "How did you do that? And before you ask, yes, I mean how did you whip the gun from his hand to yours?"

Aw, crap, her life was so over.

She heaved a heavy sigh and flopped onto the nearest bed, placing the gun gently on the bedside table. She couldn't look at him as she began. "I don't know. I can move things with my mind, I guess."

"Like Caia?"

No, not like Caia! she wanted to scream. Caia could do that because she was born to do it. Half magik, half lykan. She hadn't been tortured to near death and imbued with her torturer's gift for "Look, no hands!"

Instead she shrugged. "I don't know. I think ..."

"You think?" he prodded gently.

She curled her hands into fists. She didn't want to talk about this. How dare he force her to talk about it! It was none of his damn business!

"Jae?"

"I don't want to talk about it," she clipped out.

"Well, you're going to have to."

Her eyes flashed up to meet his, blazing with shame and fury. "Go to Hades, Ryder!"

He flinched, obviously taken aback by the venom in her voice. "Jae—"

"What, are you deaf? I don't want to discuss it. Not with Caia, not with my dad, not with Lucien, and most definitely not with a Rogue Hunter who takes nothing seriously."

A growl that built into a near roar ripped out of him, and he suddenly had her by her upper arms, shaking her like a rag doll.

"Let go!" she yelled, pulling and twisting in his grasp.

"No! You're going to tell me what is going on. Now!"

She'd never seen Ryder angry before. He was the most

together male lykan she'd ever met. She began to tremble. *Oh goddess, don't let me cry. No!*

The tears streamed down her face with a mind of their own, and she felt Ryder's death grip ease. Abruptly, she was pressed against him, her face snuggled into his chest while he stroked her hair.

"Damn it, don't cry, Jae, please don't cry. You know I can't stand to see a woman cry."

"I'm s-s-sorry," she managed, hiccupping. But the tears wouldn't stop. She continued to sob in his arms as he cradled her against him, whispering soothing words in her ear.

She cried all the tears she hadn't allowed herself until now. She cried for the way her captivity had broken her innocence and faith; she cried for letting fear get the best of her; she cried for the sharp, breathless pain any remembrance of Sebastian brought; and she cried for the shame of having the telekinesis as a permanent scar from Ethan's torture.

After a while, her tears subsided, her trembling eased, and she managed to catch her breath.

"I'm sorry," she apologized hoarsely, trying to pull away. But Ryder wouldn't let her. Instead he brushed her hair aside, stroking her face tenderly. His warm eyes seared into her own cool ones.

"Don't be. I think it was a long time coming."

She nodded, unable to tear her gaze from his.

"Jaeden ..." He seemed reluctant to continue.

She decided to put him out of his misery. "I have telekinesis because of Ethan."

He shook his head. "How did that happen?"

Sucking in a deep breath, she prepared herself to say the words out loud. Admitting it all would just make it ... real.

"He tortured me for weeks. He was a fire magik. A good one. Very inventive ... creative." She laughed bitterly. "He used fire as a whip. He lashed me dozens of times and then allowed me a day to heal before he'd start again. Sometimes he didn't use fire ... he would just use his energy to slice me open."

"Oh god—" Ryder's hold on her tightened, his lips pressed thin with white fury.

"He used to play bloody tic-tac-toe on my stomach, or quiz me about literature, movies ... whatever. And if I got the answer wrong, he'd score my skin ... everywhere. My back, my legs, my breasts, my face, my arms. Sometimes he would use this illusion on me, make me think my body was burning from the inside out. I'd scream and scream until I passed out with the pain, and then when I woke up ... I-I was okay again. Then he would start all over, laughing the more I screamed, the more—"

"Sshhh." He crushed her so tightly against him, she could hardly breathe. "I don't know if I can hear anymore."

"I'm just trying to explain." Her voice was muffled against his throat. "He used his energy on me so much that I think it seeped into my blood."

"Can you do anything else?"

"No." She managed to pull away. "Just telekinesis. I ran away because I couldn't control it."

"And now?"

"I'm getting better. When I have nightmares, I can't control it at all."

His jaw clenched, his eyes blazing. "Do you have nightmares often?"

"Sometimes."

"Jae ..." His eyes glistened and he abruptly looked away, fighting his emotions. "We should have gotten to you sooner."

"No!" She grabbed his arm, tugging him back to face her. "Don't. You all saved me. Don't do that."

"I can't help it. I had no idea it ... I knew it was bad, but that—"

Panic shot through her. "Ryder, you can't tell. Please," she pleaded.

"What do you mean?"

"I don't want anyone to know how bad it was. I don't want them to know about the telekinesis."

"Why? It's not your fault."

"I just don't."

Please, please, please, please.

He took hold of her shoulders and shook her gently, his expression darkening. "You better not be ashamed, Jaeden Rodriguez, because you have nothing to feel ashamed of. You are the strongest person I know. I'm proud to know you."

Oh goddess. She felt tears choke her again. Why did he have to be so perfect?

"Please don't tell," she persisted.

Ryder shook his head. "I won't. But it's not something you can hide easily, Jaeden. And no one will care. The pack is just happy to be getting you back."

"Still ..."

He held up a hand in surrender, smiling gently. "I promise I won't tell."

Relief flooded her and then immediately dissipated when his expression sobered. "But Caia already knows everything. She could see your ... torture ... through Ethan's eyes."

The blood drained from her face.

CHAPTER 9

Darker Side

She felt awful.

Sleeping had been an issue after Marita and her "operatives" had worked out a plan of defense against du Bois and his gang of rebels. And it wasn't because her body had still been pumping with the adrenaline of doing so well in classes at the Center. It wasn't because she was juiced with excitement over how efficient and determined the team had been when discussing the MacLachlan attack. It wasn't because she was nervous about her next day of classes.

It was because of the beautiful redhead who had disappeared into Lucien's room with him last night so they could "talk."

All night she tossed and turned, straining to hear any sounds from next door, fearing what she would do if she did. Finally, she used the telecom system by her bed to contact

Noble and ask him if it was possible for her to have private use of the woodland simulator so she could go for a run.

Of course, it wasn't a problem.

As she stood there alone, breathing in what she knew to be fake, fresh, woodsy air and yet exhilarating in it anyway, Caia willed her body just this once to change like it used to. She remembered how afraid she'd been of telling Lucien and the others that her body slipped into wolf like magik. Remembering the day they were scheduled for their first pack run together since *it* had happened, Caia felt her anger build irrationally. Lucien had been so kind as she explained the situation, and she'd been so scared he would look at her as less of a lykan because of it. No one in the pack had sneered at her, or condemned her, and she knew it was because of him.

So, why did he have to be big jerk now—taking some, six-foot-nothing bombshell back to his room? A bombshell she most obviously had a sexual past with, she rippled with fury, her eyes glaring at a large tree in front of her.

Rose had clung to his arm like a burr the entire evening.

A growl ripped out of Caia's chest, and she felt white heat building from her toes upward.

No, no, no, no, no! she cried. But too late, she was stumbling back blinded. Afraid of what she would see, her eyes opened slowly, and she grimaced at the large pile of ash in front of her. She had destroyed the tree. She was really going to have to work on that.

Although most of her pent-up frustration had expelled from her, she still shook with the agony that Lucien had been in love with someone; that he loved another woman and couldn't be with her because of *her*. Did he resent her? *Please, Artemis*, she pleaded silently, *let the change be slow. Let my bones crack and my muscles ache, and my eyes tear.*

She stripped naked, folding her clothes at her feet. And

then she pushed the change. All too quickly she was a wolf, her hard paws sinking into the dirt. No cracking, no aching, no tearing.

Caia pelted straight into the heart of the woodland, the added feeling of impotence peddling her speed. She hated that she felt this way, hated the rage that gripped hold of her until she was almost blind with the pain. This was what it meant to be his mate. To hurt with a jealous longing so intense, it was as supernatural as the world she lived in. Jealousy, she was beginning to realize, was like a cancer. It ate at your very being.

She ran around the arena until her anger subsided to a thrumming beneath her skin, until it was somewhat manageable. Once she had changed back, and had her jeans and T-shirt on, she turned around to squint at the pile of ash. With a flick of her wrist, the tree rematerialized.

"Good as new," she whispered.

If only she could do that for herself.

* * *

GLAMOUR WAS EASY FOR HER, and Caia could tell Mordecai was becoming worried that she was bored.

"There really is no challenge in it for you, is there?" He watched as she glamoured an apple to look like a banana.

She shook her head. "Nope."

Usually, she would have been apologetic, but in truth, she *was* bored, which meant her mind was too easily on other things. Like Lucien ... and his *lover*.

Mordecai rubbed his bristly cheek in thought. "*Well* ... we could try the martial arts class. Or we could go back to natural materialization ... damn. I just wasn't expecting you to pick things up so quickly. Marion did warn—"

"Martial arts sound good. Do I get to kick someone's ass?"

He laughed. "Yeah. Mine."

She chuckled, not really seeing Mordecai as the Jackie Chan type. *This should be funny*, she mused.

* * *

THIS WAS SO NOT FUNNY. Caia groaned as her back grumbled in complaint, her eyes glazed at the ceiling as she lay prone on a mat.

Mordecai's head popped into her vision, smiling down at her. "Looks like we found something that doesn't come so easily, huh?"

"If I were a wolf right now, your jugular would be mine."

He chuckled and grabbed her wrist, pulling her to her feet. "That would be unsportsmanlike."

She grunted. "What, in comparison to flipping me over your shoulder and grounding me into the floor?"

"It's called judo."

"It's called whaling on a ninety-pound, nineteen-year-old girl and being smug about it."

He laughed and shrugged. "What can I say? It's nice to be good at something around you."

She frowned. What did that mean? That she made people feel inadequate? Did Lucien feel that way?

"Did I say something wrong?" Mordecai asked. "I was just joking with you."

She turned away, pulling her ponytail back into place. "No, I guess I just didn't realize how annoying it is to be around a freak like me."

"Hey." He whirled her around, his eyes wide with concern. "Caia, I was kidding. Your abilities are exhilarating to be around, I promise." He chuckled. "That doesn't mean it isn't funny that someone as graceful as you is as hopeless as you seem to be at judo, tae kwon do, and aikido."

"Don't forget jujitsu."

Mordecai let out a guffaw of laughter. "I didn't, I was being kind."

She smiled and shoved at him playfully, although her mind still buzzed with insecurity.

He seemed to sense it. "Is this about Lucien?"

"No," she said too quickly and then laughed at herself when she saw the disbelief in his eyes. "Maybe."

"Is it about Rose?"

Caia shook her head frantically. No, no one could know about her hopeless unrequited infatuation. It was too, too sad. "No. It's just ..." She flopped down on to the mat. "Lucien is my best friend, you know. Sometimes when Marion or I talk about my magikal abilities, he goes all weird and quiet. What you said ... I mean ... I don't know. Do you think he might ... resent me?"

"Resent you how?"

"He's the Alpha of our pack. And he's been through a lot and deserves that position. He's the most powerful lykan among us, except—"

"That he's not. You are."

She nodded reluctantly. "Yes."

"You think it bothers him?"

"I don't want to lose him."

Mordecai smiled kindly down at her. "I don't think you need to worry about that, Caia. The way he looks at you ... he cares a great deal about you, I'm sure of it. I think you are as much his friend as he is yours."

His friend. Wonderful.

"Now, if you are done having your ass kicked, might I suggest you shower and then join me for the afternoon lecture on the element of water?"

"Sure. Whatever floats your boat."

"Was that a joke?"

"A poor one, but yes."

He laughed and pulled her to her feet. "You'll learn a lot. It's a beginner's lecture, but it's useful, I promise."

Caia would never know if her first beginner's lecture in the practice of water magik was useful. After Mordecai had led her to the lecture halls in the basement level at the back of the building, an increasing sense of unease trickled down her spine, an unease accompanied by a familiar icy, tingling sensation.

The feeling grew stronger as she followed him into lecture hall A and took a seat in the back row of the semicircular theater room. She blankly took in the younger magiks who sat talking and laughing, notepads at the ready in front of them. Numb, she was barely aware of a short magik set up down in the center of the room, where he had a laptop connected to the projection screen behind him. The magiks quieted as he began to speak, but Caia was no more aware of his words than of Mordecai's concerned stare.

There was a Midnight at the Center.

Caia homed in on the trace and found the female. Because the girl was young, unpracticed, and afraid, her connection was strong. She was somewhere dark and cold. Trapped and bitter. Feeling stupid.

For what? Caia snapped internally. She pushed harder with the trace until she made a connection to the girl, the strongest she'd felt since her horrific invasion of Ethan's conscience. The young girl had fled from someplace where there were many Midnights. She'd hated them. She had found a Daylight.

She had come here to join the Daylight cause.

Caia gasped and tightened her hold on the connection. Could this be right? She scrambled like an excited child through the trace, trying to find evidence of this girl's duplicity, of her malevolence. She found none. Only a bitterness that she had naively wandered into the Center and been imprisoned.

No! Caia shook her head.

Who was this girl? Where did she come from?

Frustrated, she collapsed back in her chair. She couldn't pick up any definitive details, but she knew enough to know that an innocent girl was imprisoned here in the Center.

"Caia?"

She suddenly became aware that Mordecai was shaking her, and others were no longer paying attention to the lecture but staring at her, bewildered by her presence and the disruption she was causing.

She didn't care about them. She turned to Mordecai. "I need to speak with Marita. Now."

* * *

HIS CELL BUZZED on the coffee table, and he grumbled when he saw the caller ID. He really didn't want to speak to that Midnight at the moment, not with what had happened. He needed Nikolai to maintain confidence in him, and this situation was only going to incite the opposite.

Sighing, he picked up the phone.

"Yes."

"I've called you twice now. Why haven't you answered?" Nikolai's thick voice queried suspiciously down the line.

He better just get it over with. "There's been a development."

"Good or bad?"

"Not great."

"Outline the problem quickly. I have one of my own."

"Du Bois?"

"Du Bois. Speak, Kirios."

He bristled at the use of his name but bit his tongue. He

swallowed and tightened his hold on the phone. "I've temporarily lost my access to Caia."

Silence.

"Nikolai?"

"I'm still here," he said wearily. "This is not a good time. Things seem to be unraveling."

"No, they are not. If you had been paying attention, I used the word *temporarily*. I'm on this, don't worry."

"I shall try to maintain faith in you, Kirios. You can't have survived the world this long without a certain amount of ability."

He grunted. "I appreciate the confidence."

"Hmm, well, I can do no other thing but trust you will take care of this. I am having enough trouble with du Bois. He has gathered some rebels, idiots who believe in his faithless words. I have one in custody—she says they are planning an attack against a pack of lykans, the MacLachlans."

"Have you taken du Bois into custody?"

"Not yet. I need verification from the other idiots who are joining his little rebellion before I can take him before the Council. I *will* put a stop to the attack in time."

Frustration rippled through his body. "You better. You realize Caia will be aware of this little attack, which means the Daylights will be gearing up to defend the pack. If Caia is caught in the crossfire, our plans will be obliterated. We need that girl alive."

"I am aware of what is at stake, Kirios!" Nikolai raged. "Do not push me. I am not the one who lost our inside asset."

"It looks like we both have a lot of work to do and very little time. And Nikolai ... don't ever speak to me that way again. Understood?"

A tense silence, followed by, "Understood, Kirios. Apologies."

"Accepted." He sighed. "Call me when you've squashed du Bois."

He hung up, threw his phone over his shoulder, and leaned back into the sofa with his eyes squeezed tight.

He had to get moving. There were too many years at stake to let Caia and du Bois control this war.

CHAPTER 10

Mate

The television flickered, lighting her face in the dark motel room, revealing her sardonic smirk as she chewed on candy and watched the soap opera. He studied her from his place on the adjacent twin bed, amazed at the feeling of peace that settled over him just by being near her, by being allowed to look at her.

Ryder closed his eyes briefly as he fought the courage to say what he had to say. Maybe he should just let it be. She'd had a rough few days.

After her revelations the night before, Jaeden had fallen asleep quickly, exhausted from her much-needed crying jag. He, on the other hand, couldn't even close his eyes, her descriptions of her torture rolling around in his brain and roiling his stomach. How had she survived it, still able to function as normally as she was?

Her strength amazed him.

Jae had been sleeping for only an hour or so before she'd started crying out in her sleep. Her bed shook, and then the telephone on her bedside table flew across the room and smashed into smithereens. The TV in the corner was just beginning to rumble when Ryder jumped across the room and slid in beside her, pulling her into his arms and soothing her away from the nightmare.

Slowly, the movements ceased and she stopped crying, snuggling into him instead. When she woke up in his arms that morning, neither said anything. Jae merely tugged away from him to sit up. Climbing out of bed, she saw the telephone smashed on the floor and turned back to smile at him gratefully, realizing the kindness he'd paid to her during the night.

After they ridded themselves of the vamp's body, Ryder let her drive to give her something to do, but the conversation had been shallow and teasing, the dramatic events of the night before studiously avoided.

When it was time to stop at another motel, Ryder refused to let her sleep in a room by herself. Despite the warnings in his brain that he might not be able to keep his hands to himself for another night, they booked a twin room.

"I can feel you staring, you know," she said softly. "Go to sleep, Ryder, and stop worrying about me. I'm fine."

He grunted and reached over to switch on the lights.

"Hey!" She turned to glare at him. "You're ruining the ambience."

"I want to talk."

"You're kind of a girl. Anyone ever tell you that?"

"And you're kind of a ballbuster, anyone ever tell *you* that?"

"All the time."

Sighing, he threw his legs off the bed and leaned toward her with his elbows on his knees. "I'm serious."

Jaeden switched off the TV with the remote before turning to give him her full attention. "I thought I'd gotten away with it."

He frowned. "Away with what?"

"Talking about last night."

He grinned. "Really? Come on, this is me, you should know better by now."

She stared at him for a long time before returning his smile. "Yeah, I guess so." She shifted so she was sitting on the bed with her knees tucked against her chest. "What do you want to talk about specifically?"

Ah, he wasn't sure she was going to like this at all.

"Well?"

Okay, man, just say it ... then duck.

"I wanted to discuss the idea of getting Caia to train you, to help you control your telekinesis."

He waited with his hands clasped tightly in front of him while she seemed to absorb this. Finally, Jae nodded, brushing a silky curl back from her face. She pierced him with her clear-eyed blue gaze, and it got him thinking about the other thing he wanted to discuss before this night was through.

"Okay." She grimaced. "Since she knows about the ... about what Ethan did, I doubt there's any harm in confiding in her. I'll talk to her when we get back tomorrow."

That had been easier than he'd expected.

Smiling, Ryder got up so he could sit on the bed next to her, especially enjoying how tense she got the closer *he* got. "I'm glad you'll talk to her, but it will have to be when Caia and Lucien return from the Center."

"Oh yeah, I forgot," she replied quietly, trying to shift away from him.

He couldn't help it. He laughed.

Her head snapped up, her eyebrows drawn together. "What?"

"You," Ryder snickered. "Could you be more uncomfortable?"

"I'm not uncomfortable. Why would I be uncomfortable?"

"You've been jittery with me all day. I don't bite ... well ... occasionally." He wiggled his eyebrows suggestively.

"Ugh, you are such a male."

He guffawed. "Yeah, thank Gaia."

"And I am not uncomfortable!"

"Then stop moving away from me!"

"Stop crowding me!"

Ryder whooped, his eyes glittering as they drank her in. Deliberately, he washed his eyes over her from head to foot, lingering on her long legs, breasts, and finally her lips. She was blushing madly by the time he was done, and the heat between them had cranked up a hundred degrees.

He stopped grinning and leaned toward her, his lips inches from hers. "I'm going to kiss you now, and I would appreciate it if you would shut up long enough for me to do that."

"How romantic—"

"Ah, ah. What did I just say?"

She clamped her lips closed tightly, glaring at him. Her rosy cheeks, however, told him she was as affected by him as he was by her.

They sat like that until her mouth opened to say what he knew would be a smart-ass comment. Before she could, he closed the distance between them, wrapped his hand around her neck and pulled her into his kiss. Satisfaction slammed through him at the taste of her, and he couldn't stop himself from crushing her against him, pressing her as close to his body as he could get her. Only one word remained prominent in his mind as he devoured her.

Mate.

SHE FELT like she was minutes from bursting into flames.

Oh my goddess.

Jaeden only put enough distance between her and Ryder to slide her hands over his chest and sink her fingers into his thick hair, anchoring his mouth to her own as their tongues mated.

Her blood bubbled under her skin, a heat so intense building inside her she thought she was going to incinerate them both.

Ryder was kissing her.

Ryder.

Wow.

One of his hands slid down her side, his thumb brushing her breast and setting off another blast of fireworks inside her. Eventually, he curled said hand around her thigh so he could wrap her leg around his waist. Automatically, she did that with her other one and found herself flat on her back while Ryder pressed his body into hers.

Oh goddess!

She gasped into his mouth.

Then suddenly a breeze blasted over her, and she opened her eyes to see Ryder pushing himself back to the foot of the bed, his hand shaking as he brushed his hair off his face.

Why had he stopped?

"That wasn't meant to happen," he said hoarsely.

With that, a crushing sense of deflation swamped her. What? Did she think Ryder ... the most notorious bachelor in the pack, would actually be interested in her? Puhlease. Of course he stopped before things went too far. He was disgustingly honorable.

Plus her father would kill him.

"Yeah, I guess not," she snapped and then bit her tongue. Damn it. She didn't want him to know he had hurt her.

"I didn't mean the kiss." He moved toward her again, and she strained back from him.

"Stay back. I don't need this kind of crap right now, Ryder."

His eyes seemed to darken in anger, confusing her.

"Hey." She shrugged, unable to meet his eyes. "Don't worry about it. I'm not going to tell my dad. You're safe."

He snorted in disgust, and she looked up to see him glaring at her—*really* glaring at her.

What was his problem? She was the one who was going to end up with her heart broken if she didn't get away from his dumb, tight ass. As if she didn't have enough pain in her life without adding him to her already broken soul.

"What?" she huffed. "What is your problem? Stop looking at me like that."

"I'm trying to decide whether I want to kill you," he growled through clenched teeth, "or haul you underneath me and finish what we started."

"Charming."

Ryder's hands flew up in a strangling gesture. "Can you shut up for one second so I can explain?"

"Explain what? Your almost molestation of me?"

"I swear you say one more word and I—"

She knew she should stop. He wasn't teasing. He was mad, and *way* bigger than she was. "You'll what?"

The next thing she knew he had hold of her, his hand clamped tightly across her mouth. She wriggled but to no avail.

"Ah, much better." He grinned down at her.

"Mm mmm hu uhh uu."

"What's that, sweetheart? I'm a little hard of hearing."

Goddess, he was a schmuck.

"Now." He pulled her closer. "Let me talk before you continue jumping to all the wrong conclusions and decide I'm a bastard and that you hate me."

What was he talking about?

His eyes had gone warm and buttery as they wandered across her face. She stilled, suddenly too intrigued to fight him. Did Ryder ...? No ... Could he?

"I stopped kissing you because I was this close to making love to you, and I would rather we did that after I've spoken to your father."

Huh?

He laughed as if he could read her reaction in her eyes. "Jae ... I think we have something. You can deny it all you want, but there's something more between us. Something real." He smiled, looking unexpectedly shy. "I think we could be mates."

Jaeden's eyes widened, and she tensed. Was he serious? Was Ryder Alexander, the biggest crush of her life, actually suggesting they were mates?

"I don't know how it happened." He unclamped his hand from her mouth and cupped her face tenderly. "But the thought of not being able to spend every day bickering with you and then kissing you quiet, it knocks the breath out of me. When we get home, I'm going to ask permission from Dimitri to court you, if that's okay with you?"

"Then why did you stop?"

He chuckled. "Because I want to do things right with you."

"Ryder." She rested her forehead against his chest. "Are you sure? I mean ... if you hadn't noticed, I'm not exactly Miss Normal right now. Are you sure?"

His cheek slid against hers, sending sparks running throughout her as he breathed in her ear. "Completely. You're mine, Jae." He pulled back. "If that's okay with you?"

As he smiled down at her, a weight she didn't even know she'd been carrying floated off her body and out of the room. She knew she looked too serious, but she couldn't help it. "I've had a crush on you forever."

His eyes widened and he appeared smug. "Oh, really ..."

She slapped at him half-heartedly. "Now don't you go getting yourself a big head there, cowboy."

"I can't help it. The untouchable Jaeden Rodriguez has a crush on me." He pulled her closer again and brushed a soft kiss across her lips. "Why didn't you say anything?"

Jae snorted. "Yeah, right. You barely even noticed me."

His hand slid down her waist to her hip and he squeezed her to him. "I'm noticing you now," he growled.

Giggling, she shifted away from him. "I think we better cut that out before you deflower me."

"Deflower you?" He quirked an eyebrow. "Does that mean ..."

She blushed. She couldn't believe she was having this conversation with Ryder. "Yes." She heaved an exaggerated sigh. "I am a virgin. Scared?"

His eyes darkened, and she shivered as he shook his head, his throat thick with a possessiveness that should have alarmed her, and yet only stirred the heat in her. "Glad," he managed, seeming just as surprised. "I think I'd have to take the head off any other guy who had touched you."

She smiled. "How caveman of you."

"Yeah, you love it." He grabbed her and nipped playfully at her lips.

Jae melted into him and would have happily let him do what he would with her, but somehow Ryder shook himself into focus enough to sit back on the other bed.

He shrugged ruefully at her questioning look. "It's safer."

She blushed again as she tried to articulate what she wanted. "I wouldn't mind, if we—"

"I would, sweetheart." He cut her off with a soft look. "I want you. But as my mate."

Jae nodded, shocked that somehow this three-day car journey with Ryder had turned into a long-ago fantasy she'd had before Ethan took her. A sense of peace washed through her as she looked at Ryder. With him beside her, maybe she really would be okay.

She snuggled deep into her pillow as he talked. For hours they laughed and chatted about everything and nothing, until eventually she fell into a deep, dreamless sleep.

* * *

RAP, RAP, RAP.

Ryder bolted out of bed, his gaze going straight to Jae to make sure she was all right. Sunlight streamed through holes in the motel room curtains, shooting shafts across her golden skin. A tingling ran through him as he remembered the night before. He smiled. She was one step closer to being his.

RAP, RAP, RAP.

Jae was coming around at the banging on the door. Ryder cursed, creeping toward the door.

"Who—"

He held a finger to his lips to cut off Jae's question as she sat up, pushing her thick hair off her face.

Who was banging on their door? No one knew they were here.

"Jaeden, it's me!" a strong male voice yelled through the wood.

Ryder tensed as Jae gasped, "Reuben?"

She flew from her bed and knocked Ryder out of the way so she could throw open the door. The next thing he knew, *his* female was in the arms of some tall, built, dark-haired vampyre. Ryder growled. He wasn't an expert on the subject, but he was guessing the vamp would be considered good-looking.

Jaeden must've heard him growl because she pulled back from the vampyre and turned to him now. "Ryder, this is Reuben. I told you about him."

Ah, yes, the vamp who talked her into breaking coven laws—the vamp who wanted something more than just friendship. He had never considered himself the possessive type, but all of a sudden, he understood why Lucien got as crazy as he did whenever another male came on to Caia. His arm shot out of its own accord, and he pulled Jaeden into his side. She groaned at his obvious display of jealousy, but right now he didn't care if it irritated her.

He glared at Reuben, whose dark eyes were narrowed on him. "What are you doing here?"

The vampyre straightened and spoke calmly, "I was worried about Jaeden. I came to check she was all right."

"Some tracking skills you've got there."

Reuben didn't respond, just stared at him with a practiced bland expression.

Jae was right. This vampyre, despite looking about twenty-four, was old. And that meant he was dangerous.

"You've seen she's all right. Now leave."

"Ryder." Jaeden smacked him lightly on the chest in admonishment. "Stop." She turned to smile at Reuben. "I'm fine. But you're here now, so why don't we grab some breakfast together?"

Reuben smiled at her. "Sounds wonderful."

"Sounds crap."

Jae snorted. "Reuben, this is Ryder. Please forgive him and his lack of manners. He's a Neanderthal."

"He's just being protective."

Hey, he didn't need the vamp sticking up for him. He was about to say so when Jaeden clamped a knowing hand across his mouth. Her eyes smiled at him, and he relaxed, wanting nothing more than to kiss her good morning.

"Can you stay quiet long enough to get dressed so we can meet Reuben at the diner?"

He nodded reluctantly and waited, secretly amused, as she turned back to the vamp to direct him to the motel's diner, her hand still tight across his mouth.

The door closed behind the vamp and she released him.

Before she said a word, he had her backed up against the door as he devoured her mouth with a hot kiss. Finally, he pulled back, enjoying the way her chest heaved from his attentions.

"Morning."

"Morning," she croaked. "What was that for?"

"Just a reminder."

"A reminder?"

"Yeah, a reminder of what we talked about last night. Of how you belong to me."

Her eyes flashed, and he waited for their fight to begin. Really, was there anything better than sparring with this woman?

"Of how I belong to you?" Her voice went up an octave.

"Yeah."

"Forget about the verbal arm wrestling! Why don't you just pee on me and everything I own?"

He smirked and turned away to saunter to the bathroom. "I will if it comes to that."

"Arrghhh!"

Ryder laughed, ducking the shoe that flew at his head as he closed the door on her.

CHAPTER 11

Misunderstood

"I'm sorry I couldn't meet with you last night, Caia." Marita breezed into her suite without knocking. "I had urgent business to attend to."

Caia nodded wearily, standing up from the window seat that looked out over Paris. "I understand."

She didn't actually, but she was trying to. The last two sleepless nights hadn't exactly improved her mood, but Marita *was* the top gun and had to be respected. Caia was going crazy wondering about the Midnight imprisoned in the Center. Her refusal to join Mordecai for training until she met with Marita was *actually* an attempt at exerting self-control over her anger.

Marita threw her a surprisingly warm smile and took a seat on a nearby sofa, smoothing her conservative skirt over her legs as she did so. Instead of sitting spine straight and stiff, however, she relaxed against the back of the seat and tilted her head casually. "Mordecai seems concerned for you. I'm worried."

The witch's tone was gentler than Caia had ever heard it —that, mixed with Marita's relaxed body language, completely threw her off. She realized this was the first time they'd ever been alone together—no Vanne, no servants, no guards. Maybe *that's* why Marita was so tense all the time. Here with Caia, on her own, she could be a little freer, not have to play the role of "in control queen of the castle" so much.

Caia shook her head with a polite smile and took the armchair opposite her. "No, I'm fine. Just ... a little anxious."

"Anxious?" Marita frowned.

She nodded and leaned forward. "Yesterday, when Mordecai took me to the lecture, I felt a Midnight. Here at the Center."

Marita froze, her expression blank.

"A girl. Imprisoned ... I'm guessing somewhere in the basement near lecture hall A."

A silence fell over the room, increasing Caia's anxiety. Marita's eyes seared through her. "You really are the Head of the Midnight Coven."

It was Caia's turn to look bewildered and concerned. "Uh, yeah. But you knew that."

"Of course." Marita's hand fluttered by her face, as if at a loss. Caia could not reconcile this magik with the woman she had met previously. "But I have actual hard evidence for myself now. I've been reading your reports passed on by my sister but ... well, it's a little strange, this situation, as I'm sure you already know. I've been Head of the Daylights for twenty-five years, and I was groomed by my father for twenty years before that. That's forty-five years of working against the Head of the Midnight Coven. To now be working *with* her is ... weird."

Caia laughed. "Yeah, I guess it would be."

Marita smiled, a smile that never reached her eyes, and then settled back into her seat. "Before I explain about the Midnight, can I ask you a question?"

"Of course."

"Your trace ... it seems different from my own."

Caia wriggled in her seat at the inquiry and the pinched expression on Marita's face. "Different how?"

Did she really want to know?

Marita shrugged, but Caia could tell it was a deliberate attempt to look casual about something she obviously didn't feel casual about. "I can only follow a trace if I am specifically looking for someone. I've heard that you can do more?"

Wow, every second at this place was making her feel more and more like a freak.

"Yeah, the trace sort of finds me. I do *that*, what you do, as well ... specifically locate someone, I mean."

"What do you mean the trace sort of finds you?"

Caia cleared her throat, shifting again in her seat. "It's hard to describe. Um, let's see. Okay, for instance, Nikolai—I have a tap on him ... yeah, I suppose you could call it that."

"A tap?"

"Yeah. His trace will alert me if he seems intense about something, whether it be a negative or positive feeling. And then I go in and check to see what's up. Nikolai is actually a tough cookie. He's good at hiding his emotions."

Marita stared at her blankly, no emotion to disclose exactly how she felt about this information. Finally, she smiled tightly. "I think what's important is you're using your quite considerable gifts to help *us*."

"So about the girl?" Caia did not intend to be sidetracked.

"The girl, the Midnight, is a spy sent to infiltrate our coven. She is very good, very convincing. Three months ago, she turned up with a young male magik she'd convinced she was from a group of Midnights from Scandinavia who ran a small army base for the Head of the Coven—Ethan. She said they were extremists and that with Ethan's disappearance, they had become even more vicious, killing anything that got in their way of the war. She said she was a disbeliever, a Midnight who actually agreed with Daylight." She stopped to scoff at the thought, and Caia's pulse sped up. "Vilhelm—the boy she met—fell for her lies and he brought her to me. I knew right away she was lying. A Midnight apathetic to the war? Maybe, although I doubt it. But a Midnight switching sides? Never."

Caia felt a wave of panic. She'd better tread carefully here, or she could find herself locked up too.

"Well," she began slowly, throwing the witch a trembling smile, "it can't be impossible, right? I'm part Midnight and I don't want to maim any Daylights. I want to end the war."

Marita seemed to look right through her, reminding Caia that she was still the pragmatic woman she'd met upstairs. "Your Daylight blood obviously overpowers the bad blood. Not to mention you were raised Daylight."

"I understand." Caia gave her a tight smile, squishing the anger that exploded through her at the "bad blood" comment. "But I didn't get a malevolent feeling from her."

"Perhaps you were too far away."

"Could you take me to her?"

Caia was again surprised by the smile bestowed upon her, her eyes trying for kind and concerned. "Will that help? Will it stop whatever anxious thoughts you've got buzzing around in your head and get you back into training? You're missing important things. Lucien is with Rose and the others, training in the simulator."

Caia tried not to feel as if she'd been slapped in the face by the mention of Rose and Lucien, together.

"It would help."

Marita nodded regally and stood, walking to the telephone by Caia's bed. "Noble, can you please alert the Containment Center that I'm on my way down with Caia?"

* * *

SHE'D BEEN RIGHT. The Containment Center—the prison—was situated one level below lecture hall A. Bars rolled down from the ceiling as you passed through the "reception," and rows of individual cells with what looked like magikal Plexiglas contained the prisoner rather than steel bars. Caia wondered at the other occupants who gave off no Midnight trace. They were obviously rogues.

She didn't have time to wonder too long because the electrifying trace sizzled through her even more intensely as Marita drew her to a halt outside a door at the very end of the corridor. It was a huge iron monstrosity with a small rectangle at the top that slid open so you could peer inside.

"She's in here," Marita sneered and placed her hand against the door. She muttered an incantation under her breath, obviously forgetting that Caia had supreme hearing.

Occultus atrum unus. Caia repeated the words in her brain, and her heart suddenly slammed at the thought of why. *You really do want to play with fire, don't you?*

The door swung slowly open with a forbidding creak, and Marita seemed to prepare herself before entering. Caia followed, only to feel the trace grow even stronger. The sound of the door had frightened the girl.

The door was the sole source of light, but Caia could see well with her wolf eyes the hideous conditions of this prisoner's cell in comparison to the others. She sat huddled in the corner of a bare square stone room, thick iron bars that crackled with electricity (more magik) separated her from any visitors. Her long, bedraggled hair covered most of her face and knees as she pulled herself tighter into a ball. The sight of Marita terrified the girl.

A rush of pain hit Caia so fast, she cried out and stumbled back.

"Are you all right?" Marita was by her side in an instant.

No, she wasn't all right. This girl was innocent. Despite her harsh treatment, she still held no ill will toward the Daylights. The only person she felt bitter toward was Marita, and yet at the same time, she understood why the witch would not believe her. Of all the traces Caia had felt over the past few months, of all the feelings of antipathy toward the war, of actual *goodness* she thought she was picking up from the Midnights ... none could touch this young woman for her purity of soul.

There was a pearl of blissful warmth in the girl's trace, something Caia had never encountered before. She tried to push the connection harder to discover what it meant, but all she received were the girl's thoughts on Vilhelm, the Daylight magik, her friend. Without realizing it, she sent Caia an image of his anguished face as she was torn from him by Marita's men.

Laila. Her name was Laila.

"Caia." Marita shook her. "Are you all right?"

Goddess, what could she say? Marita's eyes were narrowed in suspicion.

"Has it done something to you?" she spat, turning to glare daggers at Laila. "If this filth has managed to get her magik past these bars, I will have her executed."

"No!" Caia grabbed her arm in reflex.

Uncertainty flickering across Marita's marble face. "What is going on here?"

Lie, Cy, lie!

Marita would have her thrown in with the girl if she knew Caia sympathized with her. Marita's prejudice was too great for her to even contemplate that the continuing war may be a consequence of a horrendous misunderstanding on the Daylights' behalf. Caia couldn't fight this war. Not like this. But what could she do? Her powers had her trapped in it; she was obliged to stay and fight.

But how? And with whom?

One thing she did know: Laila's time was running out, and somehow Caia had to get her out of the Center.

She cleared her throat and stood up straight and determined. "I'm sorry. The feelings ... she reminded me of Ethan."

Softness slid back into Marita's features. "Of course."

"You were right. A Midnight's a Midnight. Let's go."

Marita nodded militantly and led her out of the cell.

Caia had to force herself to not look back at the young woman she was now determined to save.

* * *

LUCIEN GLANCED FRETFULLY DOWN at Rose, curled up on the leather sofa in his suite. They had just finished training with Anders and Phoebe, who butted heads so often it was a wonder they were getting anything done. Lucien was worried about Caia. Mordecai mentioned an incident yesterday, but she wouldn't speak to anyone except Marita, who hadn't been able to schedule Caia in until today. *What is going on with her?* He paced back and forth, running an anxious hand through his hair. She'd avoided him all day yesterday.

"Lucien, sit down, you're making me antsy." Rose laughed and pulled him down beside her. A wash of guilt ran through him that she was in his room again. Caia wouldn't even look at him when Rose had insisted on coming into his suite the other night. Nothing had happened between them, but Rose had revealed how terrible she felt for the way she'd treated him, now that she knew his not mating with her was because he couldn't, not that he wouldn't. Talking with her had been as easy and as natural as it used to be. She'd listened patiently while he told her the story.

"So you and Caia aren't together?" she asked quietly once he'd finished.

"No. We're not."

Her smile had been so wide, guilt crashed around him in waves. But he had nothing to feel guilty for! Caia was not his, and he was not hers.

And Rose ...

He'd been crazy about Rose. Being with her the last couple of days only reminded him of the good times they'd had. And she was making it obvious she wouldn't mind taking a physical trip back down memory lane.

Thing was ... Lucien wasn't sure if he was ready to give up on the hope that Caia would come to her senses and realize they should be together.

"Seriously, Lucien, what is up?"

"Just a little worried about Caia."

He watched as her full lips fell into a pout. "From what I've heard, your worry is redundant. She's a big shot around here. An all-powerful genie. Why don't you stop worrying about Caia and loosen up a little? I could give you a massage." She grinned suggestively.

That did sound tempting ...

A knock at the door.

"Lucien?"

"Caia?" He shot out of his seat and rushed to the door, throwing it open.

His relief at having her in his sight was washed away by her appearance. Her gorgeous eyes were round with worry and sadness, and her long, pale hair looked as if she'd been tugging on it in exasperation.

"Thank goddess," she muttered when she saw him and walked past him with a familiar caress on his chest that sent heat rushing to his good-for-nothing places. "I need to talk to you. Lucien, some—"

She stopped, and he turned to shut the door realizing the cause of her disruption.

Rose.

"Oh." She threw her shoulders back. "I didn't realize you had company."

Rose stood from the sofa and smiled weakly. He quirked an eyebrow as he walked toward her. That wasn't like her. Was she frightened of Caia? Lucien almost laughed out loud at the thought but then realized it wasn't so funny. He guessed if he hadn't known her personally, the idea of Caia— a Midnight/Daylight lykan/witch—was intimidating, if not a little frightening.

"You remember Rose?" he came to a stop by his ex-girl-friend while trying to catch the eye of his mate so he could determine her feelings. Caia stiffened, and her eyes narrowed on Rose, an Amazon compared to her. If he wasn't so worried this was going to cause the rift Marita intended, he'd actually find it funny how unintimidated Caia appeared by Rose's height and build.

"How could I forget?"

Was that a sneer? Aw, crap, she *was* pissed.

He felt Rose stiffen next to him and was afraid to look at the expression on her face.

"I'm Lucien's ex-lover."

Ex-lover? That word, it was just so ... *graphic*.

"I see." Caia nodded, flashing him a hateful look. "Not so ex by the look of things."

No, no, no, no! He took a placating step toward her. "Now, Ca—"

"Actually," Rose interrupted, placing a hand on his arm

and drawing him back toward her. "We were just discussing that. After all, you two aren't going to commit to your mating, and Lucien and I would have been mates if he hadn't been obligated to fulfill his father's betrothal to you."

Someone shoot me. Just put a gun to my head and pull the trigger. It would be more humane.

He squeezed his eyes closed as the words tumbled spitefully out of Rose's mouth. How could he have forgotten the word *bitch* was invented by competitive female lykans?

The deafening silence became too much, and he finally worked up the courage to look at Caia.

He wished he hadn't.

A look likened to anguish and regret glittered in her eyes, but her face seemed pinched with resentment at the same time. Classic Caia. She never failed to surprise him. She fixed that gaze intently upon him and said, "I always seem to be apologizing to you these days." She shrugged so wearily, he wanted to pull her into his arms. "I am so sorry."

"What ... Caia?" He frowned, gently knocking Rose's hand from his arm as he approached her. Worry, panic almost, washed over him as she retreated from him.

"I'm sorry ... for a lot of things. But mostly, I'm sorry you got caught up in this, more than you ever should've been. My father and yours ... what they did was unforgivable—"

"What they did was for the best ... to protect you."

"What they did was take away your choices."

"And yours."

She shook her head, her eyes flickering bitterly to Rose and then back to him. "I haven't lost what you have. I'm sorry you can't be with the person you want."

"Caia—"

"Well." Rose swaggered forward, cutting him off. "We can't have kids together, but that doesn't mean we can't be together. You can still do the right thing here, Caia."

Irritation ripped through Lucien as he watched Caia grow paler by the second. "Rose," he warned, a growl rumbling from the base of his chest. She stared at him, all wide-eyed innocence.

"I'm going to go," Caia replied softly and started for the door.

That was enough.

Lucien took three long strides toward her, grabbing her by the arm and turning her around. Still she refused to meet his eyes until he gave her a little shake.

"I have a meeting with Mordecai. Let go."

"Lucien?" Rose asked uncertainly from behind him. He tried to ignore her, concentrating on getting Caia to acknowledge that she was pissed at him and there was a reason. She was jealous. Because *she* was his mate. Not Rose.

"Caia, you're being an idiot."

She flushed red, and he realized he'd said the wrong thing. With a strength belying her size, she ripped herself from his grip, her green eyes blazing with renewed energy. "Yeah, I guess I was. But I'm all good now."

"You've obviously gotten the wrong—"

She laughed humorlessly, cutting him off. "You know what, Lucien? I think you're forgetting that I'm in the middle of a war here. I'm a very important person, don't you know. I don't have time to deal with your guilt issues over moving on from our little mating. I moved on months ago, and now you have. Nothing to feel bad about." She tilted her head to smile at Rose. "I'm happy for you both."

And with that, she was gone.

She thought he loved Rose? She had moved on? She thought he had moved on? How could she think that after everything …?

The pack means everything to me, and I won't have anything to

*do with someone who puts it last. I don't want a mate like you. Not
ever.*

He'd said those awful words to her in the motel room
before they rescued Jaeden. Could she really have believed
he'd meant them?

Yes.

Shit.

Marita—1, Lucien—0.

* * *

SHE COULDN'T BREATHE. The pain was that bad. She couldn't
cry. The heat of her anger had dried her tears.

Lucien loved Rose.

A brittle disquiet had captured her body as she perched
on the side of her bed. She could feel herself shutting down,
her walls shooting up, locking her soul in and the world out.
A deep retreat was in progress and she shivered, feeling the
icy blockade settle around her.

In that moment, she loathed her magik blood. A lykan
would be tearing the room to shreds, expelling their ire from
their body like sucking poison from a snake bite. Half-heartedly, she turned to the lamp that sat on her bedside table and
lifted it slowly with her magik. With a flick of her eyes, she
sent it speeding into the fireplace and took a momentary
satisfaction in the way its destruction caused the flames to
flare up and out, displaying their anger in the way she
wanted to.

But there would be no white heat from this pain, no
involuntary destruction of property. This was a kind of
suffering she wanted to hide from.

With a shuddering breath, the tears began to fall.

So it had happened. She had fallen in love with Lucien.
Maybe she'd always been in love with him. How could she

love him when he didn't love her back? How could he stand to be around her when she was the reason he couldn't have children with the beautiful redhead?

It felt like she sat there for hours, broken porcelain badly glued together. She could either fall deeper inside herself to escape the thought of Lucien with Rose, or she could fall deeper into a problem she might be able to fix. Laila's image wavered in her mind. She went to Lucien to confide in him, finally, to ask him to help her get Laila out, to tell him that after they helped the MacLachlans, she was leaving the Center, that she was no longer fighting for Marita. The beginnings of a plan were forming in her mind—it wasn't much, but so far it was all she had. It was all Laila had. It was all the next generation had if she was going to be able to enforce the beginning of the end of a millennia-old racial war.

"Caia?"

She bolted upright at the sound of Mordecai on the other side of her door, and jumped off the bed, flicking her wrist to replace the lamp she'd broken, wiping her hand across her face to glamour away any evidence of her crying.

"Mordecai," she greeted brightly and gestured for him to come into the room. He regarded her with an odd smile as he took a seat.

"Are you all right?"

"Of course."

"Marita said you visited the Midnight."

Caia's smile tightened. "Yeah. I was curious."

He grinned back at her. "I wondered what happened in the lecture hall. I keep forgetting you're the true Head of the Midnights."

"I've been hearing that a lot."

"I just came up to fill you in on training today."

Caia nodded and listened patiently as he explained the strategies that had been used in the woodland simulator.

"I've never worked with Anders before, but he's an extremely good leader." Mordecai laughed as if remembering something. "Of course, he and Marion have been placed in charge of the task force, but Phoebe has other ideas. I don't think she and Anders like each other very much."

"Sounds like I missed some drama."

He nodded and then grew quiet.

Eventually ... "Caia?"

She frowned. This was the first time the self-assured magik looked uncomfortable and unsure. "Yeah?"

"The simulator ... well ... after your run in it the other night, there was some *energy* picked up around a certain oak?"

She flushed. Oh dear. How to explain that one?

"I, uh ..."

"Was it you?"

There was nothing to do but be honest. And she knew she could trust Mordecai.

"Yes. I'm so sorry. I just ... got angry. And killed it. I replaced it, though." She threw him an imploring smile.

Mordecai grinned back at her. "Yes, you did."

Caia watched as he took off his glasses to rub a smudge from the lens. "Was it deliberate?"

"No."

"Cy, I know what you did to Ethan."

"Do you, 'cause I don't," she quipped, but he only smiled like he pitied her.

"The tree? Was it an unfortunate victim of your anger over Rose and Lucien?"

This was even worse than she thought.

"Maybe," she managed through clenched teeth.

"Does that happen a lot, when you get angry? Can you not control it?"

How to explain something this weird?

"It just happened with Ethan and the tree. And once with a female from my pack. It's a white heat that just explodes out of me. But I think I'm beginning to control it. With Alexa, the girl from my pack, I blew her across the room—I would never hurt a member of my pack intentionally. With Ethan ... he was going to kill Lucien, and I knew he was evil, so I guess it made whatever it is stronger. Marion thinks it's something to do with my water element. The tree ... my focus was on it when I let myself get mad enough about the Rose situation."

He nodded. "You don't think it's a problem?"

"No. I was going to talk to you about it, but I think I'm getting a handle on it now."

He appeared uncertain, as if he had more questions. Instead he settled back to ask why she'd blown Alexa across the room. Soon she was telling him all about the pack.

"They sound great." He grinned. "I wish I could meet them."

"Maybe you will."

"Jaeden sounds like a riot."

Melancholy swept over Caia. She wondered how Jaeden was, if Ryder had managed to get her back to the pack safely.

"She was."

"Don't you mean *is*? She sounds tough, Caia. She'll be all right."

"I hope so. What she went through was unbelievable."

Mordecai's expression twisted in sympathy. "What did he actually do to her?"

She shook her head. That was nobody's business but Jaeden's, and no matter how much she liked Mordecai, she wasn't going to give him the sordid details.

"I'd rather not talk about it."

He snapped back in his seat, looking abashed. "Oh, of course. I didn't mean to pry."

"I know." She smiled kindly.

He stood. "You look exhausted. I'm going to leave and let you get some sleep so that you're prepared for the training tomorrow."

Yeah, like she was going to sleep with Lucien, Rose, and Laila rattling around in her mind.

And then there was Vilhelm.

Don't forget Vilhelm.

Because first chance she got, she was going to find that young magik and see how *he* felt about Laila's imprisonment.

CHAPTER 12

Homecoming

"*H*e knows you're okay, better than okay, actually, so why isn't he hightailing it back to the city? I thought he was your little gang's leader?"

He waited for Jaeden's answer as they passed the sign welcoming them into town. Ryder was angry. Not only did he sit through breakfast with that chump while Reuben oohed and aahed over Jae but the idiot couldn't take a hint and had traveled behind them all day, stayed at the same motel, and took a room next to theirs.

That was when things had started to get really irritating. Reuben wasn't happy that Jae was sharing a room with Ryder and had gotten even unhappier when Ryder had less than politely told him Jae was going to be his mate. Jaeden explained the situation, assuring Reuben that this was what she wanted. Hearing her say that had gone a long way to smoothing Ryder's ruffled fur.

His calm disposition lasted all of five seconds.

Reuben had insisted on staying the night in their room so he and Jae could talk and reminisce. Come morning, the vamp had decided he wanted to come back with them to visit the pack. Ryder still didn't get why.

"Stop being condescending," Jaeden muttered, her head turned away from him as she gazed out the truck's passenger window.

"I'm not."

"Yeah, you are. Why are you so jealous? You know, if I wanted to be with Reuben, I would've done it back when we were in our 'little gang' together."

"I'm not jealous. I just don't get why the guy is still hanging around. Why he wants to meet your family."

When he was met with silence, he threw her a longer glance before turning his attention back to the road. She was tense as Hades, her body stiff, jaw clenched. Concern—choking, unfamiliar concern—hit him hard.

"Jaeden, are you okay?" This was what Lucien was always going on about with Caia. This overwhelming protectiveness that he knew was irrational and yet was too powerful to control. Having always known when to stop pushing someone when they didn't want to talk, Ryder found it unpleasant to realize that with Jaeden, he no longer had the option of politely backing off. He *had* to know what was going on with her. His grip tightened on the wheel again.

"Jae ..." he warned, his lykan entering his voice.

She huffed beside him, but the noise immediately relaxed him. That huff usually signified that she was ready to talk.

"I'm nervous, okay? No, not nervous." She sighed. "Nervous doesn't cover it. I haven't seen my family in months, and I'm a five-minute drive from them. Reuben is hanging around because he knows about the telekinesis. He knows how worried I am about it ... all of it."

That annoying possessiveness surged inside him. "Yeah, well, I know too. I get it. But I also know something neither of you seem to grasp. The pack—your family—will accept you, no matter what."

Jae snorted. "Like they accepted Caia?"

It was true that some of the pack was still unsure of the half lykan, but for the majority, she was a welcome addition to their pack.

"That's different and you know it. Caia was a near stranger to us, but you've always been here." He chuckled. "And let's not forget you were quite the favorite little brat of your generation."

"That's not true. I was never a brat."

Ryder slowed his truck as he turned onto Dimitri's street. He felt, more than heard, Jaeden's intake of breath.

He glanced briefly in his rearview mirror, a sneer curling his top lip. "Vamp boy is right behind us. What, is he intending on being there for this family reunion?"

"Actually, yes."

His heart slammed in his chest. "Why?"

"Because he's my friend, and I'm sure my parents would like to meet the person who has been there for me these last few months."

"*I'm* sure Dimitri's gonna want to tear the face off the vamp who nearly got you thrown into a Daylight detention center for breaking coven laws."

They stopped outside the two-story house that belonged to Jaeden and her parents, parking behind her brother's Volvo. Ryder glanced from the clear view he had of Reuben in his wing mirror, taking a parking space a little down the street, and then to Jaeden who had gone as pale as a white moon.

"I never thought of that." Her eyes widened in panic. "Oh goddess, what if he kills Reuben?"

"Would that really be so bad?"

That earned him a wince-inducing punch to his upper arm. "Ryder!"

He unclipped his seat belt. "Fine, if it's *that* important to you that the vamp lives, I will intervene in the instance of attempted murder."

"Uh, you will intervene in the instance of attempted assault or I will break the news quite bluntly to my father about *our* little situation."

Not many people on this planet had the ability to intimidate or frighten him.

Dimitri?

Definitely one of the few.

Ruthless, blackmailing wench.

He clenched his teeth. "Fine."

At her grateful smile, he ignored the little flip his stomach gave when she looked at him like that. He got out of the truck and made his way around to the passenger door, all his senses alerting him to Reuben's cautious approach. Jae made a face at Ryder as he took her hand, believing he was making a point to Reuben, but in truth, he just wanted to comfort her.

He could actually smell her fear.

He squeezed her hand and gave Reuben a nonchalant nod in greeting.

"Ready?" Reuben rubbed her shoulder affectionately, setting Ryder's teeth on edge.

The nod she gave them wasn't exactly confident, but Ryder tugged her forward anyway. She had nothing to worry about. He just wished she'd realize that.

They hadn't even stepped onto the path that led to the house when the front door blasted open and Julia came running out to throw herself into her daughter's arms. Ryder felt an unexpected pain in his chest at the way the fear melted from Jae's face, replaced by silent tears as her mother held her fast and sobbed in her ear.

A click sounded in his head as everything fell into its natural place.

Jaeden was home.

* * *

HER HEART BANGED LOUDLY, and she knew that not only could everyone around her hear it but her mother must feel it slamming against her own as she hugged her close. Jae inhaled Julia's damp-earth-and-peaches scent that flooded her with warm memories.

It hurt to remember how loved she was.

How could she have ever thought it was for the best to leave them?

"Mom," she whimpered, nuzzling into her mother's shoulder.

"Sweetheart, sweetheart," Julia gurgled happily between sobs.

And then another scent flooded her senses as solid arms came around both her and her mother.

"Dad," she gasped and peered up at him from her crushed position.

His dark eyes shone down from his rugged face as he pulled her close, and that ache in her chest sharpened as she saw how much those eyes and that face had aged since she'd gone.

She had done that to him.

Julia sidled out from their embrace to allow Dimitri to envelop her, and she held on to his huge frame like a little girl.

"I'm sorry, Dad," she whispered, choking on the emotion.

"It's okay," he said, brushing her hair back from her face,

drinking in every feature, assessing her to make sure she was all in one piece.

Finally, he tore himself from her to stare over her head at someone else.

"Thank you."

Ryder.

She winced at the reminder. She had no idea how her dad was going to react to that piece of news.

"No thanks necessary."

"Let's all go inside where your brother, Lucia, and your niece are all waiting for you. Maybe once inside, you can explain the vampyre ... and that guilty look in Ryder's eyes."

She groaned inwardly. Her dad had always seen too much.

EVERYONE JUST STARED AT HER. No questions, no prodding ... just staring.

It was disconcerting.

It was good to see her brother and Lucia again. Good to hold Jaela's warm little body and inhale damp earth and baby lotion. Christian had frowned at her even as he hugged her tight, but Lucia and Jaela had welcomed her home with broad grins and lots of bubbling happiness. She'd always gotten on well with her sister-in-law, who had been born to a different pack. When Lucia married Christian, her sister Cera and husband Michel had decided to move into Pack Errante with her. Dimitri had requested the inclusion from Lucien, who of course said yes, respecting Dimitri's judgment and wishes.

After losing Michel to a gun-toting mugger, Cera and her children had become a huge part of their family and a protected member of the pack. Julia, Jae, Lucia, and Cera were especially close.

Somehow she had forgotten that.

"Where's Cera?" Jae asked, lowering a now-wriggling Jaela to the ground.

Lucia picked up her daughter and strode over to place her in her playpen. "She wanted to be here, but she has the kids and ..."

"We thought there might be a discussion that wasn't ... suitable for young ears," Christian finished, still staring at her, his eyebrows pulled together. She might have known he would be the one to not let any of this go.

Not that she'd been expecting to get off easy.

"I'll visit Cera in the morning."

Julia smiled softly. "She would like that."

All of them stood on the opposite side of the room, except for Reuben, who stood close by her shoulder. Ryder was more in the middle, watching her worriedly. Never in a million years would she have ever thought he would look at her like that. Heaving a sigh, Jae swung around to look at her family.

"You're staring."

"We're waiting," her brother snapped.

"Christian," Julia said.

"Well—"

"Christian," her dad warned, "give your sister time."

Aw, jeez. They were waiting for the answers. Why had she run off? Why hadn't she gotten in contact? Why had she broken coven law?

Craning her neck, she sought Reuben, sought his comfort and his go-ahead that she could explain. After all, he was an implicated villain in this story.

His dark eyes caught her blue ones, and for some reason, she felt ... relaxed, filled with a sudden desire to tell them everything.

"Dad." She turned back around with her shoulders braced.

Just say it. It's no big deal. Ryder is right.

"Yes, sweetheart?"

The relaxation started to tighten back into anxiety until she felt Reuben's comforting hand on her shoulder and looked back at him. Swimming in his gaze, the mellowness returned. The words tumbled from her mouth. She didn't pause once to catch her breath. "I was tortured by Ethan. You know that, and I won't go into the details because that's not something you need to hear, but whatever happened to me, I think part of his powers transferred to my blood because when I got home, I was able to move things with my mind and I couldn't control it and I was scared and I was ashamed, so I ran away. I met Reuben, a rogue vampyre hunter, and I joined his gang and helped him but it really helped me deal with a lot of anger and I've managed to bring my telekinesis under a kind of control and please don't blame Reuben for any of this because he has been a very good friend to me."

Silence.

"Jae! O-pen! O-pen!" Jaela slapped her ineffectual hands against her playpen walls.

Lucia blushed at her daughter's bad timing and rushed over to her. "She wants you to open the pen. Sorry."

"Well." Christian looked back from his mate and child to his father and then to Jaeden. "Looks like you had a reason to run off, then. A crap reason, but one nonetheless."

"It wasn't a crap reason." Jae bristled.

Her brother snarled and made a move toward her. "Do you know what this family has been through? Do you know what you did to us? Or are you really so selfish you can't process what these last few months have been like for us, not knowing if you were alive or dead!"

A growl ripped through the room, and before she knew it,

Ryder had her brother by the shirt front, his teeth bared. "Do you have any idea what *she's* been through? No! So back off before I make you." He pushed Christian away with a disgusted snort.

Jae watched in shock as it unfolded, waiting for her father's reaction. Instead of getting angry, however, Dimitri merely placed a placating hand on Ryder's shoulder. "Christian doesn't mean any harm. He's just been worried sick about his sister."

"Jaeden's been through hell. I won't have her attacked."

Her dad quirked an eyebrow. "Oh, you won't, will you? And *why* is that?"

Julia sighed impatiently. "Boys. Arrggh." She turned to her daughter, her eyes bright with love. "I think it's best someone says the right thing." Her mother strode toward her and gripped her by the arms. "I'm sorry you felt you had to go through this alone. But you're not alone. You're home now, and we are going to help you get through this. We love you. Nothing could ever stop us from loving you."

Jaeden felt that ache in her chest implode, the remnants spreading out into a tidal wave of relief.

"Thank you," she managed.

Julia nodded, tears glistening in her eyes, and then turned to gaze kindly at Reuben. "Thank you, Reuben, for being there for her when we couldn't."

"It was my pleasure. You have an extraordinary daughter."

Jae blushed at the compliment before looking anxiously toward her father.

"You're home now, sweetheart. That's all that matters."

"Thank you, Daddy."

"Jae." Christian brushed past Ryder, who still looked ready to pounce on anyone who caused her any harm. "I'm sorry," he grumbled and then pulled her tight for another hug. "But I swear to Artemis, if you ever pull anything like that again, I will kick your ass."

"Like you could."

He laughed weakly and pushed her playfully.

"So"—her father's voice brought all eyes back to him —"now that that's settled, I want to know what on earth is going on between my daughter and you." His eyes burned into Ryder, who blanched and threw Jae a helpless look.

"Dad ..."

"Because if it's what I'm thinking it is, I am not going to be happy." He clamped a hard hand on Ryder's shoulder and tugged him threateningly close. "Either you've done some- thing that's going to get you killed, or you're *about* to do something that's going to get you killed. I just got her back, Ryder. I'd hate to think you're thinking what I think you're thinking."

Lucia snorted. "Am I the only one confused?"

She was met by a chorus of nos.

Julia wandered cautiously back to her mate. "Dimitri, would you care to tell me what's going on?"

His gaze was firmly locked on Ryder, and Jaeden began to worry for his safety. "Dad, maybe you should let go of Ryder."

"Dimitri, tell me."

"Dad—"

"Dimitri—"

"Ryder!" Her dad yelled, causing Ryder's eyes to widen and then wince as if waiting for the blow. The only one he felt was the huff her father expelled before releasing him with a beleaguered sigh.

He knew.

How did he always know these things?

"Ryder here is going to ask our permission to court Jaeden. They think they're mates," Dimitri finally said.

Everyone exploded into conversation, except Reuben,

who actually appeared to be watching on, fascinated. That confused Jae, who would've thought the reminder that she belonged to someone else would piss him off. However, he didn't look at all bothered, merely bemused by the ruckus her family caused.

She didn't have time to ponder how weird that was because Julia and Lucia hugged her, exclaiming happily. Her father and brother, on the other hand, glared at Ryder like they wanted to rip off his head. She couldn't leave him there to stand alone. It wasn't right.

She marched across the space to take hold of Ryder's hand. He nodded gratefully and squeezed tight. "This isn't exactly going to plan," he murmured, even though everyone could hear with their supersensitive ears.

Jae chuckled humorlessly. "Nothing ever does."

CHAPTER 13

The Proposition

Strange how over the last few days, she'd become something of a favorite at the Center, and with that newfound status, her loneliness had only intensified.

After one young magik approached Caia on a dare, and then been surprised and relieved to find out how friendly she was, word had spread that the half Midnight in their midst wasn't actually the daemon they'd thought. Gradually, others had come forward to talk with her, and now she found herself with a constant cloud of groupies under her feet.

The silence here was particularly wonderful.

She rested her head against the pew she crouched in front of, hidden from anyone who decided to enter. Desperate to breathe air that others weren't sucking out of her immediate vicinity, Caia had remembered Marion telling her about the altars. Maybe she should've paid a visit to Artemis, but she'd found herself entering the quiet marble sanctuary of Gaia instead. This was the goddess who'd made her existence possible, after all.

There was no doubt in Caia's mind that in this place of worship, Gaia could hear her. But what was there to say? She had only questions that required answers and being trapped on Mount Olympus kind of cut off Gaia's vocal cords here on Earth. If Caia wanted something, perhaps then Gaia could see that it was done, but what she wanted even Gaia couldn't give her.

Not being able to confide in anyone had brought on a fresh wave of grief over losing Sebastian. If she'd been given the chance to tell Seb she thought Midnights might not be so bad after all … he'd have believed her. No questions asked.

A flash image of him lying on the truck bed with his stomach torn to pieces, telling her he loved her, burned behind her eyelids, and Caia felt her chest tighten around her lungs. She found herself dragging in air just to catch a breath.

Sebastian.

She choked on a sob, clasping her hand against her lips to quiet the sound in the peace of the altar. What she wanted was her friend back, the most loyal friend she'd ever had, but Gaia couldn't give her that. And truthfully, she didn't deserve him back. She was failing miserably at whatever it was the prophecy said she was supposed to be doing.

She'd begun to fail when Sebastian had drawn his last breath.

Prying open her eyes, Caia slowly lifted her eyes to the marble statue of Gaia that presided over the altar in its center. Her face, though cold to the touch, was lit with a warmth that should have soothed a desperate soul. Instead it only frustrated Caia more. Gaia's eyes bored into her with a mix of sympathy and impatience.

"Tell me what you want from me."

"You know, there was once a time the goddess herself would have answered you."

Caia gasped in fright and looked up from her crouched position to see Vanne staring down at her.

"You scared me." She drew in a shuddering breath as she clambered to her feet. Even when Caia was standing, the elder magik towered above her with almost as much intimidation as Lucien.

His mouth quirked into a small smile, his eyes soft on her. "I'm sorry."

A moment of awkward silence ensued.

Vanne cleared his throat and glanced from her to the marble statue. "I didn't mean to disrupt ... I like to come in here and gaze at her when things feel ..."

"Overwhelming?"

He threw her a self-deprecating smile. "Yes. Overwhelming. She has such a soothing presence for a piece of marble."

Caia nodded. "I thought so at first."

"Caia." He suddenly leaned in close, his strong hand gripping her upper arm. "I think Gaia would tell you the one simple truth that we all like to pass off as cliché."

Caia found herself leaning closer to him, desperate for any kind of guidance, no matter the source.

"She would tell you that in the end, we only have ourselves, no matter how many friends, allies, or loved ones are in our lives. You have to trust yourself before you can trust anyone else. Trust yourself, Caia. Do what *you* think is the right thing to do."

"And the prophecy?"

"Why don't you stop looking so far ahead? Stick with the now and see where that takes you."

* * *

VANNE WAS RIGHT. Caia had already decided she needed to find the boy, Vilhelm, so she could determine how he felt about Laila; maybe find an ally in him and get him to help her free Laila. The last few days, that resolve had withered under paralyzing self-doubt, but surprisingly, and completely out of nowhere, *Vanne* had helped her.

Who saw that coming?

"Ooh, Caia!"

She turned and pasted on a bright smile as she entered the communication hall, only to be set upon by a couple of her groupies. Desdemona and Ophelia were nineteen-year-old twins who looked a little like her. They were both small in stature with long, blond hair and green eyes and had decided that this made them all like sisters.

Caia wanted to grimace at their puppy-dog enthusiasm but managed to control the urge. The girls were Caia's complete opposite—bubbly, outgoing, perhaps a little annoying ... but they were sweet. And they actually thought they had something to learn from Caia, which was just so—

"Ooh, Caia!" Desi repeated, rushing at and throwing her arms around her, causing all her classmates to stop and stare. Once Caia was free, Ophelia entrapped her in one of her own girlish hugs.

"I can't believe you've come to one of our classes!"

It was true she'd spent all her time in the advanced classes, such as natural materialization and water element lectures, but after spending the last day and a half strolling through them all, trying not to make it obvious she was looking for someone, she still hadn't found Vilhelm.

It occurred to her at lunch yesterday, when Ophelia had bemoaned her and her sister's loser-like place in the Center's posse system, Caia had only been in the beginners' and intermediate classes for communication spells. Apparently at the Center, there was an advanced communication spell class and an advanced specialist communication spell class. Desi and Ophelia were advanced specialists, meaning that neither of them had shown much aptitude in natural materialization or glamour. They were extremely adept at using their element—air—and excellent at communication spells. They were what the Center called Travelers.

While most magiks used the communication spell to journey quickly between places they were familiar with to relay information, Travelers could journey anywhere for long periods, whether they'd been there before or not. Caia thought it was pretty damn neat, but other magiks were snobby. Because they couldn't really do much of anything else, they were, well, outcasts.

Hence why they were so eager to please Caia.

"You know I'm in awe of you people." Caia swept her arm around the room, trying not to be embarrassed that she was the center of attention. She really should be used to it by now. "I just wanted to stop by, thought you could introduce me to your class?"

In truth, I just wanted to stop by and see if there was a tall, cute Scandinavian kid hanging around.

Desi laughed excitedly. "Uh, ye-uh!"

With that Caia found herself doing the uncomfortable task of pretending to be sociable. But while investigating, it suddenly occurred to her that dropping by had its upside.

Allies.

The whispering that met her sensitive ears told her she had just become the coolest kid on the block for these students. No other VIP magik had ever taken an interest in them before. *She* had given them hope that maybe things could change around the Center. Maybe people would open their minds and stop clinging to traditional thought.

I couldn't agree more.

Moving on to another group of magiks, Caia began to feel ... good?

Yeah, *good.*

She almost laughed out loud at the thought. These were exactly the kind of people she needed on her side: nontraditionalists who were prepared to welcome a new outlook.

Okay, so maybe they were only referring to the inner workings of the Daylight Coven, but if they weren't completely satisfied with how things were running at present, then maybe they would be the first to believe the war with the Midnights was based on misinformation and misunderstanding.

She smiled brightly, genuinely, as she talked with the Travelers, a small weight lifting from her shoulders.

She could do this.

She had to believe she could do this.

"And, Caia, this is Vil." Ophelia turned her around to face a tall magik. "He's my secret crush," she whispered in her ear.

Her heart pounded immediately as she took in the sight of the Scandinavian. His ice-blue eyes were nothing like their color; instead they were soft and shy, as was his smile as he reached out a nervous hand.

"It's an honor." He quickly pulled back from her clasped hand.

"Vil?" Caia breathed. "Is that short for Vilhelm?"

He nodded, blushing as Ophelia sidled up to him to squeeze his arm affectionately. "Vilhelm is the best Traveler here. We can all go places we've never been before, but we can't track a person or anything using the communication spell. Vil can."

Caia's mouth fell open a little as her eyes washed over him. "Like trace?"

"No, no," he quickly refuted, his eyes wandering nervously. "I can't feel a person's thoughts or energy ... but if you tell me to go to someone in particular, I get the impression of them from you and I can travel to wherever they are."

Was that right? Caia mused. *That might just come in handy.* "Impressive."

"I told you he was, like, totally cool."

A queasy, icy feeling enveloped her as Desi and her sister chattered away, her brain and senses battered by new information from Nikolai. Jeez! She fought to catch her breath. *This was good news.* She shook her head. *Good news.* Or was it? It kind of meant her time at the Center was up.

Her attention snapped to Vilhelm and the girls who were staring at her wide-eyed.

"Caia, are you okay?" Desi whispered.

She nodded, throwing them a tremulous smile. "Just tired. It was nice meeting you, Vilhelm. Ladies, nice to see you again, but I'm going to go lie down for a while."

"Do you need anything—?"

"Can I get you—?"

"No!" She raised her hands in supplication. "Please. No. I'm just … gonna … go."

Outside of the communication hall, Caia strode determinedly to the telecom system mounted on the wall next to the elevator.

"Center Reception, Chloe speaking."

"Chloe, it's Caia Ribeiro. I need to speak with Marita immediately."

"One second, please."

This gave her very little time to rescue Laila. She had to think fast, think fast, think fast, think fast, think fast …

"Miss Ribeiro, Marita will see you. If you please make your way to reception, someone will be there to escort you up."

That someone was Marion.

"What's going on?" she asked, her pixie face creased in concern.

"I'll explain once we get there."

"Lucien and Anders were with me when Marita called to say you had news. Lucien is already up there waiting. I didn't know what it was about so I didn't see the point of letting Anders in on it."

"This affects Anders."

"The MacLachlans, then?"

"The MacLachlans."

Marita and Vanne stood at their dining table, Lucien off to the side, his dark face brooding and troubled. Caia had only seen him during training sessions for the defense of the MacLachlans and had skillfully avoided talking to him. Not that it mattered since Rose was constantly attached to his side. In fact, this was the first time Caia had seen him alone since Rose's arrival.

Avoiding his eyes, she strode resolutely to the head of the table, Marion's soothing presence beside her.

"What has happened?" Marita frowned impatiently.

"The attack is off."

A shocked silence resonated around the room.

"How?" Lucien managed.

"Nikolai must have become aware of du Bois's plan. He's rounded up du Bois's rebels and given them immunity in exchange for their evidence against du Bois. Du Bois is now in prison, and the attack has been stopped."

Marita moved forward, her lips pinched in anger and confusion. "And you can't feel any plans from any other Midnight for the go-ahead on the MacLachlans?"

Caia shook her head. "I've been searching, but there is nothing. The attack is definitely not going forward."

Lucien frowned. "Well, that's good news, right?"

Marion seemed to agree. "Indeed."

"Caia and I will return to the pack tomorrow." Lucien strode toward her, and at his declaration, she couldn't stop herself from raising her eyes; they clashed with his. He seemed tired, angry, frustrated, and concerned all at the same time. Surprised at his words, she could only stand gaping at him. She thought he'd want to stay for Rose. His impatient bristling, however, told her that Lucien was clearly missing the pack and ready to get back to them as soon as he could.

The problem was that no matter how much she might want to go back with him, she had a little prison break she needed to orchestrate, and leaving before that wasn't really part of the plan.

* * *

"Leave?" Marita snapped. "I don't think so."

Lucien's hands curled into fists at her tone.

"We came here to do what were asked to do. Now we're leaving," he said between clenched teeth, watching in annoyance as the Head sauntered past him with barely a glance and came to a stop before Caia. Her usually frozen face had softened in a way he hadn't seen before. Her eyes washed over his mate imploringly.

"Caia, you can't leave yet without considering a proposition I have for you."

"Proposition?" Lucien asked, as did Marion and Caia.

The witch nodded. "I wasn't going to mention it until after the defense of the MacLachlans, but since that's not happening ... I wish to sit down and discuss the possibility of you staying at the Center."

Caia narrowed her eyes. "For what reason?"

Relief washed over Lucien. It was good she was just as suspicious of the magik as he was. He didn't want her rushing into anything that might take her away from the pack. And these days, who knew what was going on in her head. He hadn't been able to get a hold of her for one second to discuss anything. Caia was constantly bombarded by magiks, lykans and vampyres alike, all eager to befriend her. Not to mention the fact that she'd been avoiding him.

Something more than just Rose was plaguing Caia, and the fact that she wouldn't talk to him, confide in him, trust him ... it killed him. That she might be running to her precious pretty boy, Mordecai, with all her troubles made Lucien want to go for the jugular, but he was holding back until he had hard evidence that his mate was really slipping from his grasp.

"I would prefer if we discussed this is in private."

"Surely we can all be trusted here."

The witch pinched her lips but didn't dispute it. Instead, she nodded. "Very well. I want you to stay and help me train an elite force of lykans I'm working with."

Lucien felt his gut twist.

"Elite force?" Caia raised an eyebrow.

"An elite force. I won't go into specifics until you agree to aid me."

"How can I agree to help if I don't know the specifics?"

Lucien growled. "Exactly."

"The special training these lykans will undertake is highly classified. All Caia needs to know is that I think she has the abilities needed to not only train them but to lead them into battle."

Red washed over his eyes. "I won't allow it," he ripped out, his chest heaving with anger. For the first time in what felt like forever, Caia's soft touch wrapped around his wrist, squeezing it reassuringly, asking him silently to calm down.

Vanne had taken up beside Marita, glaring at him. Marita herself was not impressed. "May I remind you to whom you are talking, Mr Líder, and that this decision will be Caia's alone. You are not her mate in actuality after all."

"You want me to head up an elite combat force?"

No, no, no, no, no, no! His mind screamed and he knew Marita must be feeling everything he was. He couldn't seem to block or conceal his panic at the thought.

Marita nodded. "You would be instrumental in bringing this war to a close."

"I have to think about this."

Had he heard her right?

"What?" he gaped.

Caia set her shoulders as she met his gaze. He was shuddering with the need to change, to either run as fast as his wolf legs could take him or turn and rip apart anyone who dared take her from him.

"Lucien, calm down," she pleaded quietly. "This is my decision."

His wolf rumbled through clenched teeth, "I can't believe you would even consider it."

"It's important."

"Maybe take a few days. Stay a few days more, think about it. Both of you." Marita nodded at him, her eyes demanding that he fall in line.

Fall in line, my ass!

Caia seemed to brighten at the suggestion. "That's a good idea."

His gut flipped with a nervous, sick feeling at that smile. He realized the truth—the truth he hadn't wanted to face. Caia liked it at the Center because she was useful here, worthy, important. She was probably one of the most powerful beings in the Daylight Coven. Did he really think the pack would be enough for her?

Shutting her out in anguish, Lucien marched from the room, away from Caia and her master puppeteers.

CHAPTER 14

Cryptic Much?

The three trees directly in front of her were severely injured, their middles pierced with knives, thick branches, and her own little ax. She stood satisfied, her hands braced on her hips, looking over her handiwork. Then her attention drifted downward and swept her surroundings.

"Oops."

"You know, when I let Caia practice out here, she had the luxury of being able to clean it up in seconds."

Jaeden turned toward the speaker to find Ella leaning against her back porch, drinking in the mess Jae had made with her telekinesis.

She threw her a sheepish look. "Caia will be home soon, right? She can fix it?"

Ella gave her a smile so she knew she wasn't that upset. "Yeah, she can fix it."

"Thanks for letting me practice out here."

"You're welcome, hon." She was suddenly distracted by the stabbed trees at the edge of the yard. "Wow, you did that?"

Nervously, Jae followed her and walked toward the trees, pulling each implement out one by one. When she got to her ax, she placed the small weapon into the belt on her dark jeans. She spun around, knowing she would find Ella right behind her. Holding out a bucket, she gestured for Jae to dump the knives into it for now. Her eyes drifted down to the ax snuggled against her hip.

"You've certainly grown up since …" Her voice trailed off at the delicate subject she had almost broached.

Jae grunted and brushed past her toward Lucien's house. It was nearly five, and Ryder was supposed to be picking her up.

"Jaeden."

She reluctantly turned around, waiting for the admonition that had yet to come from anyone in the pack, but she knew was bound to soon. Ella, however, strolled toward her, eyes warm with motherly affection. She brushed her hand down Jaeden's face and smiled into her eyes. "I can only imagine how proud your mother is of you. I know because *I* am so proud of you. You've taken all the horrors you've been through and become fierce, strong, someone to be reckoned with. *I* think … that you are very brave."

Don't cry, don't cry, don't cry.

Jaeden laughed at herself, her throat closing with emotion as she turned away and forced her tears back. "I'm not brave. I'm scared all the freaking time."

Silence fell between them.

Ella sighed. "When Lucien was a boy—after everything that happened with Rafe and Griffin—he was so confused and scared. He knew something was terribly wrong. For a while he used to check the house over before he went to bed.

Every closet, every nook, every window, every door. And then he'd get angry because he thought he was being a coward. Albus took him aside one day and told him that courage was not the absence of fear, but the ability to walk into unknown territory despite it."

"Didn't Mandela say that?"

Ella pursed her lips at the interruption. "An abridged version, but that's not the point. The point is Lucien checked over the house each night, prepared to take on whatever bad thing he thought was waiting for him, even though he was scared. *That* was what made him brave. And you're the same, Jaeden. You of all people have every reason to curl up and hide under your bed … but you don't. You get up and you ready yourself for whatever might come your way. As I said, you are very, very brave."

"Or just crazy."

Ella laughed and chucked her under the chin. "Or just crazy. Anyway, is that a car I hear?"

Jae heard the gravel spinning under a wheel from the front of the house and her pulse picked up speed. She grinned. "Ryder."

Ella grinned back at her. "It's a good match. And when you mate, we really will be family. Have you seen Irini and Aidan yet?"

Jae smiled. She'd caught up with Ryder's brother and his mate the day before. The entire encounter had consisted of Aidan ribbing Ryder for falling prey to the mating when all along, he'd bragged about his bachelor lifestyle. The meeting with Yvana, however, hadn't gone as smoothly.

Apparently the relationship between sons and mother was not nearly as good as everyone had believed. It seemed Ryder and Aidan had taken more of Lucien's side over the whole Caia thing than anyone realized. Thus, the dinner Yvana hosted was stilted and cold. She was no longer the woman she'd once been, and what little remained of that woman had disappeared when Caia arrived, bringing with her the remembrance of what had happened to Yvana's mate.

Throwing another quick thank-you Ella's way, Jae jogged around the house to the driveway where Ryder was parked, listening to Nirvana. She shook her head, smiling. From Lynyrd Skynyrd to Nirvana, from *Top Gun* to *The Godfather*, he really was a mass of amusing contradictions. Unsurprisingly, when she jumped into the truck, Ryder pulled her over to the driver's side for a long, breath-stealing kiss. She should be used to his casual public affection by now, but every time he touched her, she still had to remind herself that, yeah, *he* was really kissing *her*.

"How was practice?" He grinned as they drove away from the house.

"Good. My aim is getting better."

"That's great! Guess who I bumped into at the diner today?"

"Hmm ... a member of Pack Errante?"

"Take the fun out of it, why don't you."

She smiled teasingly. "Sorry. Who did you bump into today?"

"I don't want to tell you now."

Feeling playful, as he always managed to make her feel, Jae reached over and slowly slid her hand up his thigh. "Please tell me."

He jumped at her touch and was now throwing her a beseeching look. "I'll tell you if you remove your hand from my person."

Grinning devilishly, her hand moved closer to the spot that would make him sweat. Suddenly the truck swerved. "Jaeden!"

She laughed and pulled her hand back. "Sorry."

He huffed, "Oh, I'm sure you are."

"Goddess, Ryder, you should be trussed up in a white chemise and a padlock covering your virtue for all the fuss you're making."

He spluttered in indignation, which only made her laugh harder. "I'm trying to be honorable here. Having your hands roaming freely over my particulars sort of makes the task Herculean!"

His exasperated tone made her feel guilty. "Sorry. I mean it. I'm sorry."

Somewhat mollified, he nodded and turned back to the road, keeping his eyes fixed straight ahead. "So, do you want to know who I spoke with?"

"Of course." She was determined to behave now.

"Alexa."

"Oh. How is she?"

"Working for my mother while she goes to community college."

"And?" If she knew Alexa, there was definitely an "and."

He coughed, looking uncomfortable. "And … a little pissed off."

Jaeden grimaced. "What now?"

"Me. You. Mating."

"What?" Jae growled. "Alexa was after Lucien."

"Apparently I forgot to mention that she was a little … interested in me … after you left."

An inexplicable jealousy ripped through her. "Did you sleep with her?"

"What, are you nuts?"

No! Alexa was the most predatory lykan out there; it would not have surprised Jaeden in the least. "No, I'm not. Alexa is attractive and easy. A lethal combination."

Ryder looked angry at the insinuation. "You know I don't mess around with our pack women. I told you because I wanted to give you a heads-up in case you see her.

She's pissed, and she's always been vindictive when she's pissed."

"Oh really, I hadn't noticed."

"What are you so mad about?"

"You! You didn't tell me to give me a 'heads-up.' You told me to make me jealous."

He snorted, his mouth twisted with as much sarcasm as his tone. "That's crazy. Why would I want to make you jealous? Look how much fun it is."

Jaeden wasn't stupid. This was deliberate. And she knew why. "Reuben. You're jealous of Reuben, and you want to inflict a little of that on me. Mission accomplished."

"That's not true. Although, since you brought it up, what the hell is the bloodsucker still doing in town?"

"He's staying in a motel."

"Yeah, in town. And he's constantly hanging out. When we get to your place, he'll be there."

"He's my friend."

He harrumphed.

A tense silence fell between them, the truck cab thick with strained animosity and sexual tension.

"We need to get this mating ceremony over and done with," he growled.

"Why?" Jae asked derisively. "Because we're so good together?"

"Because I have a feeling we'll be arguing a lot."

"Oh, great reason for mating!"

"And if we're going to be arguing a lot, that tension has to go somewhere."

Immediately his meaning dawned on her, and she turned, blushing, to meet his gaze. His eyes burned as they washed over her. "I swear to Artemis, Lucien is dead if he doesn't get back here soon to authorize this ceremony."

Feeling shy, Jaeden mumbled, "We don't have to wait."

Ryder heard her anyway. "You know we do."

"I told you it doesn't matter to me."

"Well, it matters to me."

Her eyes drifted over his strong forearms and the large hands that gripped the steering wheel. She felt the tension in the truck thicken, and her face heated. "Maybe we shouldn't spend too much time together until then."

"Uh, you think?"

* * *

DESPITE THEIR DECISION to not be around one another, Ryder found himself following Jae into the house when they arrived at Dimitri's. The fact that Reuben's car was there had nothing to do with it whatsoever. He shrugged off the annoyance he always felt when the vamp was around and greeted everyone with an impression of his old laid-back self. *Ha*, he inwardly snorted. He wondered if he would ever be that guy again.

Sure enough, he found Reuben in the kitchen with Julia, helping her with a recipe.

"I would never have thought of doing that," Julia exclaimed happily as she read over a piece of paper. "However did you come by this recipe?"

Reuben smiled. "I was friends with a very good chef once."

"How many years ago was that?" Ryder couldn't help himself.

Julia and Reuben turned, and Jae's mother grinned happily. "I knew I heard you come in." She sauntered over to him and patted a floury hand to his cheek before leaving the kitchen to see to her daughter. He winced at the sound of major hugging in the sitting room. Poor Jae. Since returning, she only ever got peace when she went to Ella's to practice. Everyone wanted to see her and check on her, and she never had any alone time in the house. He understood her family's anxiety, but she must be going crazy. Nothing to be said, though, he reminded himself. He had to stay on Dimitri's good side or he might not give his blessing for the mating.

"How was practice?" Reuben asked in his sober way. Ryder disliked the way his eyes darted past his shoulder, obviously looking for Jae.

"Good."

"I better say hi."

"Why don't we take a minute outside?" Ryder gestured to the back door.

This was a conversation long coming.

He knew the vamp got why he insisted on some privacy, his dark eyes glittering with anticipation.

Once outside, Ryder cut to the chase. "Why are you still here?"

Reuben laughed. "You know, I actually like your forthrightness, lykan. It makes your unnecessary jealousy a little less tedious."

"Unnecessary. You sure? Why. Are. You. Still. Here?"

The vampyre moved farther into the darkening backyard, his face tilted toward the sky. "For Jaeden. I want to make sure she's okay before I leave."

"She's fine. She's got me."

Reuben chuckled. "As if you're enough against what's coming."

"What the hell does that mean?"

The vamp seemed to remember himself, and he shook his head, a smile of apology on his lips. "Nothing."

"It wasn't nothing. What the hell is coming?"

Holding up his hands in surrender, Reuben approached Ryder slowly. "I didn't mean anything you don't already know. I know about Caia, that's all. Jaeden told me everything. I can keep a secret. But we all know that Caia's presence in this war is only the beginning of the end of a very old story. The penultimate episode is encroaching, and the action in that is always as bloody for the minor characters as it is for the major ones in the final. Who knows how bad it will get. Jae—all of you—will need all the friends you can get."

The vampyre brushed past Ryder and into the house, leaving him feeling unsettled. That guy was so weird.

Sighing in frustration, Ryder turned and followed him back into the house. Immediately he went on alert at the silence that greeted him and raced toward the sitting room to find Jae. She was there, safe and sound with her family and Reuben, but everyone was gazing toward the doorway on the other side of the room where a familiar being leaned against the doorframe.

Saffron.

"What's going on?" he demanded, striding into the room to stand by Jae.

Saffron's mouth twisted into a moue when she saw him. "Ryder." She heaved a sigh. "I should have guessed you would be here. Always sticking your nose in."

He ignored that, knowing her propensity for childish argument rather than getting to the point. "Why are you here?"

She seemed surprised by his complete disregard of her attempt to rile him but straightened and stared at Dimitri. "I'm here to kill two birds with one stone. Lucien wanted to convey a message to the pack *and* find out if Jaeden was returned safely home."

"I'm Jaeden." She wiggled her fingers at the faerie.

Saffron rolled her eyes at her. "I'm aware. I killed the spy who was pretending to be you."

He bristled at her blasé tone and the way the blood

drained from Jaeden's face. He growled in annoyance, as did Dimitri.

The faerie raised a delicate eyebrow. "Was that insensitive?"

"Just a little," Julia said.

"Sorry. Old habits and all that. Anyhoo, she's safe and sound and hunky-dory. I'll tell Lucien. And Lucien wants you to know that the attack against the MacLachlans has been stopped by the Regent of the Midnight Coven. However, he and Caia will be remaining at the Center for a few days more while Caia considers a position Marita has offered her."

Position? Ryder shook his head in confusion. What the hell kind of position would Caia possibly consider taking after she had promised Lucien she was staying with the pack? That didn't sound right.

Something was up.

"Position?" Reuben asked quietly. Ryder frowned, wondering why the vampyre wanted to know.

Saffron blinked, and Ryder was sure he saw a flash of familiarity flit across her eyes as she stared at Reuben. When he stared harder, however, all he found was the polite mask frozen on her face whenever she was talking to a stranger ... hell, when she was talking to anybody.

"What position?" the vamp repeated.

Ryder was surprised the faerie didn't take offense at Reuben's authoritative tone. "Leader of some elite force of lykans, apparently."

"What?" Ryder snapped. "That doesn't make sense."

"I'm surprised anything makes sense to you, what with your brain being the size of a peanut."

Jae growled and stepped toward the faerie. "Watch it, Tinker Bell."

Ryder smiled smugly at her protectiveness and the look of astonishment on the faerie's face.

"That's the thanks I get for unmasking the bitch pretending to be you?" She sulked and looked back at him. "Well, the little ones will be double the morons when *you two* mate."

"Hey!" Julia took offense.

Saffron grimaced. "Looks like I've outstayed my welcome, then." And just like that, she disappeared.

"What a snotty—"

"Pain—"

"In the ass," Dimitri finished.

* * *

HE RUSHED from the bathroom at the sound of his cell ringing and snatched it up, his heart faltering at the caller ID. What had happened now?

"Nikolai. Problem?"

The Russian sighed down the line. "Why do you think so? You're always looking at the bad in everything, Kirios."

"Something has happened."

"Da. It's that insect du Bois."

"I thought you handled that."

"So did I. He's more powerful than I realized, and his hand reaches further than I thought."

"Where is he?"

"I can only imagine at this moment he is on his way to attack the MacLachlans."

"Then Caia knows. She'll be preparing for war."

"Da."

"Do you not realize how disastrous this is, Nikolai?"

The magik cleared his throat. "Actually, I was thinking we have been looking at this all wrong. This attack, this defense

… is it not the perfect opportunity to test Caia? To see exactly what she is capable of?"

"If we start thinking that way, we will be just like them. That is not what we want for the future, Nikolai."

"I know. But to win this war, we must know exactly what our weaponry and the enemy's weaponry is capable of."

He squeezed his eyes closed, feeling a metaphorical headache coming on.

"Very well. Send in a spy."

CHAPTER 15

Breaking Out

A trickle of sweat slid down her back, hidden from
view. Thankfully, they were all aware she'd rushed
to this meeting, and she hoped the lykans who could smell
the sweat would mistake the cause of it. Caia held her breath
as her gaze swept Marita and Vanne's sitting room, battle
plan central as it was now. She coached herself to remain
outwardly calm, to keep her eyes from widening, her chest
from heaving. Her face was a frozen mask.

Marita, Vanne, Marion, Lucien, Rose, Mordecai, Anders,
Michael, and Phoebe stared at her in frustrated confusion,
wondering why they had been called, probably guessing, but
still annoyed by her silence. She was preparing her voice to
come out steady, not high and squeaky like she felt inside.

Finally, she drew a breath and announced. "Pierre du Bois
has escaped imprisonment. Petrovksy has no clue as to his
whereabouts, but I've picked him up with a few of his rebels

that have remained faithful. The attack against the MacLachlans is going ahead. Which means the attack is tomorrow
evening in Remnant Forest."

There were growls, hissing, and expletives as they
received confirmation of the news that had been clear the
moment they'd been called together. To them this would be
the reason for Caia's frozen anxiety; to the lykans, the reason
they could smell the sweat that trickled under her shirt; to
the vampyre, the reason he could detect the quickening of
the pulse in her neck with his razor-sharp eyes.

They would be wrong.

Suddenly the double doors to Marita's suite banged open,
and in hurried a worried-looking magik. At the same
moment, a feeling of triumph mixed with fear rushed
through Caia when the trace she was holding on to disappeared from the Center.

The magik's eyes swung wildly until they found Marita,
who rounded the table with a look of outrage pasted on her
face.

"How dare you barge in here uninvited!" she exclaimed,
glancing behind the magik to find Noble pale and beseeching. "How did she get in here?"

He blanched and gestured to her. "This is Blair, the
warden at the containment center. She said it was an
emergency."

Marita whipped toward the warden. "What is it?"

Blair gulped, smoothing her hair into its severe bun with
shaking hands. "Madam, I'm afraid it has come to my attention that the prisoner has escaped."

Marita jerked as if she'd been slapped. "Prisoner? You
mean the girl? The Midnight?"

Blair nodded frantically.

"Have you searched the entire Center?"

"All of it, madam. There is no sign of her."

Marita shook her head in disgust and then closed her eyes. "Caia?"

Her pulse sped up and she willed it to slow so the lykans present would not hear it. "Yes?"

"Can you feel the girl?"

She pretended to take a moment and then shook her head gravely. "No. She's not at the Center."

"Well, where is she?"

Okay, Cy, time to draw on your best acting skills. Channel Meryl Streep. "I-I don't know. I-I can't feel her," she said, pretending to be panicked by the thought.

"What do you mean you can't feel her? You told me you could find anyone in the trace?"

She pushed a few tears into the corner of her eyes, brushing her hair off her face, making her hands tremble. "I'm sorry. I don't know why ..."

"Argh!" Marita threw up her hands in exasperation. Then she took a calming breath, turning back into the ice queen as she menacingly glanced at Blair, her voice low and terrifying. "How on Gaia's green earth did this happen?"

* * *

FORTY-EIGHT HOURS earlier

AVOIDING LUCIEN WAS PROVING EASY. Avoiding everyone else?

Not so much.

It was easy with Lucien because he was angry at her, and he had reason to be. She *had* promised she would stay with the pack rather than fight at the Center. On the other hand, if he wasn't being such an idiot, he would realize she would never go back on her word and realize that something was up. At the moment, his misunderstanding was working more in her favor than if he was questioning her motives. She needed him well and truly out of this.

This being …

Her, trying to build up the courage to confront Vilhelm. The idea of encouraging someone to break a Midnight out of prison and out of the Center was insane.

Maybe I've got Marita all wrong. Maybe it's me with my stupid trace. Maybe being a half Midnight means my trace is broken. Maybe I'm the delusional one.

The truth was that she didn't want to believe all these people she trusted were wrong and she was right. What about Marion and Magnus?

What about Albus?

What about her father?

Were they wrong? Did they give their lives to a lie?

Goddess, it was too awful to conceive.

Then she let herself feel Laila's trace, and her gut twisted.

Could her trace really be so off that she would feel this sweetness from a girl who was evil? Was there ever really just good and evil?

Ethan had certainly been evil.

But was that like condemning Austrians because Hitler was a soulless fiend?

My head hurts.

She flopped back on her bed, staring up at the heavy silk canopy above, wishing she were anywhere but where she was.

"You have to make up your mind, Cy. Time is running out," she snapped at herself. At this moment she was supposed to be at a water lecture. That's what she had told Mordecai, anyway. When he realized she wasn't there, he'd come looking for her. She was surprised, in fact, that there wasn't a gaggle of bodies outside her room, but she guessed the ordinary candidates couldn't access her floor.

Muffled voices suddenly floated through her walls from the hallway and she moved quick and quiet to press her ear against her door. Sure enough, she could hear voices coming from the elevator, which was at least fifteen meters around the corner and down the hall.

She recognized them. Mordecai and Marita.

Artemis, she loved her lykan hearing.

Grinning jubilantly, she pressed harder and felt her pulse race at the conversation.

"I don't know what this plant of yours is going to pick up, Mordecai. From all accounts, she has had no one in her room."

"The lykan. Lucien. Surely she'll invite him into the room. We should learn something from that conversation."

"And this plant? You're sure it will go undetected by her?"

"Well, you could put a faerie in there if you aren't confident in me."

"One: Stop being impertinent. Two: You know why I can't put a faerie into her room. It's that bloody faerie of my sister's, Saffron. She's too influential among the faeries here and she happens to hold Caia in the deepest of respect, which is saying a lot for the sarcastic relic."

"This will work, I promise."

"And you're sure you personally can't learn anything more from her?"

"I told you, Marita, I got all the info I could on her special ability. I tested that tree she blew up and still nothing of any consequence. We won't know for certain until we see it in action. But I maintain that I believe her when she says she has it under control."

"And Jaeden?"

"I'm not going to get anything more out of her on that subject. Hence the plant."

"Do you think she's even aware of Jaeden's ... abilities?"

"I don't know. But we'll find out."

"You better. We need that information if we want to be successful. So far the children are not reacting in any way."

"Yes, well, this bug should tell us what we need to know."

"And if it doesn't?"

"Then we find another way to get what we need. Perhaps a more direct solution, such as the one I suggested earlier."

"It's too risky. I told you it's a last resort ... impertinent ... "

Shock reverberated through Caia's body. She pulled back from the door, staring at it in disbelief. Mordecai was working with Marita, trying to unearth secrets from her. What did they want with her? With Jaeden? What abilities? What children?

Oh goddess, she cupped a hand over her mouth to silence her snarl of frustration. Something seriously weird was going on here, and her spider senses were telling her it was something bad.

Enough was enough.

She straightened and glared at the doorway.

No more second-guessing herself. No more doubt. She'd been right all along. Something wasn't right at the coven, and there were innocent people feeling the consequences, including herself and more importantly, Laila. She was getting the girl out today.

Mordecai's and Marita's footsteps grew closer, and Caia panicked. They couldn't barge in here because that would be suspicious of *them*, and she had to maintain the cover that she trusted Mordecai completely. She began to sing loudly, making them aware of her presence. There was silence for a moment and then a soft tap on her door.

"Come in."

Alone, Mordecai strolled in, a breezy smile on his face. "Hey, I wondered where you had gotten to. You weren't in the lecture."

Caia shrugged, holding her claws in tight so she wouldn't attack the traitor right. "I just wanted to catch a breath before I head down to see Desi and Ophelia."

He looked momentarily bewildered. "It's just like you, Caia, to take people like Travelers under your wing."

You smug son of a bitch.

She smiled tightly.

He strolled around the room making small talk, and if she hadn't been looking for it specifically, she never would've noticed the ultra-subtle move he made, dropping something tiny and weightless into a vase by the fireplace.

So now her room was bugged.

His eyes creased in concern. "You're sure you're okay?"

"I'm fine. Honest. Just taking some time."

"Well." He grinned and headed toward the door. "Just checking up. Come get me if you need me."

"Will do."

"Oh, and Caia … have you thought any more about Marita's offer? I think you should really consider it."

I bet you do.

"I'm definitely giving it serious thought. Wouldn't be here otherwise. You know, there's just so much more to learn."

Like just how sneaky and conniving the Head of the Coven is.

He smiled again and left.

Jeez, that magik was a great actor. She'd had no idea he was a scummy little toad working for his mistress. She withheld from snorting in disgust in case the bug picked it up and instead headed for the door.

She had a prison break to put into motion.

* * *

TWENTY-FOUR HOURS later

"THERE YOU ARE."

She tried not to groan at the familiar voice that sent shivers down her spine no matter the occasion. And right now, she did not have time to deal with the person belonging to that voice.

"Ssh," she hissed at him, sliding the actual book she'd been reading under a copy of *Practical Tae Kwon Do: Back to the Roots.*

"What are you doing here?" Lucien whispered, sliding into the chair beside her and leaning over to check out her reading material. He raised an eyebrow but made no comment. And then he lifted his silver gaze to hers and she had to force herself not to look away.

"Why are we whispering? There's no one else in here."

Caia glanced around the small, empty library and shrugged. "There could have been."

Lucien stretched back in his seat, pinning her with a look of frustration. "I've come to a conclusion after our little meeting with Marita."

"Oh?"

"At first I was angry. And then angrier. And then today I let my brain take over and I thought, no—Caia wouldn't abandon the pack after what happened with Sebastian. She still feels raw about that, still feels guilty even though it's not her fault." He heaved a sigh, running his hand through his hair, before setting his elbow on the table and leaning toward her. "You still grieve for him. You would never leave us. So why did you tell Marita you would consider her job offer?"

Crap. She had so wanted his obtuse lykan self to not figure out this part.

Even though her heart was determined to race, she held tight in her seat, her butt clenched with the tension it took not to give anything away. "I don't know what you're babbling about."

He smirked, unconvinced. "You're delaying leaving here. Now, again, when I first came to that conclusion, I thought it was because you were kind of a rock star—enjoying the glory of being a mega-being." He guffawed. "Then I came to my senses, and thought no, this is Caia, the girl who blushed at her first pack run, the girl who looks as if she would give anything to melt into the wallpaper every time we meet in Marita's suite to discuss the MacLachlan attack."

Oh Gaia, she really wished he hadn't decided to get all perceptive where she was concerned.

"Lucien—"

He held up his hand to cut her off. "So that leaves me with one question."

She waited.

His eyes narrowed dangerously and his head lowered in mimicry of his lykan when going on the attack. "What the Hades are you up to, Caia?"

"Lucien—"

"I am still your Pack Leader and I demand to know what you're planning here."

She wanted to tell him, she really did. But without knowing how he really felt about her, how could she trust him with this before she actually did it? If her plan went accordingly, she would have to tell him eventually. But now, when there was still so much at stake?

"The Center has made me see things differently. I really am considering Marita's offer."

He growled. "I don't believe you."

"It's the truth."

"Caia—"

"Lucien, I'm telling you the truth, so drop it."

His nostrils flared and he pushed back so hard from the table, his chair flew out behind him and smashed against the wall at the opposite end of the room.

Caia scowled at him. "Nicely done."

"Don't even start. Do you know how close I am to ... to ..." He made a choking gesture with his hands and bared his teeth at her. Instead of responding to him, she glanced in what she hoped was a casual manner behind him and flicked her wrist, setting the chair to right and returning it to the table.

He grunted at her use of magik and then turned on her, his eyes glittering as he leaned down so close to her face she felt his warm breath whisper across her skin. "I will get to the bottom of this."

Trying not to blink, Caia eased away slightly but kept her own challenging gaze locked on his. "Good luck with that."

With a harsh curse, Lucien jerked away from her and marched toward the double doors that led out of the library. She watched as he hesitated and half turned to glare at her. "Thought you might like to know that Jaeden is home safe and sound."

Jae? She was all right? Marita had said ...

"Is she okay?"

Lucien twisted his mouth in derision. "Safe and sound generally implies such."

"Sarcasm. Wonderful."

He grunted and turned to the door.

"Lucien!"

Heaving a melodramatic sigh, his shoulders hunched in defense, Lucien refused to turn and look at her. He threw out an exasperated "What?"

"Is … is Jaeden … has Jaeden … Was there any mention of Jaeden having … abilities?"

He curled his head toward her, enough to raise a mocking eyebrow. "Such as the ability to morph into a wolf?"

She grimaced. "You really are unpleasant when you're not getting your own way."

"No. I'm just used to having my orders obeyed."

"There's a difference between that and abusing your position to nose into my privacy."

Scowling, he made to turn away from her, and before he disappeared with a banging of the doors, he murmured, "Don't think I don't find the Jaeden question weird."

When he was gone, Caia blew out a weary breath.

Jaeden was okay.

And she would remain so as long as Caia had any say in it.

* * *

TWENTY-THREE HOURS later after that

VILHELM STARED BACK AT HER, wild-eyed and shaking.

"You're sure this is going to work?"

Caia nodded, poker face on, her body steady as a rock. If they were to pull this off, she needed to project a calm confidence that he wouldn't question.

She had to hand it to the kid—he was either extremely brave or stupidly in love. After hunting him down, it had taken very little to convince Vilhelm to break Laila out of the Center and take her to Ryder's. It seemed they were both desperate enough to place their trust in a stranger. They stood now in a janitor's closet, a few corridors away from the prison.

"You ready?"

Vil nodded excitedly. "Do it."

With unruffled nerve, Caia raised her hand so that it hovered an inch in front of Vil's face. Slowly and carefully, her fingers crackling with energy, she swept the air in a vertical motion from the tip of his hair to the tip of his chin.

"Is it done?"

She bit her lip, staring at Vil who was now the exact image of Vanne. "Not quite."

Softly, she placed a hand on his neck, over his voice box.

"Cold," he chuckled nervously.

With a satisfied nod, Caia pulled back. "Say something else."

"I can't wait to see Laila." His eyes widened. "I can't wait to see Laila. Wow, I sound exactly like Vanne."

Caia nodded. "Remember, you have thirty minutes to get in there and get out of the Center before your face and voice return. Hold out your hand, palm forward."

He did as instructed and she placed her small hand against his large one.

Lucien had almost caught her researching this act she was about to perform: the transfer of a small amount of her power to another magik. The transfer would last only ten minutes at the most, but they needed this so Vil could break Laila out of the bars in her prison.

Yesterday morning, Caia and Vil had managed to sweet-talk a junior officer at the containment center into giving up the name of the spell wrapped around the bars holding Laila in. He'd been more than happy to show off how the facilities worked for the VIP magik.

With the help of a little something Vil had picked up during an air element lecture, he was able to stop the memory of their having been at the containment center by temporarily starving the oxygen flow to the hippocampus of the officer's brain, where memories were consolidated from short to long-term.

It tended to be a little painful and cause confusion for a moment, giving them plenty of time to get out before he came to his senses.

Lucien had then interrupted Caia's research in the library where she'd discovered what kind of spell to counteract the one keeping the magik up around the bars. It was a small incantation that needed to be said while focusing the energy used to produce glamour on the bars. The temporary transfer of her power to Vil was necessary, since he wasn't really good at anything but using his air element and being a Traveler.

"You remember the password and incantation?"

Vil tapped his brain. "Locked in tight."

It was weird talking to him when he looked and sounded like Vanne. Filled with trepidation, Caia jerked her head toward the closet door. "You better get going. Remember you can trust Ryder—he'll keep you safe. Don't mention Laila being a Midnight just yet."

"Got it."

"Tell him what I told you to tell him."

"Don't worry, I will. I trust you."

She guessed it was easier to trust the person who tells you they think the girl you love is actually a good person than the person who imprisoned her and forbade you from ever seeing her again.

It was at that moment the familiar, sickening, icy feeling shuddered through her body, and a wealth of new information poured into her.

"Crap," she whispered.

"What, what?" Vil asked, frantic.

"Nothing. Nothing. It's not about this. It doesn't affect this. Go!" She pushed him toward the door and watched impatiently as he ducked his head out to make sure the corridor was clear. Caia closed the closet door behind her and nodded at him. "See you soon."

He smiled tremulously. "Hope so."

With that, they spun away from each other and headed in opposite directions. At the elevators, Caia picked up the intercom system.

"Center Reception, Chloe speaking."

"Chloe, it's Caia Ribeiro. Can you put me through to Marita?"

"One second, please."

The line was silent for only a moment.

"Caia?" Marita's imperious voice rang down the line. Caia felt her face grimace in anger; she scolded herself for being obvious even if the witch couldn't see her.

"Could you please gather the tactical team for the MacLachlans?"

"What's going on?"

"I have some important news."

CHAPTER 16

You

"I thought we were going to spend more time apart until Lucien gets back?"

She stood slouched and languid against her doorframe, her mouth twisted in mockery, her tone suggesting irritation. But Ryder was not deterred. He grinned cockily into her dark blue eyes and found in them attraction, happiness that he was on her doorstep.

He mirrored Jaeden's pretended indifference. "I'm bored. Thought you might be bored, maybe desperate to get some air." He nodded behind her shoulder, his eyebrows raised pointedly. He watched, amused, as she struggled to hide her smile of relief.

Yeah, she would definitely enjoy escaping her parents for a while.

"Come on, Jae," he taunted at her hesitation. "You know you want to."

She huffed in response, "You are such a tease."

Grinning wolfishly, he gestured with a sweep of his hand to his truck. "Not tonight."

Her eyes lit up, and he had to stifle his groan of frustration. He had no intention of doing what she thought he intended on doing. The truth was, he couldn't seem to last a few hours without her, despite the restrictions he put on the activities allowed during their time together. But he'd rather she was alone with him than Reuben, who was constantly in her kitchen.

"Fine," she pretend-grumbled and then shouted inside as she shut the door, "I'm going out with Ryder for a while."

Grabbing his sleeve, Jae tugged him at full speed toward the truck. "Hey, where's the fire?"

"We need to get out of here in the next ten seconds or the—"

"Jaeden!"

"Oh, great."

They both turned at the sound of Dimitri's voice. He glared at them from the doorway, his arms crossed over his chest, feet spread apart.

"Where are you going?" The question was directed threateningly to Ryder.

Great. He scowled at Jaeden as if to say, "nice going." He really hoped her dad would back off once they were actually mated.

"With it being such a nice night and all, I asked Jaeden if she would like to go for a run."

"We're going for a run?" He was relieved to hear that her surprise was tinged with pleasure.

"What about asking me?" the Elder grumbled.

Ryder straightened his shoulders. "Well, sir, I never thought. Would you like to come for a run?"

"Not me going with you, you idiot." He shook his head in

disgust. "How on earth did you make it to Rogue Hunter status?"

"Dad," Jae warned.

He gestured toward Ryder. "He's the one asking the stupid questions. I *meant* … why did you not ask permission from me to escort my daughter on a run?"

"Dad, I'm eighteen."

Dimitri snorted. "Yeah, and that makes you mature."

Ryder stiffened, feeling Jae's bristling between them. And Dimitri thought he was the dumb one.

"No," she snapped, stepping menacingly toward her father. "But weeks in a cage at the hands of a psychopath and then months living by myself hunting kind of does."

Dimitri blanched. "Sweetheart, you know I didn't mean—"

"Dad, I don't want to argue." She threw a meaningful glance at Ryder, one he couldn't help but enjoy. "I just want to spend some time with Ryder."

The Elder stared at them for some moments and then nodded stiffly. "Okay." He pointed a finger at Ryder. "No funny business, though, or I'll kill you."

"Daddy," Jae groaned, "Ryder is a perfect gentleman." She lowered her eyes, blushing and murmuring, "So embarrassing."

Ryder struggled not to laugh as he grabbed hold of Jaeden's hand. "I'll take good care of her."

"You do that."

* * *

THEY LAY side by side on the hood of Ryder's truck, their limbs torpid and warm from their run in her father and Lucien's woods. She smiled, comforted by the heat of him next to her, by their recent playfulness in their wolf form. Ryder was a big gentle beast; no matter how hard she came at him, he would just shrug her off and tickle her with his snout. It wasn't like Lucien with Caia. She'd watched them play together, and Lucien was a rougher kind of guy, nudging Cy as hard as she nudged him, nipping, biting, tumbling. Ryder just seemed happy to be there with her, despite the bruises she inflicted.

Jae giggled.

"What was that for?" Ryder asked in an amused, sleepy voice.

She shook her head and watched him from the corner of her eye. His eyes were closed, his arms locked behind his head.

"You're not what I expected."

"Hmm, no? I guess I wasn't expecting you at all."

She chuckled and gazed at the stars, distant lights in the dark ceiling over their heads. "Fair enough."

"You glad to be home?"

It was weird how glad she was to be home. Having been so set against coming back, having been so determined to leave in the first place, she still couldn't quite work out her own sudden feelings.

"Very."

"Told you."

"Yeah, there's no need to be smug." She edged a little closer to his body heat. "It's still weird, though."

Jaeden almost laughed at the way one of his eyes snapped open in alert. "What is?"

"Like I said before, I was so set against coming home and then ... just as suddenly, I couldn't believe I had ever thought leaving was the answer."

He rolled onto his side, his head propped in his hand. "You went through a lot, Jaeden. You keep saying you're okay, but maybe that sudden switch in feelings is just part of what you're dealing with."

No, she thought inwardly, *no, I really am okay.*

As if he could hear her thoughts, he reached out to stroke her cheek. She curled into his touch.

"How can you be okay, Jae? I don't understand how you can be okay."

With that she withdrew, her eyes fixed back on the sky. She didn't want to pull away from him, but she didn't want him thinking she needed help when she knew she didn't.

"I thought we'd been over this already. You're starting to sound like a broken record."

"We've not been over it to my satisfaction."

It bothered her that he wanted to talk about all the bad stuff when all she wanted was to forget it. And she could; she could do that now that she had him, now that she had something to look forward to, something to work toward.

At her silence, she could feel his tension build, his frustration pulling tighter and tighter until—

"For Artemis's sake, Jae, talk to me."

With a huff, she drew herself up on the truck, tucking her legs in close to her body. Finally, she allowed her gaze to drift over him. As his eyes blazed with a mixture of emotions, she was reminded how lucky she was that someone like him cared enough to keep asking, despite her stubbornness each time he did.

"What is it you want to know, Ryder?"

He sat up, his huge body taking up most of the hood, drawing her closer toward him.

"I want to know if you really are coping with what happened with Ethan. Are you still having nightmares?"

She clenched her teeth, grinding them back and forth as she squeezed out, "You really are trying to embarrass me to death."

"Why is this embarrassing?"

She dodged the question. "I thought we talked about this that night in the motel room. I told you I was fine."

"Yeah, and I ... I don't *get* how you *can* be."

Goddess, he was a frustrating pain in the ass. No wonder he was a Rogue Hunter; he was completely relentless.

"I told you I don't understand my change in feelings."

"I told you that's not what I'm asking about."

"Ryder ... " She threw him a pleading glance. "This is what I'm afraid of. You're doing what my parents are doing."

"What?"

"Trying to decide if I need access to a mental health professional."

"Well, do you? Lykans have their own therapists, you know."

"Ryder!"

"Jaeden, I just need to know you're okay."

"Yes, I'm okay!" she yelled at him. "I'm okay because of you. Because I love you! You big ass!" Face pulsing with heat from the blood rushing under her skin, Jae made to throw herself off the hood only to struggle against a steel hold wrapped around her waist. She yelped as it dragged her and slammed her none too gently on her back. Ryder held her down, his eyes bright as they roved over her, red face and all. He looked ... surprised.

This is it. It's true. You can die of embarrassment. He thinks I'm insane.

"You ... you're okay because of me?" he asked incredulously.

"Well, not *just* you," she said, still pinned under him. "The fact that I might be useful to Caia in the war is also keeping me sane."

"You plan on fighting?" He frowned.

"What did you think I've been practicing for?"

"Huh." He looked off into the trees and then his eyes narrowed back on her. "I don't know if I like that too much."

"You can just take a flying—"

"Now, now, I said I didn't like it, but I get it." He nodded and pulled back, allowing her to scramble up and regain some equilibrium. "It makes sense that it would help."

Great, he's not going to say anything. He's just going to ignore that little announcement.

I thought he had to love me back if we had any chance of being mates?

She felt like killing him.

Matters weren't helped by the way he stared at her for a long moment, his expression quizzical.

"It's more than you," she reiterated. "When I was in that cage … I gave up on life." Her voice cracked. "And when Sebastian died, I felt ashamed for feeling that way. I've promised myself that I will live … because he can't."

For a moment they sat in heavy-hearted silence.

"Maybe you should take me home," she whispered, looking away, an ache throbbing in her chest.

"Jaeden?"

"What?" She refused to look at him.

Gently, he took her chin in his hand and forced her to look at him, his eyes searching. "I'm not ignoring what you said—"

"Ryder, don't—"

"Shut up for a second. Jaeden, I wouldn't have suggested we might be mates if I hadn't been falling in love with you. I love you." He grinned ruefully. "Despite the fact that you make me crazy. I'm just … awed that I could do that for you, that I could help you that way."

Relief flooded her, and she let him draw her in for a long, comforting kiss that heated up too quickly. He withdrew, laughing shakily. "I'm going to kill Lucien for extending his trip."

Jaeden laughed at his belligerence, her doubts melting into the shadows of the surrounding forest. "Yeah, 'cause I'm sure Lucien is enjoying being away from the pack."

"Point taken." He looked around them. "I suppose I better get you home."

"Can't we stay ... just for a little longer?"

He smiled. "Sure."

They settled side by side, listening to the sounds of the insects in the nearby woods, the chirping of birds that should have been asleep.

"So, you really want to fight, huh?"

Jaeden laughed. "Yes. I'll be fine. You'll be there."

He chuckled and put his arm around her, drawing her in. "Nice try."

"Ryder?" she asked after a few moments of delicious silence.

"Hmm?"

"Why did you decide to be a Rogue Hunter?"

It took him a moment to answer and then he squeezed her closer once more. "Because of my dad."

Her heart thudded a little with the sad remembrance that Ryder had lost his father when he was a young boy. "Your dad?"

"Yeah. Because of what happened to him. What he couldn't prevent from happening. He was strong, don't get me wrong, but he was always just a family man. However, he loved Caia's father, respected him a great deal. Rafe was a Rogue Hunter, and a great one at that. But for the most part, I remember Rafe being the guy everyone turned to, you know. He was a good guy. A truly good guy.

"I remember my dad defending him when he brought Adriana into the pack. A lot of people back then were already sore over Mikhail's stupidity and betrayal. When Rafe fell for Adriana's lies, only a few stuck by him. People left. Of course, Magnus and your dad were two who stuck by him—so did Lucien's. And my dad. Jeez, my mom would rag on Rafe so badly, which would just end in an explosive argument between my parents. My dad would take me and Aidan aside and tell us quietly that Mom was just upset, but not to listen to the pack's tales about Rafe. Or Caia. My dad was really fond of that kid."

Jaeden quietly placed her hand on his chest, feeling it thud quickly into her palm.

"That's why he was there when Adriana came back for Caia. He was at their house. He told Rafe to take Caia and run, he would hold her off." He cleared his throat, and she hurt for the way it still hurt him now. "My dad was a brave guy, strong, and he did a heroic thing. But he wasn't trained to fight. And he especially wasn't quick enough to fight a magik."

"So you became a Rogue Hunter."

"I became a Rogue Hunter. So I could fight and give myself a better chance of staying alive to keep protecting the people *I* cared about."

"That's why you're so protective of Caia."

He nodded, clasping her hand tighter to his chest. "My dad didn't die for nothing, Jaeden. He died to keep her alive. She's here for a reason, and I trust that. I've come to trust *her.*"

"So you'll fight for her?"

"Yeah, I will."

Jaeden felt an overwhelming respect for him in that moment, a feeling so strong, it actually took an unyielding grip on her chest. "I said I would fight with her. But *I* trust *you.* I guess I'll fight *for* her as well."

She felt his smile without looking for it.

186

* * *

"Why don't you just give him the tools tomorrow?" she asked in a "guys have no logic" tone.

Ryder shrugged. "I'm trying to stay on his good side."

"Getting me home at a decent hour would accomplish that."

He jumped out of his truck. "Come on, I'll just be one second."

Jaeden hopped out of the passenger side and came around to meet him as he walked toward the main door of his apartment building. As he was driving Jae home from their unbelievable night together, Ryder remembered the toolbox Dimitri had asked to borrow. He detoured, thinking it prudent to do everything he could to be a dutiful son-in-law. Jaeden was still teasing him as he put the key in his door and pushed it open.

Immediately he felt something unfamiliar in the air, and his arm flew out, pushing Jae behind him, shushing her with a finger to his lips.

She nodded, telling him she understood.

Slowly, they crept down the hall and turned to stare into his living room. In the dark, they could clearly see with their wolf eyes the two figures huddled together by the window. Their body language didn't suggest menace. Curious and furious at the same time, Ryder hit the switch and flooded the place in light, eliciting a high-pitched squeal from the girl. The boy blinked in fright, holding the girl closer.

"Who the hell are you?" Ryder growled, hoping to scare the truth out of them. Jaeden seemed to sense what he had—they weren't a threat—and pressed a halting hand on his arm.

The tall boy edged a little closer, drawing strength from somewhere as he straightened his shoulders, bracing himself. "We're from the Center. Caia sent us."

Well, *that* he hadn't been expecting.

"What?" Jaeden asked.

"I'm Vilhelm, this is Laila."

They were Scandinavian by the look of them, and by the boy's accent. Ryder glowered, bewildered by their appearance here.

"Sit down," he ordered, ignoring Jaeden's continued attempt to make him be nicer to their "guests." Obediently, the two fell onto his sofa, and he felt a twinge of regret at his tone when the girl cowered as he strode toward them.

"Why would Caia send you here?"

The boy looked quickly between the two. "You are Ryder?"

"Yeah."

"Caia said to come here. That she trusted you."

"That doesn't answer my question."

"She's a Midnight."

They all swiveled around at the voice, and Ryder narrowed his eyes suspiciously.

Reuben.

"What the Hades are you doing here?" he snapped.

Even Jaeden gazed at him warily. "Reuben?"

The vampyre moved fluidly from the hallway to stand by her. "I came to speak with Ryder."

"Maybe we should leave." The boy stood abruptly, his eyes now wild with fear, his grip on the girl white with intensity.

"No." Ryder gestured them back and then glared at Reuben. "What do you mean she's a Midnight?"

"Please," the girl whimpered.

Ryder's mind whirred. "Reuben?"

"I can feel it."

"I thought only the Head of a coven could feel trace?" Jae interjected.

The vamp shook his head. "I don't have trace. I can't find

188

supernaturals. But I can feel whether one is a Daylight or a Midnight when I'm in the room with them."

"How freaking old are you?" Ryder snapped, not for the first time.

Reuben's gaze was fixed on the young couple. "I don't think she means any harm."

Jae turned to Ryder in equal bewilderment. "Why would Caia send a Midnight to you?"

The boy shook. "She told us not to tell you Laila was a Midnight ... but now that you know"—he threw a skeptical look at Reuben—"I will explain."

What followed was a tale Ryder couldn't believe he was hearing. Caia rescued this girl from a Daylight prison because she believed the Midnight was good? Were they kidding?

"You expect me to believe this?"

Vilhelm held strong. "She should have been following us, but I got the impression before I left to get Laila that something had happened. I swear I'm telling you the truth. Caia just wanted you to keep us hidden until she returns."

"To hide you from the rest of the pack?" Jae asked.

Vilhelm nodded. "For now."

Ryder growled. They all seemed to have forgotten one thing. "And what about Marita? Surely she would just follow your trace here?"

However, the magik shook his head. "She will not know it was me until they scour the Center. It would take enough time for Caia to return."

"But Marita will still find you here."

"Caia intended to protect us from her."

WHAT?

He felt a rush of inexplicable fear, fear that something beyond his belief and capabilities was occurring.

"Does this mean," Jae whispered, "is Caia ... turning

against Marita?"

Good question.

"Caia is kind, good." Vilhelm shook his head vehemently. "I'm a Daylight, and I believe what Marita did was wrong."

"But she's a Midnight!" Jae spat, glaring at the girl, despite how weak she appeared.

The boy twisted his face in disgust at her outburst. "And that gives you all the right to condemn her?"

"But, but ..." Jae spluttered, mirroring Ryder's own turmoil. It was like they were on the high seas, being rocked violently from side to side, waiting for the boat to overturn.

"How do we know it was really Caia who sent you here?" Ryder threw out in desperation.

Vilhelm nodded, as if expecting that question. "She said to remind you of a conversation only you and she know of. She'd just started working for your Alpha in his store, and you sat with her in the showroom. You told her about your friend, David, who mated with a faerie. She hadn't known some supernaturals could mate outside their own race, and you told her all about it. You told her stories about hunting, about a faerie who tricked you three times."

Dread settled throughout his body. It seemed the boy might be telling the truth.

Goddess, he hoped Lucien knew what Caia was up to, that Caia knew what kind of fire she was playing with.

Wearily, he nodded. "I believe you."

"I could hide them," Reuben suddenly offered.

"What do you mean?" More than ever, he didn't trust this guy.

"I can hide them so Marita doesn't follow them to the pack."

Before he could jump on this, Jaeden stiffened and turned to regard her friend in annoyance. "And how can you do that? She would come after you."

Reuben smiled arrogantly. "I'll be fine. I've been around, I have my ways."

"No. You're being an idiot," she snapped.

As much as Ryder was glad to see Jaeden jump aboard the anti-Reuben bandwagon (even if it was out of some misplaced sense of concern), he had to settle with the boy and girl. "We'll discuss that later. For now, they stay here. Caia entrusted them to me and to me alone."

Visibly trembling, Jae approached him, her hand reaching for his. "Ryder, what's going on? What is Caia doing?"

He shook his head. "I don't know."

Jaeden looked at the girl, a mixture of sympathy and fear in her expression. "She saved me too."

"What?"

"Caia," she groaned. "She saved me too."

"Still trust her?" Ryder asked.

"Do you?"

He chuckled humorlessly, looking back at the magiks who were listening intently. "Call me crazy, but … yes, I still trust her."

"Alright then," she agreed.

"I guess I'm not needed," Reuben muttered from behind them.

"Hey." Ryder stopped his departure. "You have to keep your trap shut about this."

The vampyre sneered. "I'm not the gossiping kind." And with his usual stealthy regality, he left.

Ryder looked down at his soon-to-be mate. "That means you too."

Jaeden shook her head. "This is going to be impossible. My dad isn't a wolf, he's a freaking bloodhound."

"Just channel pre-Ryder Jaeden."

"Oh, har de har har."

CHAPTER 17

Soldier

The last meeting had dispersed and Caia stood in the main reception hall waiting for the others to join her. The Center was abuzz with anticipation. Even though the students didn't know exactly what was going down, they knew it was something big. The hype level was agitating an already nervous Caia. She was thankful for Marion, who stood close by her side, watching as the others arrived. She was barely aware of Mordecai and the five magiks he had chosen from his unit to help take out the spies watching the MacLachlans.

Her mind unfortunately was all over the place. One, she was terrified their carefully strategized plan would fall apart in action; and two, she was worried how Vilhelm and Laila were faring with Ryder. Caia was supposed to have returned home almost immediately where she would've put her now-fully formed plan into action. When it became apparent that the battle was back on with du Bois, she forced herself to remain confident that it would still take Marita at least the length of the battle to figure out it had been Vilhelm.

For a start, they were focusing their investigation on the idea that a Midnight had somehow infiltrated their facilities to break Laila out (which was sending them into a massive panic). Because of this assumption, Vilhelm wouldn't even be a suspect yet, not to mention he was a Traveler, a magik without the kind of power needed to do the glamour she had done to disguise him as Vanne.

Caia wasn't stupid. Eventually someone would report Vil gone, but by then, she was hoping she would be back with the pack and there to take the heat off him.

She sighed heavily, watching as Michael appeared around the corner, body strapped with guns and knives. Behind him were the four other vampyres he had selected who were partnered with a lykan to take out the four Midnight guards du Bois was placing in a sort of rhombus formation around the edges of the forest.

Moments later, Anders emerged from one of the elevators with nine other lykans from his unit. Four of them would take out the guards; the other five would attack the spies sitting outside the MacLachlans'. The plan was, the MacLachlan pack would pretend to depart for their pack run. All of them would leave their houses and get into their cars and drive away. In truth, they would be heading to Magic Fitness where a magik would be waiting to transport them through the portal to the Center for protection.

The spies watching the houses were to contact du Bois as soon as the MacLachlans were off the street. Caia would be listening in on du Bois, and once the spies had done this, she would send in the paired lykan and magik to take out the spy. She'd given each team the description of the car the spy would be in and a description of the spy themselves and the element they used. The magik was to open the car door for the transformed lykan and cloak the vehicle while the lykan turned the Midnight into a chew toy. This way, there would be no human witnesses wandering around.

Once this was done, four teams of two, consisting of one vampyre and one lykan, would take out each guard around the forest perimeter quickly and silently. Caia, Lucien, Rose, Phoebe, and Anders would head in, in wolf form, along with Michael, Marita, and Mordecai. Each had been given a magik to take out—they were situated toward the north end of the forest where the pack met in a clearing and changed before the run. Du Bois had decided to outflank the MacLachlans by encircling the clearing, ensuring his magiks could attack from all sides.

Caia knew exactly what position each would take. To Caia's chagrin, Marita had ordered that Mordecai take out du Bois. She'd wanted Pierre for herself, mostly because he was an extremely powerful water magik and she was afraid for the person who would be attempting to attack him.

Even if that person was a treacherous man-whore.

Speaking of which …

She was sure she'd caught a glimpse of familiar jet-black hair on top of brawny shoulders. Squinting, she pressed gently against Marion to get the magik to budge a bit so she could see around one of the reception's steel pillars.

Her heart literally stopped.

Rose was pressed against Lucien, who had his arms around her waist, and they were kissing … quite passionately.

She felt sick to her stomach.

Trembling, she pulled back so she didn't have to look anymore. Gaia, how had her life gotten here? She flexed her hands, trying to force the trembling to subside.

"Caia, you have to forget what you just saw and focus.

You have a long night ahead of you," Marion whispered in her ear.

"I'm fine," she assured her mentor.

"No, you're not. But you will be."

Surprised at her cryptic comment, she turned to look at the witch only to see her glaring at Lucien and Rose as they came into view. It almost made her smile. It was nice having friends who cared.

Blowing out a troubling breath between her lips, Caia focused beyond the couple and watched as Phoebe appeared behind them.

That was everyone, then.

"We're all here." Marion nodded around at the tactical team. "We're all aware of our parts in this?"

A lot of murmuring and nodding offered confirmation.

"We all have a set of comms?"

Caia nodded with the rest, hardly noticing the small earpiece that would allow her to communicate with the others.

"Remember, the portals that have been opened transport us out very close to the Midnights, so stealth is of the utmost importance. Unit One." Marion turned to the magiks and lykans who were teamed together. "You'll each take a portal to the street your target is on. It will open in a secure location where you are hidden from Midnight view. You all remember which team you are? Caia, do you?"

She nodded, trying to ignore the sickening butterflies in her stomach.

"Caia will prompt you when your Midnight has made the call to du Bois, and you go in, quick and quiet." Marion stared at them a few intimidating moments at a time before turning to the teams of lykans and vampyres. "Unit Two, you'll go through the portal with us. You'll take position near your Midnight and after the spies are out, Caia will send you in to take out the guards." She smiled dryly and turned to Anders, Mordecai, and the others. "Unit Three, you're with me. We'll head in once Unit Two confirms the guards are down. Everyone clear?"

The back of the reception area had been sealed off. Shimmering against the wall were six portals. The colors and shapes they made up were merely a warped version of reality; it was the wall, but it swirled and glittered and pulsed invitingly.

Caia looked on, barely listening as Marion directed each Unit One team to the correct portal; then they began following the witch to the portal reserved for Units Two and Three. The others strode ahead and through, the vampyres holding their weapons high just in case they encountered any Midnights on the other side. She could've told them they wouldn't; she knew where every single one of them was, and they had no idea a battalion of Daylights was on their way to ruin their night.

"Caia?"

She started at the warm hand on her shoulder and looked up into Lucien's concerned face. Out of the corner of her eye, she saw Rose glide past with the others, her gaze washing over them as she did so. Lucien had obviously asked for a moment alone to talk to her.

"What?" She didn't mean to snap. There was just too much to concentrate on; her self-control over this issue didn't seem important at the moment.

He blinked, seeming surprised by her tone. "I just wanted to say good luck and please don't do anything stupid."

His concern, his tenderness, created an urge to scratch her claws across his face and spit and growl and snarl until she was hoarse. She didn't want to see that he worried about her. She didn't need the confusion.

She twisted her mouth in derision and jerked away from

his grasp. "Why don't you save the concern for Rose? I can handle myself."

Dark uncertainty fell over his features. "Caia, wh—"

She didn't stay to hear the end of that question. Instead she almost ran for the portal, knowing he wouldn't be able to plague her with his questions once they were through. A rush of pressurized air blasted her hair back, almost as if she were on a roller coaster ... on a roller coaster in a very, very dark place.

A feeling likened to seasickness engulfed her, and she knew she was through the portal. Hesitantly, she opened her eyes, taking in the sight of Remnant Forest, which, even with her lykan vision, seemed to swallow them in its alien blackness. She could feel the energy of the amassed Midnights beckoning from the north like tendrils of hair blowing in the wind. It was strange to equate the usually familiar and welcoming smell of a damp wood with this adrenaline-charged anxiety.

Ducking to the ground, Caia took in their position. Unit Two was already making its way through the woods toward the perimeter guards. She turned to Marion huddled behind a fallen tree in which the growth covering it created a wall of defense.

Lucien was the last to come through, and he snapped down to the ground behind the tree so quickly, she heard Anders laugh and whisper, urging him once more to join his unit at the Center. Marion shushed them and turned to Caia. Her eyes closed, and she called on the trace to do its job. She was able to hold on to the five spies' energy in sync, each like a different window on one screen of a computer. The first members of the MacLachlans left their house, followed closely by the three other families on that street. As their cars pulled away, the Midnight watching sent a text message to du Bois. Caia almost smiled at that; their outfit wasn't quite as swanky as the Center's.

Remembering what all this meant, her amusement quickly faded, and she pressed the earpiece. "Unit Three, you're safe to proceed."

"Roger."

Wow, that was loud in her ear.

Anders and Phoebe were grinning in anticipation of the fight.

Within a few minutes, each Midnight spy had completed their task. Caia sent in all of Unit One, each asserting within minutes of her order that the Midnight was dead. After watching the first magik being chewed from the inside out, after the reminder of her own fight with a daemon not too long ago, Caia had been blasted with empathy a soldier couldn't really afford. The surprise and shock, the undiluted fear, the panic, the horrendous pain, and the awful realization of approaching death clawed at her throat. She knew they were magiks bent on doing a despicable thing, but it didn't make it any easier to watch them die.

She'd pulled out of the trace and hadn't watched while the other Midnights were killed. At the confirmation of their deaths, Unit Three exhaled a unanimous breath of relief and triumph.

"Unit Two," Caia whispered over the comms, "proceed to the guards."

"Roger."

The sounds of all those voices whispering down their comms made them flinch, and she hoped to Artemis that it hadn't distracted Unit Two. She felt her unit staring at her as she observed through the trace. It was done so smoothly, so perfectly executed. The magik distracted the Midnight momentarily, while the vampyre, without a ruffle of clothing or intake of breath, surreptitiously slipped up behind the Midnight, clamped a hand over their mouth to occlude any warning shouts, and slit the guard's throat. It was gruesome and underhanded, and Caia experienced more pangs of disgust that this was even necessary. Feeling their stares on her burning cheeks, Caia ignored her regrets, and gave them a brittle nod at the exact moment the teams began confirming the guards dead over the comms.

Now it was their turn.

Mordecai, Michael, and Marion were to wait as the lykans changed into wolf form. While they stripped to nothing and initiated the change, Caia was already there. With her magik, she could transform within seconds to wolf without having to strip. Using glamour, she could transform back fully clothed. She waited, however, until Lucien, Anders, and the women were done.

They took off simultaneously.

Caia was heading for her magik, an older female fire magik. At her speed she came upon the woman hiding with her back to Caia behind a large tree. She turned a few degrees at the last second as she heard the cracking of bracken, but it was too late. Caia was already clambering up her back and taking her slender neck in her jaws.

As the warm blood pulsed into her mouth, Caia pushed away the fresh memory of this woman's vertebrae snapping under the clamp of her teeth, the feel of her warm flesh piercing under her claws like the skin of a peach. In fact, it was easier to forget reality altogether as she waited for the magik's heart to stop.

It did. And what seemed like hours had merely been seconds.

Caia backed off the falling body and searched the other Midnights. Lucien must have gotten to his magik almost at the same time and had killed him, but not before the magik had let out a roar. The others were now aware they weren't alone.

Luckily, Anders had taken his magik unawares and was just now finishing him off.

Phoebe was in the middle of a physical fight with her warlock, an air magik who attempted to suffocate her; she struggled violently against his power and proved herself determined to win the fight as she viciously bit down on his privates to loosen his grip. Caia winced at the excruciating pain that ripped through his entire being and reminded herself never to get into a fight with Phoebe. The Hunter fought dirty. At his weeping, the magik finally let go long enough for Phoebe to go in for the kill. Caia turned away as his heart stopped.

Rose didn't appear to be getting anywhere near her magik. He had put up a shield around himself at the sound of his comrade's roar, and now Rose kept bouncing off it uselessly. Caia wished she had her comms so she could tell her to conserve her energy, to wait for him to let go of the spell holding her off.

Michael was in an intense fight with his fire magik, but he managed to dodge the hits from the Midnight and had even shot the bastard in the arm.

At the same time, Marion was struggling with a female earth magik. She couldn't get a hit in—the woman kept dousing it with earth and creating weapons out of rock. Poor Marion was covered in lacerations and bruises.

Caia continued sifting.

Du Bois.

Through his eyes, she saw him empty water from Mordecai's dead body. He had suffocated the magik, had enjoyed every moment of taking down "the inept boy," as if he were any older or wiser than his adversary. Hatred for him, and regret and fury over Mordecai's demise, flooded her, propelling her through the forest toward the Midnight responsible.

Still tracing du Bois, she saw Anders tear around the corner and confront him, his jaw dripping with gore, his huge wolf body an impressive sight. She thought she would feel fear in du Bois. Instead, as previously shielded thoughts poured out of him in his excitement, the fear belonged to her.

No!

It wasn't possible. How could he have hidden this so successfully from her?

She burst into view behind him, in time to see for herself the contents of a vial he had produced bursting open. Liquid gold streamed through the air, actuated by Pierre's water magik. The horror of what that liquid meant unfolded before her as each drop brought about Anders's transformation back into human form. He lay there, naked and confused, as he stared at his human hands curled into the dirt of the forest floor. His eyes flashed up in panic, just in time to see the water rush at him and force its way into his mouth, flooding his lungs and drowning the life from his body.

And Caia hadn't been able to stop it. Instead her trace had automatically taken her to the magik Rose was fighting off, and he was in the process of doing the same thing. Lucien pounded into view and battered at the shield as the magik transformed Rose back.

Crippling panic would not do.

Caia concentrated and changed back into human form, a shield automatically up and around her in order to confront du Bois.

He stared, dumbstruck. "That's some trick."

She glanced by him to Anders's lifeless body. Two of them were dead.

She narrowed her eyes in loathing at this man who'd created this devastation. "I was going to say the same thing."

Du Bois grinned unapologetically. "Just a little something I picked up."

Caia nodded, filching through his mind with the trace. "You and your lover—Thierry—the Midnight who is, at this second, inflicting burns on a female lykan while my Alpha watches on helplessly ... you did this together. You hired humans to experiment on kidnapped lykans. They came up with that concoction to transform them back to human so you could hurt them. You killed the human scientists. I marvel at how well you hid it from Ethan. But then Ethan barely knew you were alive. When he disappeared, it was *the* opportunity. But I've been watching you carefully, for weeks. How clever of you and Thierry to keep those thoughts so tightly locked. And me ... I didn't know to look, to kick down the door ..."

Pierre had paled considerably; he fisted a hand that seemed desperate to tremble. "How do you know all that? Who are you?"

"The same way I knew where you all were this evening." She felt her skin tighten as the trace told her the fighting was intensifying, the Midnights triumphant. Michael's and Marion's wounds were getting worse; Rose was bleeding out. Thierry was going to use the liquid on Lucien to change him, too, to kill him. "Your spies outside the MacLachlans' homes are dead. Your guards are dead. Three of you here have been taken out."

A tube of water shot toward her with the force of a speeding train, but she blasted it back with a flick of her wrist and it lost its form, splashing onto the forest bed before it even touched her skin. Thierry laughed as Lucien transformed; he was sure Rose was dying, and he was just about to set Lucien on fire.

Feeling the white heat, so familiar now, building through her body, Caia grabbed hold of it, determined to control this force that was so powerful. Focusing her mind on du Bois and the other Midnights' locations, Caia pulled on the white heat and the energy she used to wield her water element and tied them together in her mind's eye.

And with that, she let it out of her body.

The energy constructed itself into cocoons of water, morphing its shape at her demand. She looked on as it wrapped around du Bois's head and chest, insisting it to do the same to the other Midnights simultaneously. As Pierre fought it, Caia squeezed the cocoon and waited as the blood vessels in his eyes popped, his face turning purple with asphyxiation. It was the same for the others, and it seemed to take forever to draw to a conclusion.

Holding tight to the four Midnights was taking its toll, the muscles in her body burning in agony, her own eyes streaming with water. All the while, she couldn't stop thinking how she was *actually* killing people, making them cease to exist. The water streaming from her eyes turned salty. But she held on, maintaining the cocoons, until one by one, the Midnights disappeared from her trace … and du Bois's heartbeat slowed to a falter, puttered, and then stopped.

Caia let go and a sob burst out of her mouth. The deaths, the killings of this evening, pressed on her chest, their overwhelming weight crushing. If only she'd looked into du Bois's trace more carefully; if she had crept into his mind like she had done with Ethan and broken down his defenses, perhaps Anders would be alive, maybe even those humans du Bois had killed. The guilt weighed on her, begging for alleviation.

Thankfully, like a prayer being answered, her mind darkened, and the last thing she saw was the ground rushing toward her.

* * *

NIKOLAI TREMBLED as he dialed Kirios's number. It rang twice and then he heard the strong voice of his partner.

"So?"

Nikolai smiled wryly at his friend's charming manners. "My faerie returned. She watched everything from the trees."

"How did she go undetected by Caia?"

"Caia was a little preoccupied."

"What happened?"

The excitement bubbling in his blood threatened to burst into his speech, but he held on coolly, trying to maintain his dignified demeanor. "Well. It went well. Caia was able to kill, simultaneously, four magiks in four different locations in the woods. My faerie has never seen anything like it."

Kirios exhaled in obvious disbelief. "I've never *heard* anything like it."

"Hmm. Apparently, two of the Daylights were taken down, and then the others were in trouble so she had to kill all the Midnights by herself."

"And her state?"

He frowned at the next piece of information he imparted. "She was visibly upset by it, and then she collapsed."

"That's not reassuring."

"Kirios, stay positive. This is good news. The girl is definitely what we need."

"She has weaknesses."

"Even gods have weaknesses, Kirios."

"Are you comparing her to a god?"

"She's the closest thing to it since the old times."

"We'll see, won't we?"

Nikolai groaned, "Why are you always so pessimistic?"

Kirios grumbled, "I'm not being pessimistic. I may even have some good news. There have been a few developments I'm not ... sure of."

"What does that mean?"

"I'll explain when I see you."

"Fine." Nikolai waved off his comments in irritation. "Just remember ... now it's all on you."

"I know. I'll be waiting."

CHAPTER 18

Spark

*L*ight burned her eyelids into opening, her vision unfocused, her mouth and throat dry. She tried to move her legs, and shards of pain ricocheted throughout her body. It felt like she'd been run over. Maybe more than once.

"Caia?"

"Lucien?"

She blinked a few times and turned her head, seeing him standing before her, Marion by his side, both of them staring down at her with worry etched in their features.

He lifted her hand into his and squeezed it. "Are you okay?"

No. She was confused. The last thing she remembered was killing five people. Had that been a nightmare?

"Where am I?"

Lucien loomed closer, drawing her hand into an almost

viselike grip. "You're in your room at the Center."

"Was it a dream?"

Sadness and fury seemed to riot across his face as he shook his head. "No."

Caia clenched her jaw, turning her head away, desperate to keep the tears locked up. A single one escaped anyway, spilling from the corner of her eye and down her cheek.

"Caia," he whispered, and she felt him catch the tear with his finger. "You did good, sweetheart."

She choked on that. *Good!* She had killed people, murdered them! It wasn't like Ethan's death. That hadn't been premeditated, and he had been a monster who deserved to die. But other than du Bois and Thierry, those Midnights were mixed-up people, looking for direction, looking for a leader again. They weren't truly wicked. And their deaths *had* been premeditated.

Goddess, she felt like such a naive fool believing she could kill those people and be fine with it ... because it was the right thing to do. Hah.

"Caia," Marion said firmly, almost angrily, "I know it isn't easy, but those magiks were going to massacre an entire pack of innocent lykans."

Aye, there's the rub.

Slowly, she turned to face them again. "I know. I just ... I hadn't expected ..."

Marion placed a comforting hand on her leg. "Taking a life is never easy. But this is a war, Caia, and we have to sacrifice a part of our souls to win it."

Lucien smiled gently at her. "I've been worried about you. You've been out for a whole day."

"A whole day?"

He grinned. "You're going to be fine. Marita's personal physician looked you over. Your body was just exhausted after what you did. Caia, what you did!" He shook his head in amazement, and she watched as he and Marion exchanged awed and excited looks. "It was unbelievable. Taking out all those Midnights in one fell swoop? You should see this place outside of these doors."

"Or inside," Marion muttered wryly.

"What?" Caia asked in confusion.

"Take a look."

Slowly, with Lucien's help, she eased into a sitting position, and her eyes widened at the sight before her. Flowers upon flowers decorated every inch of the room.

"Get-well flowers from your fans." Marion shook her head and laughed.

Uh-oh.

"Fans?"

Lucien grunted. "Some of the others couldn't keep quiet about what you did. The Center is in an uproar over you. You're like a damn rock star to these people."

She gulped. This was kind of what she wanted—no, *needed*. Still scary, though.

They both seemed to understand and threw her sympathetic looks. Marion shrugged. "We knew your power could be limitless and turns out it just might be. This"—she gestured to the flowers—"might be the price you're going to have to pay for it."

Caia chuckled humorlessly. "And here I was thinking it was the bone-weary exhaustion, loss of consciousness, and oh, let's not forget the bit about losing a piece of my soul."

The witch frowned. "Caia, this is important. Two members have come to the Center representing the entire council. They want to meet with you."

The news hit her in a wave. This was good. No, this—this was great. With a little self-control, she managed to keep the relieved grin off her face.

She nodded calmly. "I'd like that. When?"

"Today, if you are well enough."

"Sounds good."

Lucien scowled. "I don't know about that. You've just woken up."

A wave of sadness washed over her. "I'm fine. Unlike Mordecai and Anders." She looked to them questioningly as they acknowledged the loss. "When will their funerals be held?"

Marion shook her head. "There won't be a funeral for either of them. We hold a ceremony here at the Center annually to commemorate the dead. We'll honor the two of them then."

"Unit Two?" she whispered, thinking of Anders's loyal men and women.

"Grieving, of course. But they're soldiers first and foremost. Lyla has been promoted to Unit Leader."

"And you? Marion, you took a few hits."

She shrugged like it was no big deal. "It's Michael and Rose who were wounded."

Rose.

She blinked up at Lucien's pinched face. "Is she okay?"

He nodded. "She's healing up pretty good. So is Michael."

She thought of the Council, of her plans. How he didn't know about any of it.

"You should go to her," Caia told him, her voice flat and emotionless.

She knew right away that her tone had sent him into lockdown. He jerked away from her, his face frozen, his eyes hard. "Yeah. Glad you're alright."

And then he was gone.

She stared at her suite door, wishing she didn't have any pride, that she could yell out after him and tell him she didn't care if he loved Rose. He was *her* mate, so he had to stay with her.

Marion clucked, "He sat by your bedside for the last few hours, you know."

"Was he with Rose before that?"

The witch's silence confirmed it.

* * *

AFTER A SHOWER and something to eat, she felt a lot more human again, enough to take a little tour around the Center with Marion. She talked to the students and candidates and answered as many questions as she was allowed to. She even signed some autographs. It was totally weird and not something she was prepared for, but at the moment, she couldn't care less because it went a long way in helping her with her plan.

While she listened to Desi and Ophelia chatter away about how jealous everyone was that they were friends with her, Marion tapped her on the shoulder, and she turned in the doorway of the classroom to see Phoebe MacLachlan waiting with a lykan Caia didn't recognize. He was a tall, well-built Elder whose soft eyes reminded her of Magnus. A pang of homesickness echoed in her chest.

Extricating herself from the young Travelers, Caia made her way cautiously over to the Rogue Hunter and her companion. Phoebe was a little intimidating, to say the least.

As soon as she reached them, Phoebe thrust her hand out to Caia, her face serious, yet her eyes were filled with what could almost pass for warmth. Gingerly, Caia shook the other female's hand, refusing to wince when Phoebe gripped too hard.

"Caia Ribeiro, I would like to introduce you to my father and pack Alpha, Alistair MacLachlan."

She'd expected the same death-grip handshake, but instead she found herself crushed in his mammoth embrace.

Caia returned his hug and swallowed her sigh of relief when he let her go.

"My daughter tells me you are the one who discovered the attack on my pack. That you're also the one who destroyed the Midnights responsible."

Feeling heat bloom under her cheeks, Caia shrugged helplessly. "I had a lot of help from Phoebe and a few others."

Phoebe shook her head, as serious as ever. "She's being modest, Father," she tutted. "I've never understood that trait."

Alistair chuckled. "Yes, we know."

Caia didn't know whether to laugh or admonish him. Didn't he know Phoebe had no sense of humor? Phoebe merely frowned at him and turned to her. "We wanted to thank you, personally."

"Yes." The Alpha grinned. He shook his head, disbelieving, as his eyes washed over her. "Such a little thing, and yet from what Phoebe has told me, I would have imagined you to be a giant. As you may have already guessed, Phoebe isn't really a people person—"

"Father!"

"—and so when she admires someone, we all know they must *really* be worthy of her respect."

"That's true." The Rogue Hunter nodded militantly.

"We're very grateful to you, Miss Ribeiro, and if there is anything my pack can do for yours, you must not hesitate to call on us."

Okay, so perhaps she might have done something truly good despite the remorse she felt over the deaths of those Midnights. She had saved this kind Elder and his valuable daughter, not to mention the rest of their pack.

Caia, wake up. Be strong. And think ... they're not just offering you a thank-you, they're offering themselves.

Allies.

Smiling warmly, she shook their hands again. "That's very

gracious of you. Thank you."

The two lykans left her to recount their encounter to Marion, who grinned proudly at her like a mother hen.

"Compliments from Phoebe MacLachlan. Now *that* should go on your résumé."

Marion left her to her fans, a decision Caia teasingly told her she would later regret, a look of dismay falling across her features as the witch disappeared out of the hall. No matter how many times she told herself that networking was good, it still left her feeling as if she were stuck in coach between a snorer and a crying baby on a long flight.

After doing the rounds Caia snuck away from the inquisitive looks and prying questions. She walked toward the elevators to head up to Marita and Vanne's suite. The Center's layout still confused her, and she found herself taking a wrong turn and rounding the corner to the altars. She stopped abruptly at the scene before her and darted out of sight, peering around the corner to watch Marita standing unaccompanied outside Gaia's altar.

The magik sent darting glances in every direction, as if checking to make sure she was alone, before stealthily creeping into the altar.

What the ...

Her behavior was so weird. What the Hades was she up to? Caia suddenly she remembered the conversation she'd overheard between Mordecai and Marita. Was this another one of their secrets ... or was this *the* secret? The thudding of her heart grew louder in her ears and her legs trembled as she took a tentative step toward the door.

Maybe Marita was just praying. *Maybe I'm being a paranoid idiot.*

Maybe you should hurry up and follow her in and find out what the hell she's up to!

Caia pushed open the door as quietly as possible, her eyes

sweeping what appeared to be an empty altar. A flicker of movement from the far right of the room caught her attention, and she stared in confusion at the sight of auburn hair disappearing in front of her very eyes. She blinked rapidly. What the ...

The front-row pew obstructed much of the view of that area, but Caia rushed forward, sure she'd seen what looked to be the top of Marita's head disappearing into the ground. She searched the area in front of the pews to the right of the statue of Gaia, scanning the floor. And there, a glitter of metal caught her eye and she hurried closer, dropping to her knees in fear and excitement.

The tiniest stud of gold metal was stuck to the floor, sitting on the edge of one large slab of marble. Tentatively, she reached forward and touched it.

Whoosh!

Caia strangled a startled cry as the slab peeled open in one fluid movement, revealing a secret entrance. She forgot to breathe as she peered inside what she was sure very few people knew even existed. A ladder was attached to the opposite wall, leading down into a brightly lit hallway that was clinical in appearance.

Goddess, Caia, what are you getting yourself into now?

With a bolstering gulp of air, Caia grabbed hold of the first rung and began to descend into an underground hallway, her footsteps light and her breathing restrained as she made her way down.

There wasn't a sound, only what appeared to be a silent, endless, white-tiled corridor with fluorescent lighting. What was this place? And why didn't anyone know about it? Or did they? She was down here now, so she might as well get on with it. Caia crept forward in quick little steps, her brain yelling *Idiot! Idiot! Idiot!* with each one.

And that's when she heard it. She stopped, wincing at the

squeak her Converse made on the tiled floor. Her ears perked up and a chill burst down her spine.

Crying. Children's cries! Snarling. Hissing. She could make out at least five different voices in the mix. Oh, dear goddess! She hurried forward and stupidly spilled around the corridor as it veered left. A figure disappeared into a door up ahead without noticing her and she continued forward at a quieter but still quickened pace.

The door, marked *Laboratory 1: Lykanthrope*, sat adjacent to a long window, and cautiously Caia strained, trying to look inside without anyone noticing her.

What she saw ...

"Oh my go—"

Marita.

Talking to a tall man dressed in a navy lab coat, their eyes going over whatever information he had on the tablet in his hands. In front of them were five children, their faces contorted with all manner of misery.

Caia felt bile rise in her throat at such a familiar sight.

She had seen this before. With Jaeden.

Each child was locked in a cage surrounded by magik, magik that kept them from changing. Rows of test tubes sat on trays attached to each cage, a variety of liquids in each. Caia felt a rush of anger as her eyes found the face of a small girl—she couldn't have been more than ten years old. Her huge eyes had a haunted look no person, much less a child, should ever have cause to feel.

White heat shot through Caia's body, and she gasped, spinning around, her body pressed to the door as she tried to gain control over herself. As she shuddered into some kind of normalcy, she saw another door farther down, another window. More children. Perhaps another race. Vampyre maybe?

At the sound of footsteps drawing closer from the other

side of the door, Caia took off, her eyes searching the ceilings and walls for CCTV cameras as she made her way back to the entrance. There was nothing.

No, she thought, her lip curling in rage, *Marita wouldn't want evidence of the existence of her little experiments down here.*

Caia clambered up the ladder and shot out of the entrance, thanking the gods for the quiet of the altar as she closed the marble slab. She hurried out of the altar and back into the halls of the Center, desperate to wipe off the invisible filth that now clung to her skin. She had no idea what Marita was doing with those children, what her endgame was. Then Marita's voice rang in her head like an alarm.

"I wanted you to stay and help me train an elite force of lykans I'm working on."

Is that what she was doing? Trying to make a stronger army by experimenting on children? Oh Hades, no. It was unthinkable.

And just a theory, she reminded herself.

But theory or no, Marita had crossed the line, and Caia's plans had instantly changed. She was in no mood to take things slowly now. No. Now she had no compunction whatsoever in destroying the bitch any way she could.

* * *

MARION WAS WAITING for her outside of Marita and Vanne's suite, and Caia called upon her best acting skills to greet her normally. Still, her mentor seemed to detect something and Caia waved her off, explaining it away as exhaustion.

She was surprised by the quick hug Marita gave her and had to hide her revulsion as she returned it. It was with deep relief that she returned the more sincere hug from Vanne. Did he know about the children? Oh goddess, she hoped not.

"We're glad you are okay," Marita said. "You are quite the

little wonder, aren't you."

It was hard to tell whether she was being sarcastic.

"Caia Ribeiro?"

Caia turned around to see two distinguished-looking people peering at her in astonishment. One was a stocky older man, perfectly coifed in a designer suit, and his companion a small, compact woman whose movements reminded Caia of a little bird.

"Caia." Marita gestured to them. "May I introduce Alfred Doukas and Penelope Argyros?"

It did not escape Caia's notice that both these council members had Greek names. Did that mean their family was from way back when? Was that what it took to be a council member? A lineage that could be traced back to the gods? If so, these were definitely the people she needed to impress.

"It's an honor." She shook their hands firmly, a deliberate soft smile playing across her lips. They seemed taken aback by her. She doubted she was what they'd been expecting.

"No." Alfred grinned back. "This is an honor for us. We came because we've heard extraordinary things about you, Miss Ribeiro."

"Please call me Caia."

"Of course."

What followed was almost like an interview. They wanted to know about her upbringing, about Ethan's death, about the attack against the MacLachlans. They wanted to know what her plans were from now on. She shoved what she'd just witnessed to the back of her brain and told them she was considering a position offered to her by Marita, but that she hadn't decided whether to take it yet. She told them about the pack, describing them colorfully, explaining how much they meant to her. It was safe to assume that Alfred and Penelope were enchanted by her, and thankfully seemed to approve of her loyalty to the pack, first and foremost.

"It says a little something about your character." Penelope nodded, smiling earnestly at her.

The "interview" seemed to be drawing to a close when Penelope twittered, "And this substance? That transformed Marita's first lykan in command, what was it exactly?"

Caia shook her head. A vision of Anders's panicked eyes when he realized he was going to die flashed through her mind like an arrow of guilt. "It was something Pierre du Bois and his partner, Thierry Cotillard, hired human scientists to work on. They had daemons on their payroll capture lykans and had these scientists working on their genetic makeup for the past five years. Impressively, they hid it from the trace, and I didn't know to look deeper. A mistake I won't make again.

"I'm sure if Ethan had known about it, he would've wanted a piece of the action, especially as they'd had a breakthrough. They were able to concoct a liquid from taking chemicals in a lykanthrope body and combine it with the magik used in natural materialization to transform a lykan in wolf form back into a human. I don't understand how it works, but there's a lab, here in Paris, where the liquid is kept. The human scientists have all been killed."

Alfred scowled. "Are we sure that their breach has been taken care of? No human is left alive that is aware of supernaturals?"

Caia shook her head. "I couldn't be sure. I just know from what I could see in du Bois's head that the men and women he was using are dead. Whether those people told others ..."

"Point taken." He shook his head, disturbed. "This lab must be destroyed."

Marita coughed delicately from behind them and they all looked to her questioningly. "Perhaps it would be prudent to analyze the lab, discover what we can about this formula?"

Oh, you would like that, wouldn't you? Caia thought,

concealing her disgust.

"No," Penelope chirped, shivering a little. "The idea of magiks experimenting on other supernaturals … I think it's best that information goes no further than these four walls. The last thing we need is giving the wrong people inspiration."

Well said.

Caia pinned Marita with her stare, hoping to see a glimmer of guilt or some kind of betrayal of her own experiments. There was nothing. She was so cool. Definitely not an enemy to underestimate.

"I agree." Alfred nodded gravely. "Best to destroy it immediately."

Marita shrugged as if it made no difference to her. "Fine. I'll have someone take care of it."

"I'll do it." Caia sprang to her feet. No way in hell was she letting Marita or one of her slugs near that place. "Right now. I'll go right now."

Penelope and Alfred beamed at her, clearly impressed with her offer. "That would be wonderful, Caia, thank you."

Marita threw a strained smile her way. "Aren't you exhausted, dear?"

"No. I want to do this. I want every inch of that place leveled."

"I'll send someone with you, just in case."

Why, so they could spy, find the information Marita wanted anyway? She didn't think so.

Caia shook her head. "I'd prefer to choose someone to go with me."

"Of course." Alfred nodded and then seared Marita with a penetrating look. "Caia should have whomever she feels most comfortable with in the field."

"That would be Lucien, then." Marita almost sneered at her.

"No." Caia shook her head. The last thing she needed was complicating this with Lucien thrown into the mix. No. There was only one person she believed could be trusted. Someone so principled, they were cold with it. "I want Phoebe MacLachlan."

Marion smiled and muttered, "Mutual respect."

"What?" Marita asked in agitation, but it went unanswered as Marion swept toward Caia, outlining the plan she had in mind. Alfred, Penelope, and Vanne thought it a sound one, and it was with great relief that she left the suite with Marion in tow.

As the elevator descended, Marion snorted.

"What?" Caia asked wearily.

She shook her head. "Nothing. I just … well, I haven't seen someone use that kind of charm since my grandmother. She was some lady when she was Head of the Coven. Had the Council eating out of her hand all the time. I knew you were likable, Caia, but I was unaware of the amount of charisma you can unleash when you want to. What are you up to?"

"I was just being friendly. I think it's important the coven believe in me, considering my lineage, don't you? Also … I'm working toward making Marita aware that I have no intention of staying at the Center."

"Ah, I see. Subtle. Nice. I'm sure my sister will be pleased to hear that. Another piece of good news," she muttered wryly.

"Marion." Caia turned to the magik, wide-eyed. "What happened with Laila?"

"Oh." Marion nodded, her eyes wide with anxiety. "Good question. They discovered it was a young boy from the Center, a Traveler. He must've been working with the girl because he's gone too. It was the boy who brought her here in the first place."

"Really?" She hoped she didn't betray herself. "Any leads?"

Marion shook her head. "That's the thing. Marita can't get a hold of his trace."

What the Hades?

"What?"

Was this some kind of trick?

"His trace has been cloaked."

"And this is a possibility? Why wasn't I told about this?"

"Because ... only a very, very old supernatural has that ability."

"How old?"

"As old as the war itself."

"Vilhelm?"

Marion shook her head. "No. The truth is, we knew there was a possibility there were beings that old still kicking around. The Midnight Coven's prophet is that old. But we thought he was the only one."

"I've seen him in the trace. I don't think it's him."

"Well ... if it's not, we have a mystery player in our midst."

Caia's mood plummeted at the thought of yet another problem.

"Not that you should worry about that at the moment, Caia, since you have another task to complete for dear old sis."

"Yeah. The lab."

"You didn't have to offer to do this. You could've just given her the coordinates on a map. Anyone could have done the job."

She nodded absently. No, not anyone. Poor Marion. She would be devastated when she learned that her sister was breaking every one of the supernatural rights laws. But now was not the time to tell her. Caia needed to get back to the pack—and to Vilhelm—as quickly as possible, and together, they could put her new plan into action. She hated the thought of leaving those children down there, but she couldn't just charge in. Marita would throw her in prison and then where would they be?

No. She needed an army. The most powerful army at her disposal. The political kind.

* * *

"And you're sure you don't want to involve Lucien?" Vanne queried, worry creased between his eyebrows.

Caia glanced around the room. "I told you, he doesn't need to do this, and he's with Rose right now, seeing her through her recovery."

Marita glowered at her husband. "The lykan doesn't need to follow her everywhere, Vanne. Caia is quite capable of taking care of this by herself."

Yeah, like that was what you wanted.

She nodded anyway, thinking of how annoyed Lucien would be when he found out. She should at least tell him before departing.

It was only a few hours after she'd met with Alfred and Penelope, and they were going over the plan to destroy the lab one more time. The lab was situated on the Left Bank in the Latin Quarter, in the basement of a disused jazz bar. It was guarded by only one daemon, but as Caia knew, sometimes one daemon was enough.

"You know, I could do this by myself," Phoebe suddenly declared, her eyes narrowed on Caia's pinched face. "Caia has only just woken up from being unconscious for twenty-four hours."

It was nice of her to offer, but Caia would not allow anyone do this alone. "No. I'm fine, really."

Caia felt bad for asking Phoebe to do this so soon after their ordeal in Remnant Forest, but she should've anticipated that Phoebe would actually be looking forward to the action.

"You're sure?" Marita hesitated. "Because I can send extra people in with you."

"No. A group going into an abandoned club would look conspicuous. Phoebe and I can handle this."

"Are we ready to go, then?" Phoebe strode toward the exit. "Marion has a portal waiting."

"Wait."

The Rogue Hunter turned with a look of irritation. "What?"

"You go on ahead to reception. I have to do something first."

Marita gave her Rose's room number with what Caia was sure was a look of glee.

Leaving to do this without informing Lucien would piss him off, and not least of all because technically, as her Pack Leader, she had to make him aware of any task of importance she was going to undertake. Slowly, she walked down the white corridor to Rose's room, feeling her nerves build. She wondered just how pissed off Lucien was going to be that he was out of the loop on this one.

"Do you have to leave?"

Rose.

Caia stopped and peered around the corner to see Lucien standing in the threshold of Rose's bedroom.

He chuckled. "I'll be back in five. I just need to order some food. You guys don't get it delivered to these parts."

"Show-off, with your fancy room and fancy room service."

She sounded as exhausted as Caia felt. Caia shook her head; Rose should never have been in that fight.

"Yeah, well, tomorrow I go back to the pack so the special treatment ends."

"Lucien ... I ..."

"What is it?" He moved back inside, leaving the door

open. Caia crept forward. She could see through the crack between the wall and where the door was hinged. Lucien bent over Rose as she sat propped up in bed, her hand in his, concern for her clearly shining in his eyes. "What's wrong?"

"I was ... thinking ... maybe ... maybe I could come back with you."

He bent and pressed a soft kiss to the corner of her mouth, an action that sent Caia stumbling back down the corridor. She fled toward the elevator, an image of what she'd just seen and heard filtering down to land like ash on her tongue.

Hitting the button, Caia refused to let go of more tears. She stiffened and stared into the mirror in the elevator, drinking in the sight of her fragile paleness. The time for heartache had to end. How many times did she have to admonish herself before that sank in? She had a witch and a war to obliterate.

Alone.

* * *

"CAIA!" Phoebe called to her impatiently, and she hurried over to the lykan as she waited by a portal. By now she was growing accustomed to the nauseating travel via portal, and they stepped out into the Parisian night with a little more ease. Caia exhaled as she straightened from behind the wall they had come out at and stared up and over it to the steps that led to Notre-Dame.

"Oh my goddess," she said, the smells and sights of the city tingling her senses.

"Caia?"

Ignoring the hunter, she walked toward the Gothic cathedral that rose up out of the Left Bank as surreal as the Center she'd just departed from. Her lykan eyes danced over the misshapen gargoyles perched upon the cathedral sides, their presence only adding more drama to the enigmatic atmosphere of the place itself.

"I can't believe this," Phoebe muttered and then she took hold of Caia's wrist in a painful grip. "We're not here to sightsee, Caia."

"But I've never been to Paris before. Aren't you amazed?"

Phoebe snorted and dragged her toward the Latin Quarter. "I've killed two lykans here in the past three years. I've seen all of Paris I'll ever want to see."

With that dose of harsh reality, Caia forgot about not having the opportunity to see Paris as a tourist and led the way to the jazz club. They were silent as they strode through the narrow streets, past excited tourists, and ignored obviously suggestive looks and gestures from men, young and old. Caia realized, as they approached the club, that she and Phoebe were comfortable in each other's company precisely because neither of them had a penchant for talking.

"Is this it?" Phoebe nodded toward the ground floor of a block of what had to be apartments—little windows and potted flowers sat on ledges edged with quaint wrought iron railings. The opening came out onto the street like black wings, the words Jazz Club written vertically in French and English. The double doors built in off the street were boarded over with a large padlock thrown on for good measure.

"Anyone watching?" Caia asked, approaching the padlock and boards.

After a moment, Phoebe gave her the go-ahead, and she pressed her hand against the padlock, her magik seeping out of her skin to engulf it. In a second, it quietly popped and dissolved into water. With her lykan strength, the boards snapped away from the door with ease. Phoebe followed and pulled the doors shut silently behind her.

Both of them could see through the shadows of the darkened room, past the little round tables and the bar up ahead, past the stage off center to the left.

"Behind there," Caia whispered, pointing to the right side of the bar where they could see a dark opening. "There's a hallway that leads to the storeroom door. In there is the door to the basement. Mr. Daemon is in the storeroom covering the basement trapdoor."

Offering a resolute nod, Phoebe removed her clothing quickly, neatly folding it as she went.

"Wait," Caia whispered urgently.

"What now?"

"I'm going to put a shield up to cloak the sounds of your change."

Phoebe's eyes widened. "Good idea," she whispered back.

It felt like forever, waiting for her change to be complete, the knowledge that the daemon hadn't heard them not lessening her anxiety.

She didn't like daemons.

Caia found it prudent to keep the shield around Phoebe as they moved through the club, afraid her claws would click against the concrete floor and ruin the element of surprise.

Together they stood outside the storeroom door, and Caia could feel the thing on the other side, standing vigilant upon the trapdoor in the floor that opened to the basement.

Phoebe turned to look up at her, her huge wolf eyes telling her she was ready. Caia nodded and pulled in her energy before pushing it back out and blasting the door off its hinges. Phoebe took off before the door was even gone and lunged at the daemon before it even knew what was happening. She knocked it off its feet and managed to cling on to its dirt-red skin, even as its ungraceful fall sent crates of bottles smashing down around them.

Caia shot in after her and blasted out a tube of water as

the daemon punched at Phoebe's sides, desperate to unclamp her jaws from his neck. As the hunter held him distracted, Caia forced the tube down his throat and held it there until he fell unconscious. Phoebe wasn't taking any chances; she chewed and masticated until his head rolled away from his body.

She backed up off him, making a hacking sound from her throat that reminded Caia of her own daemon takedown and how she'd retched after decapitating him. Once Phoebe was clear of his body, Caia thought of the daemon who'd wounded her that night in the mall lot, and more usefully, she dragged up the memory of Sebastian dying in her arms. Just like that, the white heat built inside her.

Taking hold of its reins, she focused it on the daemon's body and watched as it obliterated it into ash, leaving just a dusty trace. Phoebe elicited a strange noise, and Caia turned to find the wolf watching her. Even in her lykan form, her expression seemed to say, "You're kind of scary, you know that?"

Yeah, she did know that.

"Stay back." Caia pointed toward the hallway, and the lykan grudgingly padded away. She stared at the trapdoor, thoughts of the marble one in Gaia's altar determinedly pushing their way to the forefront of her mind. How could Marita justify what she was doing? Marita hated Midnights and everything they were about ... and yet wasn't what Pierre had done exactly the same as her own crime?

At the impatient sounds Phoebe made from the hallway, Caia shook off the thoughts. The trapdoor lifted easily, and a set of very unstable-looking stairs descended into darkness. The smell flooded her nostrils and she gagged, pressing her shirt to her nose. Phoebe whined from the doorway. That smell was enough to make every small move after filled with trepidation. There was no mistaking the stench of death—mixed with an obvious array of chemicals.

Taking off the backpack Marion had given her, Caia found the flashlight and dipped its light into the basement, leaning over to get a better look at what she was walking into. It seemed safe enough.

Safe perhaps physically, but emotionally ...?

Swinging the light from lab post to lab post, her shirt still covering her nose and mouth, Caia willed away the emotional reaction her body was so ready to give into. There were five morgue slabs in the room, each with a decaying lykan sliced open in varying manners upon it. The vile stench emanated from their exposed innards. Metal chains were still wrapped around their limbs from when they'd been alive and chained down. She didn't even want to think of a lykan being awake and aware during such experiments, such torture.

Moving away from them, she swung the flashlight beam toward the end of the room where a row of cages sat, some empty, some housing more dead lykans.

Memories of another basement and other cages threatened to overwhelm her.

"I have to find the liquid," Caia reminded herself and made to move toward the end of the basement behind the stairs. Sure enough, a glass cabinet against the wall held rows upon rows of vials of liquid gold.

Now all she needed to do was destroy it.

Silently, making her way out of the basement, Caia pulled another gift from Marion out of her backpack. To her it appeared to be a large crystal with a gold stopper plugged into the top. She wasn't quite sure of its mechanics, but apparently it was an expensive member of the Daylight arsenal.

"Just pull the stopper out and drop the crystal into the base-

ment. *The device will go off within five seconds of landing. You'll hear a soft pop.*"

"What does it do?"

"*Don't worry, it can't hurt living things. It merely cleans up the mess around us.*"

Caia did as Marion had instructed, closing the door after it.

"Wait, I wanted to see!" Phoebe hissed as she marched into the storeroom in human form.

As Caia stared into the lykan's angry face, a sound like an ear popping at high altitude could be heard from the other side.

"Sorry, it's too late."

"What was down there?"

She could tell her the truth, about the atrocities those two Midnights had committed with the help of humans; she could describe that reprehensible scene and wave goodbye to a potential ally. If Phoebe had seen it with her own eyes, there would've been no way to convince her that not all Midnights were bad. Describing it would just be another nail in the coffin of Caia's plan.

"But this is a war, Caia, and we have to sacrifice a part of our souls to win it."

"It was just a lab. Chemicals, test tubes ... that sort of thing."

I am so going to Hades.

"What about that goddess-awful smell?"

"Sewage," she lied, "guessing from the daemon."

"Ugh, charming."

Confident that she had convinced the hunter, Caia pulled at the trapdoor. Together she and Phoebe leaned in as she opened it, their flashlights illuminating the darkness. There was nothing there.

"What ...?"

Eyes wide, she trembled down the stairs and swung her light around.

"What do you see?" Phoebe called to her.

"Nothing."

It was like none of it had ever happened. Just an empty basement, clean of any activities. Four walls, a ceiling, and a floor.

"It's all gone. No mess," Caia told Phoebe as she climbed the stairs. "I have no idea what that thing was Marion gave me." She glanced at her watch. "Come on. We better go. Marion is opening the portal in ten minutes."

They made their way back out of the club, Caia replacing the boards and the padlock while Phoebe stood guard. Just as silently as they arrived, they returned to the spot they emerged from at Notre-Dame. Caia sidled toward the entrance of the cathedral, staring up at its two towers, wishing she could step inside and disappear behind its arched doorway, to curl up in what promised to be a mystical haven. Could she hide in there, in the arms of another god?

Phoebe tapped her shoulder, and she half turned to see the portal open on the dark street.

No. The war would still be out there, taking innocent lives and perpetuating into eternity. There was no hiding for her. She had a job to do.

A few humans strolled by, and up the way a café was still open with people outside at the little tables drinking coffee and eating dessert.

"I'm going to cloak us so they can't see us disappear," Caia warned Phoebe and shielded them both as Mordecai had taught her in glamour class. And just like that, they stepped back into the Center, leaving behind a loathsome sight that only Caia would ever carry in her memories.

CHAPTER 19

Sweet Midnight

"*A*rgh, I knew this was coming," Dimitri groaned.

Ryder raised an eyebrow expectantly. "Is that a yes?" He glanced between Dimitri and Julia, knowing his hope was out in plain view, so easy to shatter with one little word.

The thought of not having Jaeden in his life was excruciating now. Despite their attempts to not see each other over the last few days, they seemed to be inextricably connected. She'd explained there had been no more nightmares since the night he suggested they might be mates. She'd demonstrated how much control she was gaining on her telekinesis, arriving at his apartment exuberant and pleased with her progress at Lucien's.

Since Vil and Laila's arrival, he hadn't been able to leave the apartment, so Jae had come over at the end of each day, bringing food for everyone and catching him up on her

230

activities. They'd only grown closer, but he hadn't been able to relieve her of her fears over Laila. The food she brought for Vil and his girlfriend was handed over quickly before she departed for his bedroom, the room farthest away from the room he'd given to his guests.

Ryder, on the other hand, had gotten to know them as much as he could over the last forty-eight hours. Vil was a quiet, staid, young warlock who was extremely protective of the fragile creature who never left his side. He told Ryder bits and pieces of his life growing up in a household where his elder brothers were respected soldiers in the Center's First Unit. Fighting wasn't really in his blood; in fact, he couldn't quite wrap his head around this inane war, as he called it, and while home for his break, he'd come across Laila.

She'd escaped from a Midnight army base under Ethan's control. She wouldn't discuss what had happened to her there, but it was enough to cement a loathing in her blood for the Midnights. Vil had found her starving to death and had hidden her and coaxed her back to health. During this time, they fell in love, and she convinced him he should take her back to the Center so she could learn to fight for the Daylights.

Marita had her thrown in the containment center almost immediately. Marita had then dismissed him, sure his had not been an act of disloyalty but naivete, and in the end, he *had* helped her apprehend a Midnight. Vil had been trying to find a way to break Laila out of the prison ever since, but he didn't have the power a magik needed to do it, and he didn't trust anyone at the Center to help him.

And then Caia had come to him, "like an angel," he described softly, making Ryder smile. The little witch had that effect on people. Caia had said she could feel Laila's goodness, was adamant the girl posed no threat to the Daylights. She wouldn't stand back and let the girl suffer. Vil had believed her since he had no one else in which to place his faith. And the rest Ryder knew.

It was hard to imagine the gentle creature that gazed so adoringly at Vil could cause anyone harm, but he knew how deceptive they could be.

Atia and Adriana Vang had proven that. But Caia believed, and strangely, he did too.

Jaeden, on the other hand, was not so quick to trust.

"Why isn't Jaeden with you?" Julia asked, seeming amused by his proposal.

He locked eyes with her so she wouldn't suspect him of lying. "I felt this was something that I ought to do alone, man to ... parents." In truth, she was reluctantly watching over his guests at his apartment while he moved their potential mating along a little faster.

Julia swallowed a chuckle, her eyes dancing with delight. "Well, I'm all for it."

Dimitri glared at his wife. "We just got her back."

"And you think denying her the right to a mating ritual with the man she loves will entice her to stay?" Julia huffed.

Dimitri pinned Ryder to the wall with his eyes, his nostrils seeming to flare with steam like a bull getting ready to charge. And then, just like that, the air deflated out of him and he threw up his hands in surrender.

"Fine!" he snapped. "You have my blessing to mate with my only daughter ... you bastard."

Ryder whooped jubilantly and grabbed the big guy in a hug. Dimitri half-heartedly growled and slapped him, *hard*, on the back, sending him over to Julia who was the next target for his joy.

"Now you have to wait for Lucien," his soon-to-be father-in-law reminded him.

Ryder's grin refused to desist. "His return shouldn't be

long now. Then we can get straight to the mating ... err ... ritual."

Dimitri glowered.

"Uh." Julia giggled nervously. "I think you better leave, Ryder. Now ... like, right now ... righ—LEAVE!"

He was out the door like lightning, Dimitri's snarls snapping at his behind until he made it to his car.

* * *

THE WITCH still made her uneasy, despite Ryder's defense of her. Jae knew the girl didn't look like much, but Midnights were slippery, vicious creatures who knew how to get under the skin. She sat stiffly in a chair by the window while Vil and Laila snuggled on the sofa, munching on the snacks Jaeden had brought with her. The reason why she was here made her smile softly, wondering if Ryder would get the answer they both needed.

"You know, you don't have to be afraid of us." Vil's serene voice penetrated her musings.

Jaeden snapped to alert and grunted, "I'm not afraid of *you. Her* ... not so sure of."

Laila's huge blue eyes widened as she looked up and over at Jaeden who felt an unexpected twinge of guilt at the hurt she saw shimmering there.

"I would never hurt anyone," she whispered.

Vil shushed her, squeezing her closer, soothing her pain.

Why can't I shrug the guilt? Jae growled at herself, looking back at Laila. The Midnight was still staring at her, and as their eyes locked, Jaeden saw something in the magik's that was intimately familiar. Familiar ... because that haunted look had once reflected back at her every time she gazed into a mirror.

Ryder's voice echoed in her head: *I'm telling you, Jae,*

they're okay. Vil seems like a stand-up guy, and Laila ... well, she won't tell anyone, including Vil, what happened to her back at that camp, but I'm telling you it was enough to make her hate them.

"Can I speak with Laila alone?" she suddenly asked, standing over the pair.

Vil frowned, eyeing her warily. "I don't think so."

"I'm not going to hurt her."

"No, she—"

"It's fine." Laila placed a placating hand on his arm, and he glanced at her sharply.

"You are sure?"

"Yes."

"Okay. I'll be down the hall if you need me." He got up and threw Jaeden a stern warning look before he left.

She settled on the arm of the sofa, scrutinizing Laila, who had retreated a little from her. "What happened at this camp, this army camp?"

The magik shook her head. "I don't talk about it."

"If I'm to trust you, I need to know about this camp."

"It was ... just a camp."

"Under Ethan's control?"

"Yes."

"So ..." Jaeden searched for the right phrase. "It was like special ops?"

"What is ... special ops?"

"You know, like a government operation designed to ... let's say, win a war when normal tactics aren't moving things along as nicely as one would like."

Laila snorted, her face twisted in disgust. It was the most negative emotion Jaeden had seen her emit. "Yes. You could say it was this special ops you speak of."

A moment of silence fell between them as Jaeden worked toward posing her next question. She blew out a shaky breath, her voice husky as painful memories swept through her. "Did it involve torture?"

The witch's mouth fell open in surprise, her eyes round with torment. "Why …?"

"I'll take that as a yes, then."

Laila shook her head. "I don't … I can't … I—"

"I've been there, Laila," Jae whispered, not even sure why she was telling the girl something so personal. Perhaps she knew it might be the only way to get information from her. "Ethan … *personally* kept me in a cage. He tortured me. For weeks. Although it felt like years."

Laila's young face crumpled in empathy, and she placed a cool hand on Jaeden's wrist. Jaeden was surprised by the gesture, for Laila had only allowed Vil near her since their arrival. As her hand withdrew, Jaeden's pain at the memories dissipated, leaving a warm peace lingering in its wake. Relaxing back into the sofa, she smiled sadly at the Midnight.

"Is that what happened to you?"

The girl nodded rigidly.

"Why?"

A tear slid down her pale face. "It was a behavioral modification camp for magiks. He took children of magiks from all over. I come from Halmstad, but others came from Grena, Oslo … all over Scandinavia. He told our parents he was going to train us to be an elite force. It was an honor to be chosen. Instead, he used all measures of control—withholding food, brainwashing—all to turn us into an elite force that would only answer to his command, no matter the order."

"Like daemons."

Revulsion passed over Laila's face. "Like daemons. But so much more powerful."

"Why the torture? Was that part of it?"

She shook her head wildly, and Jaeden was surprised to

see an almost smug smile form on her lips. "His men couldn't break me. So they tortured me in an attempt to subdue me."

Horror rippled through Jaeden at the thought of what this girl had gone through.

"How did you escape?"

A cold, ferocious look froze her face. "The oldest trick in the book."

"Being?"

"One of the warlocks had an ... unhealthy interest in me."

No, no, no. Jae pulled back. *He didn't ... oh goddess.*

"Don't worry," Laila assured her. "They had orders not to touch us that way. It could have a disturbing effect on the controls. But this one"—she shuddered—"he would sneak in some touching, petting."

"Bastard," Jaeden snarled.

The witch looked startled at her vehemence before throwing her a grateful smile. "I used it against him, though. I pretended an interest in him, which is probably the most difficult thing I have ever had to do, and he took me from the cage and snuck me out toward the back of the camp. He turned his back for a second, and I knocked him out with a spell my mother taught me years before. Stupid man." She shook her head in disgust. "I stole his keys to his car, got a few miles away before I abandoned it and set off on foot, confusing my trail as I went. I thought Ethan would find me ... but he never came."

Jaeden snorted. "Yeah, 'cause he was dead."

"He *is* dead, then?" Laila asked quietly, her haunted eyes begging for an affirmative.

"Caia killed him."

"She helped save me from prison ... and now this news. It seems I will be forever in her debt."

A sense of connection threaded between them, and

Jaeden smiled warmly at her for the first time. "The way that girl is going, we're all going to be in her debt."

The sound of the front door slamming pulled them from Laila's tale, and Ryder strolled in, an obvious look of surprise on his face at the sight of them sitting together.

"Everything okay?" he queried.

"I was just going to ask that." Vil hurried in, his anxious eyes locked on Laila. She smiled, holding her hand out to draw him to her.

Visibly relaxing, he moved toward her like a magnet. Jaeden huffed in amusement at the suspicious look he leveled at her. She jumped up to go to Ryder, wrapping her arms around his waist, snuggling close to him. "Everything is good, actually." She searched his eyes, looking for the answer he'd received this evening from her parents. "Everything *is* good?"

"What did I miss?"

"Ryder?" she whined.

"I'll tell you if you tell me what happened here."

She pulled away from him. "You're a pain. Fine. Laila and I understand one another now, and I believe Caia when she says Laila is a good Midnight. Who would have thought? Now tell me what my father said."

All of a sudden, he laughed and grabbed her, whirling around the room. "Yes!"

"Yes?"

"Yes!"

"Oh my god—"

He smothered her words with a passionate kiss. A discreet cough pulled them apart a few seconds later and they turned, smiling, to see Reuben lounging in the doorway. Jaeden felt Ryder tense.

"What are you doing here?"

"I came to see how your guests were faring, but obviously, I'm interrupting a celebration."

Vil grinned. "Jaeden's parents are allowing them to mate."

Reuben remained passive, not giving anything away. "How nice for them."

"Reuben." Jae made a move toward him, hating to hurt her friend. "I'm glad you're here. I want you to be here for the ceremony. You've been through so much with me, it would feel weird without you."

"No, it wouldn't," Ryder growled, brushing past her to stand bristling at the vampyre. "For a start, my guests are none of your business."

"I was merely curious. She is a Midnight, after all."

Ryder scoffed, his fists curling into knots. "We both know why you're here, you son of a bitch."

Jaeden fought an oncoming headache. "Ryder—"

"Son of a bitch?" Reuben stood straight now, all evidence of passivity gone and replaced with a stony anger. "I'm the son of a bitch? You've done nothing but hassle me since I got here."

"Because you're always here!"

"I'm her friend. I'm not going anywhere."

"We'll see—"

"Guys!" she shouted, looking desperately to Laila and Vilhelm for help. They were no good, already sliding quietly away to disappear into their bedroom.

"You have no right turning up all the time, that's all I'm saying."

"I came here to see if the boy and the girl were okay. That they weren't causing any trouble, that's all."

"That's what you can't seem to wrap your thick skull around. This isn't your business."

"Whatever's coming, I'm more equipped to deal with it than you, lykan."

"Enough with the prophet crap. It's wearing on my nerves, vampyre."

"You're such a child."

"I'm—"

Their argument drifted from earshot as Jaeden slammed out of the apartment and down the stairs, out of the building. Half the time, she didn't think their inane arguing even had anything to do with her. Her headache throbbed harder as she got into her car.

A run.

A run would be good to work out everything that had happened this evening. Laila's sorrowful tale, the bond that she'd felt forging between them, the idea that Midnights might not all be bad, her official engagement to Ryder, and his inability to function normally in a room with Reuben.

Yeah, a run would be great.

Trying to throw off her irritation at Ryder and Reuben, Jae mused over Laila as she drove to Lucien's house and felt an impatience growing for Caia and their Pack Leader to return so they could work this all out. Parking on his drive, she got out and walked around to the back yard. She didn't bother going through the house, knowing they would hear her strolling around to the back and would work out for themselves who was there.

That impatience she felt bubbling in her skin changed into an impatience for the run. Jae jerked out of her clothes and suddenly wished she could be like Caia. Ryder had described how she could change into a wolf instantly now, how she could run into the woods on human legs and soar into the change. It sounded wonderful.

But as Jae's muscles strained with the burn of the change, and as her bones cracked with eye-watering satisfaction, she knew she wouldn't give up this feeling for anything. Distantly, she wondered if Caia missed it. The cool night air rushing through her pelt was exactly what the doctor ordered. She crunched through pine cones, ran at full speed toward a tree and launched herself at it, only to bound off and race in the opposite direction.

With the run, her mind cleared, replete and calm.

After a while, she grew exhausted, and so made her way back to Lucien's yard, leisurely and purposely slowing the change into human form. Jaeden smiled, stretching her muscles from top to bottom, yawning. With a final roll of her neck, she shuffled back into her clothes.

On the last button of her shirt, her ears pricked up at a loud crack from the woods close by. She sniffed the air, and an unfamiliar sweet scent she couldn't identify swam up her nostrils. She hadn't quite turned around to investigate when pain shot through her head and dark spots clouded her vision, swallowing her whole as they multiplied into a thick black tar.

* * *

"I CAN'T BELIEVE THIS. It's all your fault!" Ryder railed at the vampyre as they followed Jaeden's scent.

Reuben glared. "You started it."

"She's probably furious at me. At you. I can't believe she left without me even knowing it. It's your fault. You piss me off past rationality."

"It's always nice to be appreciated."

"Don't make me come over there, vampyre."

"I'm shaking in my boots."

Ryder bared his teeth and swung the truck viciously into Lucien's driveway next to Jae's car so that the vampyre slammed against the passenger door with an *oof*.

"Childish, immature—"

Ryder ignored him as his eyes narrowed on two figures

he saw at the side of the house. Two figures who appeared to be struggling.

"Jaeden!" he bellowed, cutting off the vampyre. Slamming on the brakes and cutting the engine, he threw himself out of the truck, running toward the dark figure that had Jaeden bundled over their shoulder. The figure stopped at the entrance of the woods, jerking toward them, their face hidden by a black hood. Unceremoniously, it dumped Jaeden's unconscious body to the ground and like a shadow disappeared into the darkness of the trees.

Reuben ran past him. "You check Jaeden, I'll go after them!" he ordered, his face set with determination. Ryder barely had a moment to register that he'd never seen anyone look quite as dangerous as Reuben did in that moment as he blurred past him.

"Jaeden." He fell beside her, turning her limp body over. He pressed his fingers to her pulse, relief rushing through him at the steady beat.

"Ryder, what happened?"

He looked up to see Ella and Magnus rushing out of the house, their faces etched with concern. "She's been knocked out. Her head's bleeding."

"Get her into the house," Magnus ordered gruffly, his eyes searching the woods. "There's someone out there."

Ryder nodded, lifting Jaeden into his arms with ease. "I couldn't see who it was. Reuben's gone after them."

Magnus frowned. "The vampyre. Sure he can handle it?"

The venomous look on Reuben's face flashed before Ryder's eyes. "I'm sure. Let's worry about Jae."

Magnus reluctantly agreed and followed them into the house. Ella cleaned the blood from the wound and Magnus checked her over.

"When she comes around, it'll heal," he assured Ryder.

Ella wrung her hands. "Must have been some hit to take one of us down."

Ryder growled in response.

At that, Jaeden stirred, her eyelids fluttering. "Ow."

He took her hand in his. "Jae. You're all right, baby, you're all right."

After a few moments, her eyes seemed to focus and she groaned in irritation. "What the hell happened now?"

"I lost them!" Reuben strode into the sitting room, his hair wild from having run against the wind, his shirt torn from obstructing branches.

"Lost who?" Jae whispered. "What happened?"

Magnus shook his head in deep concern. "Someone tried to take you."

Horror flitted across her eyes before she could stop it. "Kidnap me?"

Ryder squeezed her hand tighter, rage unlike anything he'd ever known desperate to explode and take everything with it. "We'll find out why," he promised tightly.

"I want to know *who*," Ella snarled.

They fell silent, and Reuben moved toward the hallway, his head down, shoulders hunched in thought. Ryder's head jerked up as the vampyre muttered, "If it's who I think it was, things are about to get very interesting."

CHAPTER 20

The Politician

"*I* don't think you understand how valuable you are."

Marita appeared to be fighting to remain calm, her words hissed between clenched teeth. "Forget even that you have trace powers leading us to every Midnight in this world, but there is not a witch or warlock on Earth who has done what you did in Remnant Forest."

She was allowing the Head of the Coven to pace and bluster and lecture, sitting on the sofa by Marita's fireplace, waiting patiently for her chance to speak. So far, the witch was not happy about Caia's news that she intended to return to the pack. Boo for her.

"You haven't even touched on some of the lessons in magik our advanced classes teach. We have no idea what you will be capable of when you have the knowledge and understanding of magik like that of my sister and my own. It would be idiotic to let you walk out of here and go home."

Caia tensed at her tone, her eyes narrowing as Marita spun to glare at her. "Last time I checked, madam, the coven laws forbid coercion and kidnapping."

Marita chuckled humorlessly. "So dramatic, Caia."

"You knew when I got here that it was merely a visit. I've been helping you quite well from my home with the pack."

"Your reports are useful. However, your soldiering is invaluable."

As the silence thickened between them, Caia could see the witch's eyes hardening with every tick of the clock.

She really thought I would stay, Caia mused, incredulous.

"What have you got to return to, Caia? Those people who don't understand you? And if the rumor mill here is correct, your Alpha, the one man who was keeping you bound to that pack, is now in a relationship with Rose Bronson."

The calculating gleam in her eye, that smug smile, knocked Caia for six.

Son of a bitch, she hissed inwardly. "Rose ... isn't a friend of Phoebe MacLachlan's, is she?"

Marita gave her a saccharine smile, folding herself elegantly into the armchair before her. "No, not really."

She didn't know whether to be disgusted or pay attention to this woman's tactics. After all, if she was to convince the Council to ally with her and go up against Marita, then she'd better learn to be just as ruthless when dealing with her.

"Why?"

"I need you here."

In other words, she had deliberately brought Rose here to separate Caia from Lucien, to make her feel isolated from him and the pack, to give her no other option but to call the Center *home.* There was an absoluteness to Marita in that moment. From the tip of her hair to the tip of her toes, she was determined Caia would remain with her, fight for her.

Did she really think Caia would agree to aid her in her experiments with children?

Time to change tactics.

Caia slumped, a small sigh escaping as she glanced up at the magik with a deliberate weariness shimmering in her eyes. "I don't know what I'm doing," she whispered.

The magik tutted and slid a cold hand across to her, patting it condescendingly. "There, there, my dear. You've had an exhausting time of it. But there is nowhere better for you than here. It will be better for you emotionally and physically if you stay. I thought you'd made friends here, people who understand you. And there's always Marion, who I know is extremely fond of you."

Caia nodded, tucking her hair behind her ear, making her fingers tremble noticeably. "I just … don't want to disappoint anyone."

"You mean the pack. Lucien?"

"Yes."

"He stepped aside so easily, Caia, when I brought Rose in. What loyalty do you really owe him?"

More than I owe you.

With her young heart in her eyes, she looked up at Marita as if a student to her tutor. "I would like to stay here."

A wide grin split her normally dispassionate face. "Wonderful. I'll take ca—"

"But I have to go back to say goodbye to everyone. To explain. I would … like to see Jaeden, as well, before I return to the Center."

For a moment, Marita's eyes washed over her, searching, suspicious. It took everything Caia had to maintain the sincere facade of a young, confused girl looking for guidance. Inside she was furious at this woman for putting her in this position, this woman who was supposed to be the protector of the Daylight Coven. How Marion's great-grand-mother would be howling from the Underworld at the way Marita had taken to running things. She was an autocrat all right—she was just better at hiding it than most.

Finally, the magik seemed satisfied that Caia was telling the truth. She nodded and stood. "Very well. You should leave today, then. But I expect you back in two days' time."

Caia forced a bright smile. "Yes, yes, of course."

Restraining the urge to run from the room, Caia sedately left Marita's suite, surprised to find Marion waiting inside the mahogany elevator for her.

"Well?" She smiled kindly.

Oh, how she wished she could confide in Marion, tell her the truth. She abhorred lying to the woman who'd been more than just a mentor, but a solid friend.

"I'm staying," she managed weakly. "I'm going back to the pack with Lucien to say goodbye, and then I'll be back here in two days."

Marion's reaction wasn't the one she'd been expecting.

"Are you sure that's what you want?"

"What do you mean? I thought you'd be happy."

The witch threw her a sad, knowing look. "It would make me happy if I thought that was what you really wanted."

Caia frowned. "It is."

They rode down the elevator, got off at floor five, and rode that elevator up to Caia's suite in complete silence. Marion stopped her before she could make her way to her room.

"I still believe you can help us win this war, even if you're living with the pack. My sister doesn't. That doesn't mean you have to feel pressured into staying. It would be against the law to keep you here against your will."

In that moment, Caia wanted to throw her arms around

this woman and cry, beg, plead with her to help her with what she had to do. But no matter how kind Marion had been to her, she would never betray her sister.

Caia smiled determinedly and lied, "I appreciate that, Marion, but there's really nothing keeping me with the pack."

"Not even Lucien?"

An ache rippled across her chest and her smile tightened. "Lucien has Rose."

"And if he didn't?"

"He does." She turned to leave. "I'm going to get ready. Maybe you could tell Lucien we're leaving now? Rose is coming with us."

Instead of heading toward her suite, however, Caia strode past it and got into the elevator at the other end of the hall. Her heart raced, and she hoped she would remain undetected as she made her way to visit the Travelers.

Luck must have been on her side. She found herself on the other side of the Center with very little trouble and was swarmed by the twins and a few others. The rest of the Travelers watched shyly from the background.

"Oh my goddess, Caia, Ophelia traveled to the top of the Pyramid of Khafre in Giza this morning!" Desi tugged excitedly on her sleeve. "We all told her not to because it's like insanely dangerous ... I mean, she could've missed the top by a millimeter and gone crashing down the pyramid. But she didn't!" She laughed, shooting a look of pure pride at Ophelia, who blushed happily. "She totally pulled it off!"

Caia chuckled. "Well done, Ophelia. That must've been some view."

She shrugged modestly. "There was a lot of sand."

Desi snorted. "I would so be bragging if I were you. I can't believe Vilhelm missed it. Did you hear, Caia? That he broke that girl out of prison, that Midnight?"

"I did."

Desi and a few others shook their heads in amazement. "We knew he was, like, awesome at traveling, but we didn't know he had the balls to pull that off."

Ophelia sniffed. "Well, all I have to say is that he really must believe the girl is innocent. Vilhelm would never betray the coven."

Oh, that's right, Caia mused, *Ophelia had a crush on Vil*.

Desi grimaced. "Or, uh, the girl put a spell on him."

"Impossible." One of the other male Travelers shook his head, scowling at her. "The girl was contained by magik. Vil did it of his own free will."

"So weird. He was always so quiet."

"It's always the quiet ones."

"Why did he do it, though?"

"I don't care why he did it," Ophelia said loudly, cutting off the chatter. "I'm just not going to treat him like a villain for it."

"Ophelia." Desi reminded her, "She's a Midnight."

Her sister narrowed her eyes. "She came here for refuge."

"Midnights are the enemy, remember," one older woman sneered.

Caia watched them argue among themselves, her confidence growing by the minute. It seemed the younger generation were more open to the belief that maybe all Midnights weren't to be condemned solely on heritage.

"I can't believe you would even suggest a Midnight could be innocent," the same woman spat at Ophelia, and the others crowded around her. Desi looked torn, and she turned to Caia as if for reassurance. As her green eyes swept over Caia, her face brightened, and she whirled back to the others. "Why not?" she demanded of the opposition. "Caia's part Midnight, and she's awesome."

Silence descended over the room as they all turned to stare at her.

Great.

The older Traveler stepped forward, and still scowling at Desi said quietly and authoritatively, "That's different. Miss Ribeiro isn't a full-blooded Midnight and has proven her loyalty to the Daylights thrice over. In fact, she, of all people, would be able to tell you that all Midnights are evil."

Sweat broke out under her arms. She hadn't come here to make a declaration on that subject quite yet. She'd only visited because she wanted to tell them they could come see her anytime if they needed anything at all. The Travelers were an important group to her ... and eventually, she would need *them.*

As Caia stared back at their waiting faces, she was loath to lie to them. If she did, they would only see it as hypocrisy later, and her hopes of winning their support would be dashed. She gave them a weary smile. "There are very few people in this world who are truly evil. That the Midnights are our enemy at the moment is all you need to know."

Before the surprised muttering could erupt into loud chatter, Caia moved toward them. "I actually came to tell you that I'll be returning to the pack for a few days." *More lies*, she winced. "But I'll be back." *No need to tell them when.* "And while I'm gone, I want you to know that you can come visit me anytime. If you need me, I'm here."

There was some gushing from Desi and her sister, and a few others, but mostly just grateful smiles thrown in with a bit of hero-worship. Normally it would make Caia want to sink into the floor to avoid such flattery. Her plans had changed all that.

As diplomatically as she could, she made her excuses and returned to her suite with a triumphant smile. Things were going very nicely. Just one last thing to do.

With her stare fixed on the offending vase, Caia practically stormed at it, upended its contents on the floor, and sifted through them with her toe.

There you are.

The tiny black chip lay before her mere seconds before she crushed it underfoot. Goodbye, bug, goodbye, Center … Goodbye, Marita.

CHAPTER 21

Finally

*H*e watched the rain, wishing they weren't stuck in this bubble at the Center so he could hear it battering his windows. The sounds, smells, and sight of rain had always reminded him of the pack, of the damp earth that told him he was home.

Lucien turned away only to glare at the wall that connected to Caia's suite. Something was going on, he knew it—that she wouldn't confide in him enraged him past all reason. Her attitude toward him before and after the attack at Remnant Forest had been inexcusable considering he was the wronged party. He wanted to throttle her.

The day he'd cornered her in the library, he'd gone snooping when she left the room, hoping to discover a clue as to what she had really been researching.

Tae kwon do, my ass.

To his ever-continuing irritation, he'd found nothing.

Then there had been her venture into Paris without him, without even telling him it was happening. Ah yeah, Marita had been particularly smug about that when he'd gone looking for her, only to discover Caia was destroying Pierre du Bois's lab with Phoebe MacLachlan and she hadn't had the decency to tell him, her pack Alpha.

Lucien growled just thinking about it. Marita was winning this stupid war with him over Caia's loyalty, and the sooner he could get her out and away from that woman, the better.

He snapped to attention at the soft knock on his door and admonished himself for hoping it wasn't Rose. Although he hadn't entered into a relationship with her, she'd been trying to persuade him otherwise, pulling him into surprise kisses and talking about a future together. When she asked if she could return to the pack with him, Lucien felt awful letting her down when she was recovering from the beating she'd taken from that Midnight. She'd been angry at his refusal, but he felt it would've been worse to commit to her when all his thoughts were centered on Caia. Not that the little she-witch cared, he grumbled, feeling her rejection like pinpricks of pain all over.

Disgruntled, he yelled, "Come in!" toward the door and hoped his visitor wasn't looking for pleasant conversation.

"Lucien." Marion marched inside, slamming the door.

His eyebrows hit his hairline, surprised by his visitor and even more so by the glare she was using to staple him to the window.

"Marion. What's going on?"

"What's going on?" Throwing her hands up in the air, she spun away from him and began pacing. "This is why I don't do romantic relationships. The male species, of any race, are a dim-witted bunch, testing the patience of saints."

Lucien tried to cover his snort and failed.

"It's not funny, Lucien. You'll be laughing on the other side of your face when I impart this next piece of news."

Just like that, he tensed. "What news?"

The magik strode toward him, her head craned back to look up at him, her eyes narrow slits. "What on earth are you playing at, young man? Kissing another lykan in front of Caia, avoiding her completely? She's been alone the entire time she's been here."

He only heard the first part of that statement. "What do you mean kissing another lykan in front of Caia?"

Marion curled her lip in distaste. "Rose Bronson. You kissed her in the reception area."

"Caia saw?"

"Caia saw."

Damn. Guilt flooded him. Rose had kissed him good luck, and he hadn't exactly thrown her off. What must Caia think? He was such an id—

"Wait!" he snapped, pushing passed her. "I have nothing to feel guilty about. I'm not the one who's been avoiding Caia, it's the other way around. She's been keeping secrets, giving me attitude. *She* made it perfectly clear that she didn't need *me*."

He expected an apology from Marion, for her to admit graciously she'd blundered and tell him how sorry she was for him.

The witch stared at him as if he was the stupidest person she'd ever met. "And when did this behavior start? Before or after Rose's arrival?"

"Well …" Lucien wasn't sure he liked where this was going.

She threw off his dithering with an impatient swat of her hand and stormed toward him again. "Just tell me this … are you with Rose now?"

"That's not really your business, Marion."

"Lucien," she warned.

He huffed, affronted at having to discuss his personal business with this woman. "I would be better off, wouldn't I?"

"That's not an answer."

"No. I'm not with Rose."

At that, Marion exhaled loudly while still managing to stare at him in disgust. "Men."

"I don't really understand the male bashing, Marion. What exactly are you doing here?"

"Believe it or not, I've come to help you stop Caia from making a terrible mistake that will affect you both."

An immediate panic set in. "What? What's going on?"

"Caia is staying at the Center."

"WHAT?"

"Shut up," she hissed, smoothing her hair after Lucien's ferocious bellow had blown it back. "It's your fault."

"My fault! I've been here! I've been trying to find out what the hell she's keeping from me."

"No. You've been with Rose."

"For the last time—"

"Lucien Líder, do not interrupt me again," Marion warned, her stern eyes gluing his mouth shut. "Good. As I was saying, I am tired of the complete idiocy you and Caia seem to share when it comes to the matter of your relationship. Caia has not been divulging any information to you, Lucien, because she was hurt and jealous by Rose's presence in your life."

Well, that doesn't sound right.

"Are we talking about the same Caia Ribeiro?"

"Oh dear Gaia, I'm surrounded by fools." Marion threw her hands up in dismay and flopped down onto his sofa. "Lucien, when you arrived at the Center, was Caia talking to you? Yes. When Rose arrived, did Caia stop confiding in you? Yes."

"What, no—" He stopped, an uncomfortable feeling telling him to take a moment. Now that she mentioned it, there had been a few times Caia had seemed to want to talk to him about something, but there had always been an interruption. And true, lately, that interruption had been Rose.

Marion must have seen the comprehension dawn on his face because she clucked, gloating. "And everything starts to make sense."

Lucien shook his head, trying to remain cool. "Are you telling me Caia thinks I've abandoned her?"

"I'm telling you that you let my sister's plot—to separate you and Caia so she would be more inclined to stay at the Center with her—work. I'm telling you that for the last seven months, you haven't been with your mate because you didn't say the one thing she needed to hear. I'm telling you what I tried to tell you the night Caia was attacked by that daemon."

"What?" he asked hoarsely.

"Lucien." Marion tut-tutted and got up off the sofa. "What do you think? Caia has never really had a family until you. Right now, she is the most valuable magik in our world, and she doesn't know who to trust. If she knew how you really felt about her, if she was secure in that, she would turn to you." Her eyes filled and she coughed, embarrassed, looking away from him. "I care about her a great deal, Lucien, but I worry for her all the time. This war is going to swallow her whole if she's not careful. She needs you. So choke on that stubborn pride of yours and tell her those three little words she's been waiting to hear."

He clenched his jaw, fear breaking out across every inch of his body. "And if she doesn't say it back?"

Marion smiled slowly, softly. "She will."

He searched her eyes, astounded by her certainty in Caia's

love. Did she know something he didn't? That certainty eased the ache that had been pressing on his chest for the last few months. He nodded, feeling an elated sense of hope. "I need to speak to Rose first."

* * *

PRESSING her hand against the glass, Caia wished the rain in Paris could hit against the Center's window. She loved the sound of the rat-a-tat-tat against the house when you were tucked inside, safe and sound, flames roaring in a fireplace.

A loud rap sounded on her door.

"Come in!" she called, keeping her back to her visitor, her eyes glued hypnotically to the blurry world outside.

She heard the door open. Heavy footsteps drew across the room toward her. She inhaled the scent of damp earth and electric air and wasn't surprised when Lucien came to a stop by her side, staring straight ahead out the window.

"I've been looking for you," he told her in a quiet, deep voice.

At least he doesn't sound angry.

She'd been waiting for the explosion to come ever since she'd gotten back from the lab with Phoebe. So far, she hadn't seen him.

There's a surprise.

"I like the rain."

"Me too."

After a moment of silence, Caia asked, "Did you hear the news?"

She wasn't looking forward to telling the truth, of explaining about Laila and Vilhelm, or her plans to stage a coup after her discovery of what lay beneath the Center.

"Yes." His tone didn't give anything away, and Caia snuck a glance at him out of the corner of her eye. His entire body was rigid with emotion. He *was* angry. *Time for the truth.*

She pushed out with her magik and wound a shield around the two of them. Lucien frowned, glancing around at it, but she refused to meet his gaze, her own eyes staring adamantly ahead.

"For privacy," she muttered in explanation. "We need to talk."

"Yes, we do," he agreed, exhaling. To her it almost sounded like he was nervous ... but what did he have to be nervous about?

Rose.

Caia gripped the ache that name created and attempted to suffocate it from her body.

"Rose isn't coming back with us."

What?

"What?" She forgot she was trying not to look at him and directed the question into his eyes.

He shrugged uncomfortably, and she thought she saw pain flitter across his features. "I just spoke with her. Everything was explained. She's not coming. We were never really together, you know."

"I'm sorry," she managed tightly. What? Did he expect sympathy for being dumped?

She flinched at his growl and returned to looking out the window.

"Caia," he said, exasperated, "look at me."

"What for?"

"You're being a child."

"I told you, I like the rain."

He let go of his growl and stared stormily ahead. "I never wanted to be with Rose," he revealed through a clenched jaw. "That kiss you saw was her, not me. I told her she couldn't come back to the pack with us. Caia, I thought you were

257

pulling away. I thought you didn't want ..." He sighed. "I'm not good at ... the word thing. I just ... I'm not with Rose."

Caia tried so hard to stamp down the little butterflies of hope that fluttered in her stomach. She tried to seem uninterested, she really did. She failed. "Why?"

At first Caia didn't think he was going to answer, but then she felt his gaze on her face as he spoke. "Do you remember that night you found me in the woods? The night we ran together alone?"

She nodded numbly, wishing she didn't.

At the touch of his hand sliding around her waist, Caia jerked in surprise, tensed as he slid behind her, wrapping his strong arms around her middle and pulling her body in close. His heat and strength, the feel of him, the scent of him, exploded over her in a riot of butterflies and shivers. She held her breath, wide-eyed, as he inhaled her, before tucking her head under his chin.

A moment of tense silence.

And then ...

"That's when I first knew." His voice had gone hoarse. "Caia," he said reverently, "I love you."

Her pulse raced as a sharp ache shot across her chest.

Love me? He loves me?

A sense of unreality descended over her, and she felt light-headed. It couldn't be true.

Lucien seemed to sense her disbelief, and he squeezed her even closer, his lips sending goose bumps down her spine as he pressed them against her ear. "Caia, I love you. Look at me." He elicited an aggravated sound when she made no move, and then whipped her around to face him, gripping the top of her arms and glaring sternly into her face as he shook her. "Do you hear me? Say something."

As she gazed, stunned, into his eyes, she saw his fear. It was etched in every one of his features and she could feel it in his painful grip. *He loves me.* Like a much-needed thaw, those words melted her defenses, and tears she couldn't hold back slipped down her cheeks. Caia sank into him, her arms wrapping around his waist and gripping him to her. Lucien would never lie about this, she was sure. *He loves me. He has always loved me.* Pain receded.

"I love you too," she whispered against his chest.

Lucien trembled beneath her touch and exhaled before bending his head, pressing his lips to hers, and tugging her feet from the floor so he could devour her more comfortably. Caia moaned happily into his mouth, relishing the taste of him, the burning heat he managed to evoke from her. It wasn't a soft kiss. It was hard and deep and asked everything of her. His grip on her hair tightened and he pulled back from the kiss to nip at her swollen lips, his eyes narrowed slits, his face drawn and tight.

"I thought you'd never be mine," he growled, and for once, Caia gloried at his possessiveness, excited by how out of control he seemed as his mouth found hers again. Her whole body felt like it was on fire, and she shivered uncontrollably. At that, Lucien finally seemed to calm, and he reluctantly stopped kissing her.

"Caia," he trailed hot kisses across her face and neck, his arms still crushing, "never leave me."

She grinned, ecstatic, feeling as if a war was finally over. "Never," she promised, curling her fingers in his thick hair.

They held each other for what seemed forever, murmuring love and promises in one another's ears, their relief palpable in the bubble they shared.

Lucien was hers. Finally hers. And she wasn't alone anymore.

* * *

"LUCIEN." Caia pulled back from his hug, his hard, warm body the safest place she had ever known. "I have a lot to tell you. To explain. Some things you might not want to hear."

As if sensing her fear, he cupped her cheek in his hand. "You can trust me."

"I'm more worried about you trusting me."

"Caia, I trust you completely. I thought you knew that."

"I guess we've both been a little blind."

"Oh, just a little," he muttered.

"Okay." She took a deep breath, preparing herself. "I'm going to tell you everything. No interruptions until I'm done."

He grinned at her authoritative tone. "Yes, sir."

"Lucien."

"I'm kidding. Please, continue."

"Okay. Okay. Okay—"

"Caia."

"Okay. Here goes. The girl who escaped, the Midnight … I felt her trace when we got here and didn't like what I found. She was, *is*, one of the purest souls I've ever encountered."

He frowned. "What do you mean?"

"No interruptions."

"Sorry."

From there, Caia went onto tell him about how she'd realized Midnights were just like them. That a lot of them were even indifferent to the war. She also told him about Laila, what happened to her, and how she'd helped Vilhelm to break her out of the Center.

Lucien jerked away from her in shock. "You broke that girl out of prison?"

Caia's heart thumped uncertainly. "Oh man, if you think that's a problem, you might not want to hear the rest."

Although he looked incredibly worried, he shook it off, pressing her to go on. She did. Telling him that she sent them to Ryder. That Marita and Mordecai bugged her room because they wanted to know secrets about Jaeden.

His brow cleared with dawning realization. "That's why you asked that question about her abilities in the library."

"Yeah." She nodded, taking his hand in hers. "They were talking about Jaeden's abilities, if I knew anything about them. I don't. I have no idea what they were talking about. After that, I was suspicious of them both. Marita was definitely up to something."

"You don't know what that is?"

Caia braced herself for the worst part of her news. She told him about the secret laboratory beneath the Altar of Gaia.

"Oh hell," Lucien said gruffly, and she felt the sofa dip as he settled beside her, his hand rubbing her back.

"I don't know what she's doing." She shook her head and turned to face him, his skin ashen from the news. "Do you remember she asked me to stay and help train an elite lykan unit?"

He nodded and slowly his eyes widened. "You don't think ...?"

"There's a possibility she's trying to create a super army by experimenting on other supernaturals. There was another lab farther up the corridor, but I couldn't get to it. I had to leave before Marita saw me."

"What the hell are we going to do, Caia?"

She turned toward him now, never so grateful for the use of *we* in that question, she gripped his knee as she spoke. "I had to lie and tell her I would stay at the Center, that I was going back to the pack with you to say goodbye, and then returning to her. I had to lie, Lucien, because I think she would've done anything to keep me here."

His face darkened. "As in threaten you? That's against the law."

"I think we can assume she doesn't give a rat's ass about the law."

"Right."

"Lucien..."

He squeezed her hand. "Say it."

"The war is a lie."

A cold, uneasy silence rippled out of him. "What?"

"The war ... it doesn't make sense. I can't knowingly help kill magiks who are innocent or misguided. And I can't help someone who professes to hate a race of people for doing things she's so intent on doing herself. This war is so twisted ... the reasons for it don't even exist anymore."

His grip tightened. "So what are you saying?"

She searched his eyes and took hold of the trust she found there. "I'm saying that I need more power to begin peace negotiations with the Midnight Coven."

"Caia ... peace negotiations? Are you sure that's not a little naive?"

Her eyes dropped to her feet. "Maybe. But ... if they knew that I'm the Head of the Coven, that I can find them anywhere ... a little fear might go a long way to negotiating."

Lucien nodded slowly. "Okay, true. But they might also just try to kill you."

She frowned in annoyance. "It's all I've got. I won't fight for a lie."

His shoulders slumped when he saw how determined she was. "What's the plan?"

"Vil ... the Traveler."

"Yeah?"

"When I was in the library—"

"I was wondering what you were up to in there." He tugged her close.

"I was researching a spell. But also the library has schedules for everything as a public reference. Classes, ceremonies, holidays, and … the days on which the Council convenes."

"The Council?"

"Yes. Did you know they have the authority to permit a challenger for the position of Head of the Coven if they have evidence that the current Head is not the best magik for the job?"

"What are you saying?"

She gulped. "I'm saying that I'm the most powerful weapon they have, and Gaia put me here for a reason. I'm saying that if they knew what Marita was up to … Vil can take me to the Council, and I'm going to challenge Marita for the post. If they agree, a political campaign will begin, and the coven will vote for their choice of candidate."

"Caia, if the Council discovers what Marita is up to, there will be no election." Lucien shook his head. "They will kill Marita."

"No, no, we're better than that, than her." She jerked her head. "I would ask for them to keep her alive. She could keep the trace, work for me, do for me what I've been doing for her."

He snorted. "Yeah, I can see that happening."

"She would have to. It would be her only choice."

Lucien was quiet for so long, she knew he wasn't as convinced as she was. Still, he kissed her softly. He wrapped her in his arms and whispered in her ear, "I'll make the badges and banners. You can write the speeches."

Caia smiled, comfort flooding her, and pulled him in for a grateful kiss.

* * *

THEY SOMEHOW MANAGED to disentangle themselves to make the difficult decision to lie to Marion. When they found her waiting in the reception for them, her bright eyes wide with hope, Caia felt awful duping her. She and Lucien walked with a deliberate distance between them, fake frostiness preceding them to the waiting magik. Caia winced, watching Marion slump in disappointment, glaring at Lucien as if he were to blame.

Tactful as always, however, she didn't mention the state of their relationship.

"Ready, then?" She heaved an exasperated sigh, gesturing to the portal awaiting them past security.

Lucien surprised her by pulling her into a hug. "Thanks for everything, Marion."

Caia wanted to slap him; he was going to give them away.

Sappy idiot.

The witch giggled at his unexpected affection and pushed him off. "I didn't do anything apparently," she tut-tutted and guided him toward the portal, missing the mischievous grin he threw over her head at Caia.

Trying her hardest to ignore him, a Herculean task since the very thought of him made her want to melt into a puddle, Caia hugged Marion and prayed to Gaia that her friend would forgive her as she lied, "See you in a few days."

"Hmm, yes, you will." Marion shook her head as she pulled back. "Silly girl."

With a vague gesture, Caia smiled and headed toward Lucien who waited by the portal for her.

Wary of Marion's eyes on them, Caia stuck her hand out to him as if it was the last thing she wanted to do. He reached for it tentatively but gripped it tight.

Relief and anxiety poured through her as the gel-like quality of the portal slithered across her skin. In moments they were blinking past the light streaming in from the lamppost outside the windows of the disused workout room in Magic Fitness.

She felt like a bird freed from a cage.

"Are you okay?" Lucien pulled her to him, wrapping her in his solid embrace.

"I just can't believe I'm going to do this," she mumbled into his chest. It rumbled with his laughter underneath her, and she buried deeper into him.

"Yeah, I can't believe you are either. But I believe in you."

Tilting her head back, she was surprised to find his eyes smoke with fierceness. "You really do, don't you?"

"You need to stop sounding surprised by that."

She smiled shyly. "But I am surprised."

He chuckled and took hold of her hand, leading her out of the room and out of the quiet gymnasium. "If you're going to be this bad mother-you-know-what, then you're going to have to start sounding like you're aware you're epic."

Caia nodded, straightening her shoulders. "I have to be confident, match my badass powers."

"Yeah." He grinned and then his smile fell. "Damn." Lucien stopped, crouching by the wheel of his truck. Heavy yellow clamps stood between them and the pack. Of course—the car had been sitting in the lot for days.

"Do you want me to …?" She wriggled her fingers.

"This doesn't need magik." He quickly scanned the lot to make sure there was no one else around and then gripped the tire clamps with both hands. With what appeared to be the gentlest of tugs, the clamp split in two and he pulled it out from under the car. He did the same with the others and gestured for Caia to get in.

"Wow." She smiled as she slid her seat belt on.

"What?"

"Was that a deliberate attempt to make me feel like the little Mrs.?"

Lucien grunted and started the engine, speeding out of the lot before anyone found them with the clamps. "I don't think that's possible. I was just reminding you that I have my uses. You don't have to do everything yourself."

Caia snuggled into her seat. "You don't know how good that is to hear."

He reached across the distance between them and linked his fingers with hers, keeping one hand on the wheel and his eyes on the road. "You're my mate."

She bit her lip, undecided whether she should ask the question that had been sneaking closer to the forefront of her mind since Lucien had declared his love.

Her mate seemed to sense it and tugged on her hand.

"Caia, I'm willing to take my pack into a political war against the Head of the Daylight Coven for you. Surely you realize you can say anything to me by now."

Laughing at her own stupidity, Caia blushed. "I guess."

"Well?"

I hope this comes out right or this might be the shortest relationship in history.

"Are you afraid that what we feel for each other is only because of the mating?"

When his silence stretched into awkward, Caia worried her lip with her teeth, her stare unblinking, watching him for signs of anger. Finally, he glanced at her briefly before returning his eyes to the road. She felt a measure of relief as he squeezed her hand.

"Does it matter if it is?"

She frowned. "Doesn't it, though?"

"No." By tugging on her hand, he pulled her closer to him, his scent enfolding her and warming her instantly. "Maybe we do love each other because of a deal our fathers made with a god, but it doesn't make that love any less real."

"So you're not worried that it wasn't your choice to love me?"

Lucien snorted. "No. And if I remember correctly, that

line of argument is the reason we haven't been together from the start, so I think it might be best we burn those thoughts forever. Seriously, Caia, do you want to give this up just because it was preordained by our dads?"

She could sense the worry in his question and felt a peculiar need to tease him. "I don't know. I mean, down that road is a dangerous journey—wanting the fairy tale because reality blows. Neo would be most unimpressed by us."

"Since his third movie sucked, Neo can go to Hades."

Caia grinned. "You got that reference?"

"Really, Caia, what do you take me for?"

"A lykan with very little attachment to the television."

"Yeah, but with a friend who watched *The Matrix Trilogy* ninety times when he should've been out kicking some rogue's ass."

"Ryder." Caia laughed.

Lucien grunted, "I should be thankful he keeps me socially adept."

She tried to suppress a grin. "But you're not thankful."

"Have you seen *The Matrix Revolutions*?"

CHAPTER 22

Loyalty

The sound of gravel crunching beneath tires was like a welcoming trumpet to Caia's and Lucien's ears. They tumbled out of his truck, tired but still filled with love-fueled restlessness. Caia mused over how strangely comfortable it was for them to walk with their arms around one another into the house. It felt like something they'd been doing forever.

They found Magnus and Ella standing in the doorway of the sitting room, waiting for them, both grinning at their return. And then Ella's eyes washed over them clinging to each other and they widened.

"Does this mean ..." She looked quickly to Magnus to see if he'd noticed, and he was grinning from ear to ear, his eyes twinkling.

"We're together," Lucien's voice rumbled with satisfaction.

The Elders launched themselves at Lucien and Caia and Magnus boomed, "It's about time!"

Caia laughed and allowed them to squeeze her to death. Noticing the tears running like twin streams down Ella's cheeks, Caia pulled her aside to hold her close.

"I'm so happy. Albus would have been so happy."

Before Caia could reply, Magnus lifted her off the ground in a bear hug, his own eyes suspiciously wet. When she was firmly back on her feet, he held her face between his hands and gazed down at her adoringly. "I feel like a proud father."

Her throat burned, and she worked her jaw, trying not to cry. At last she managed a hoarse, "You have been like a father to me, Uncle Magnus. Thank you."

The best moment in her life so far, a moment when she finally felt she was part of a family, was cut short by a shrill ringing. Cursing, Lucien pulled out his cell phone.

"Ryder," he muttered and hit the answer button. "What's up?"

"You're back!" They all heard Ryder. "When?"

"This minute. How did you know?"

"I've been trying your cell for the last twenty-four hours."

Lucien frowned and hunched into the conversation. "What's wrong?"

"I'm guessing you know already. You and Caia too tired to come over to my apartment?"

"No, we'll be right there."

Ella didn't look happy when Lucien hung up. "Surely he can let you two get some sleep before you visit."

Lucien shrugged like it was no big deal. "Sounds important."

Magnus chuckled. "Oh, it is."

Wait, what? Caia glanced sharply at her uncle. What did he know?

Her expression must have mirrored Lucien's because

Magnus laughed harder. "I'll let Ryder impart the news. But here's a clue ... Dimitri isn't happy."

"Magnus." Ella swatted him. "You'll give it away."

"Give what away?"

They remained silent and Lucien huffed, "Need I remind you I'm your Alpha. I have a right to know what's going on in my own pack."

"Well, you're about to find out." Magnus shot a look at Caia. "Now that he's your responsibility, maybe you can pull that stick out of his ass."

* * *

THEY WONDERED ALOUD AS to what Magnus and Ella could've been talking about, but their worries were so focused on Vilhelm and Laila, they were already at Ryder's with still no clue. Ryder threw open the door with a huge, relieved grin and clapped Lucien hard on the shoulder before dragging Caia into a tight hug. She suppressed a laugh at the feel of Lucien's hand on her waist, drawing her forcefully out of his friend's grip and tight to his side, possessively cupping her hip.

At first Ryder stumbled back, a little confused, and then his expression cleared, and he whooped, "All right, about time!" and held out a hand to Lucien. Caia looked on as they did their manly handshake and hugged quickly, a hug that was mostly battering of hands on each other's back.

"Congrats, guys, really. Very relieved." He grinned and then gestured for them to come in. "Actually." He followed them down the hallway to his living room. "I have some news of my own."

Caia's view was blocked by Lucien as he entered first, and she was surprised at the soft sound he made as his pace picked up, striding deeper into the room. Her eyes widened as she glimpsed Jaeden before she was swallowed in Lucien's tight hug. Her pulse leapt. It had been a long while, and she and the real Jaeden hadn't really spoken since her rescue. Caia glanced anxiously at Ryder who gave her a reassuring smile. His focus returned to Jaeden and a feeling rippled out of him. Caia caught it on the air.

"Ryder," she said, disbelieving at the intensity of it. "Jaeden?"

His eyes widened as he realized she comprehended the truth. "How did you know?"

"Know what?" Lucien asked.

Caia locked eyes with Jae, feeling awkward and useless. There was a time when she had thought of this girl as the greatest friend she'd ever had. It was difficult to remember now if there had been any truth in that, and what she felt toward her likened to grief.

Jaeden appeared to not know what to say either, her body rigid at first. And then she visibly relaxed, surprising Caia by hugging her, if a little awkwardly. "Cy, good to see you."

Caia smiled. "You too. You look great."

"Know what?" Lucien growled.

Jaeden giggled, a sound Caia never thought to hear from her again, and then danced into Ryder's arms, kissing him affectionately. "Ryder and I want to be mates."

Lucien's emotions veered from gobsmacked, to confusion, and then delight when he realized his friend was serious. He'd never seen Ryder look at anyone the way he looked at Jae, obliterating his predictions that Ryder would be a perpetual bachelor. Sitting on Ryder's sofa, he and Caia watched and listened as Ryder and Jaeden told the story of their return to the pack. Lucien grinned at Caia as the two of them bickered like an old mated couple. They didn't even

have to ask if he would give them permission to have a ceremony, and anyway, Ryder probably would've killed him if he
didn't.

Lucien was not surprised, however, to hear that Dimitri
was having a difficult time with the idea, considering Jaeden
had only just returned to him. As his attention fell on his
own mate, he was glad there was no waiting involved to be
with her truly, as there was for his friend. It still amazed him
how easily Caia had come to him when he told her he loved
her, and ever since, he had to stop from kicking himself that
he hadn't said it sooner.

Knowing what the Hades was going on in a female's mind
had never been his strong suit.

As Caia laughed at something Ryder said. It had been a
long time since he'd seen her look this happy.

At that, a darkness, like a silent snowfall shrouding his
world of color and warmth, settled over him, sending chills
across his skin.

She'd better enjoy it, he thought somewhat bitterly. This
battle she wanted to wage against Marita to win the war was
going to siphon that happiness out of her. He was terrified
for her. That the majority of Midnights could be misunder-
stood was inconceivable, but Caia saw it, felt it, and he
believed in his mate.

A flare of pain radiated from his chest. He believed
enough to drag his pack into a coup against the Head of the
Daylight Coven.

"Lucien?" Caia was gripping his hand.

He blinked away his contemplation and found the three
of them staring at him in concern.

"You okay, man?"

"Fine." He shook it off gruffly.

"You looked a little put out, that's all," Ryder said.

"I said I'm fine."

Caia squeezed his hand and then released it, turning to Jaeden with a curious smile. "So, this Reuben character?"

Ryder growled and spun away from Jaeden, his body bristling. Obviously, the vampyre was a problem for his friend, Lucien concluded. He could relate with the whole possessiveness thing—a genetic defect of their species, if you asked him.

Jae hid a grin at Ryder's attitude. "Yeah, there's not much else to tell except that he's here, offering his help—"

"Sticking his nose in," Ryder interrupted.

"No. Being a friend. He and Ryder don't exactly get along. Especially since my attempted kidnapping the other day."

Lucien flinched like he'd been hit. Why was this not the first piece of information relayed to him upon his return. "What?"

His friend's face reddened with anger as he glared back at Lucien. "Yeah, someone tried to snatch her off your grounds. I got there with Reuben just in time. The vamp chased the person into your woods but lost them."

"Did you see what they looked like?" Caia asked, her face drained of color.

Jaeden shook her head, her lips pinched. "They were apparently dressed in black. Another kidnapping attempt. I'm beginning to think someone doesn't like me."

"The Midnights?" Lucien asked Caia, immediately regretting his accusatory tone.

She snapped up off the couch with a disdainful look. "I would've felt it if it were the Midnights."

Jae crossed her arms over her chest defensively. Her eyes, which just moments ago had sparkled happily, were narrowed, trying to mask her vulnerability. "Well, maybe you missed something. Can't you double-check?"

Caia bit down on her lip as all three of them stared at her in expectation, and Lucien detected the shudder that ran through her body. "Caia, no pressure," he assured her.

"I'll check. I'll be back in a second."

When she was gone, Lucien skewered the two of them with a look. "Ease up on my mate."

"You just like saying that, don't you?" Ryder grinned. "*My mate.*"

"That's beside the point. There's a lot going on that you aren't aware of."

"Oh, like the Midnight Ryder's keeping in his guest bedroom for Caia?" Jae asked dryly.

He had no idea how the two of them had found out that Laila was a Midnight, and no idea how to explain the situation to them. More than that, however, he was curious as to why Ryder would keep Laila under his roof if he was aware of her heritage.

"How did you find out?"

"Reuben." Ryder curled his lip in distaste at the mention of the vamp. "The guy is weird, Lucien. Knew little Laila was a Midnight right off. I think you should interrogate him."

"Oh, there will be no interrogating of anybody," Jaeden snapped, "except perhaps Caia. We've been waiting for what seems like weeks for an answer to why she sent a Midnight to us and how she knew Laila was a good guy."

His ears perked. "So you believe Caia?"

Jaeden snorted. "Have you met Laila and Vil? There isn't a bad bone in that girl's body, and I don't have to be a tracer, or whatever, to know that. Plus, she told me what the Midnights did to her. If anyone has a reason to go AWOL and join the other side, it's that girl."

"What happened to her?"

She shook her head, her face taut with restrained emotion. "That's her private business."

Lucien scratched his cheek, bemused. "I'm shocked. I thought when we told you, I'd have a battle on my hands convincing you Caia is right."

Ryder shook his head, sitting back down beside Jaeden. "Nah. Little Laila is a sweetheart. Anyone can see that."

Hmm, he wasn't just talking about little Laila.

"What about other Midnights?" Lucien ventured tentatively.

"What do you mean?"

Their expressions changed often as he told them about Caia's certainty that the war as it stood made no sense, considering there were Midnights who did not believe in the destruction of other supernatural races. And then he broke the news of what Caia had found in the basement of the Center. They listened attentively, their eyes round with disbelief and fear.

"Wait a minute," Jaeden choked out when he was finished, "Caia's going to usurp Marita?"

"Well"—Caia's voice caught hold of Lucien like a hand at the back of his neck—"when you put it like that, it sounds crazy."

"Cy." Ryder stood. "Are you serious? Are you really going to the Council to do this?"

At first, Lucien detected the uncertainty in her face. Then she looked at him, and he could tell she was remembering what he told her about confidence. She straightened her spine and swept her hair off her shoulders. "Yes. I'm completely serious. It's the only thing to be done."

Jaeden snorted. "Oh yeah, 'cause there aren't any other options here. It's too risky, Caia."

"You would rather I aid Marita in killing hundreds of thousands of innocent people?"

"Innocent according to you."

Caia's eyes softened. "It wasn't a Midnight who attempted to kidnap you. And these people aren't my uncle, Jaeden."

"How dare—"

"I don't mean to upset you. And yes, many of the older families abhor us. Some are just following a faith—it's a religion to them—while others think it's moronic and xenophobic. There are Daylights who are beginning to feel the same way. But there are also little kids being experimented upon, and the only way I can get to them is with some major political backing. I can win this. *We* can win this."

"We?"

Lucien cleared his throat. "I'm in this with her, which means the pack is. If you don't want in, you leave the pack."

Ryder grinned at him. "Final word of the Alpha, huh? You know I'm completely in, right?" He nodded to Caia. "I've seen this girl in action. My bet is on her."

"Jaeden?" Caia asked tentatively. "I know it's not the war you thought you'd be fighting. It shocked me too. I want to go back to everything being black and white, but it won't. There *are* no other options."

He watched Jae as she turned to lock eyes with Ryder. Whatever passed between them drained the tension from her body, and she turned to Caia. "I can't believe I'm saying this, but … fine. I believe you. I'm in. I won't stand by and let her get away with this."

Caia nodded, only a slight curve to her mouth betraying her relief. "Good. I guess that means it's time for me and Lucien to check in on Laila and Vilhelm. I need Vil to take me to the next Council meeting. It's in two weeks' time. Actually, you guys have done me a favor."

Ryder smiled. "How so?"

"I can use your mating ceremony as an excuse to stall returning to the Center."

Lucien chuckled. "Crafty."

"Nice to be of help," Jaeden said wryly.

Caia jumped at the sound of a door slamming and turned as Vil slowly entered the living room, his hand tangled in Laila's. The girl looked much healthier than the last time Caia had laid eyes on her. Caia would even go so far as to say she looked radiantly happy. Ryder and Jaeden really must've been treating them well.

"Caia?" Laila asked Vil.

Vil smiled at Caia and nodded.

The next thing Caia knew, the girl had her delicate arms wrapped around her, hugging her close.

"Callan." Laila eased away from her, her eyes shimmering with gratitude. "There are no words to thank you for what you have done."

Caia's whole body thrummed with a golden peace at Laila's proximity, and once more that intangible quality in her trace flummoxed her. The girl was like sunshine and air, her presence so relaxing and sweet, Caia couldn't believe anyone could ever wish her harm.

Uncomfortable with the gratitude, Caia shrugged, considering she now needed a favor from Vil.

"It was nothing," she mumbled and held her hand out behind her for Lucien, knowing he would understand. At once she felt his warm, calloused hand engulf her small one, and her breathing eased. It was wonderful, after weeks of feeling alone, to finally trust someone, to be able to lean on him.

"It's good to see you again, Caia." Vil smiled warmly at her. "I was afraid something might have happened to you."

She shook her head. "The attack went forward with the MacLachlans. We dealt with it." She didn't want to think about that night. "You should know that Marita can't pick up your trace."

The two magiks frowned, glancing at each other questioningly.

Caia grimaced. "I guess that means neither of you know why."

Laila floated back to Vil's side. "No, Callan. I've heard only a very old supernatural can mask their trace, and Vil is just a boy."

"Nearly a man," he mumbled, drawing her close and puffing his chest out a little. Caia tried not to laugh.

"Why are you calling Caia *Callan*?" Lucien asked in his usual tone, which to outsiders could sound a little reproving.

"Looks like I'm interrupting," a new, unfamiliar voice greeted from behind Vil and Laila.

They moved out of the doorway to reveal a tall, good-looking young man with dark hair and eyes. His youth could be attributed to his cool, unkempt appearance, the dark jeans and black T-shirt, the silver thumb ring on one hand, the tattoo on his forearm, the silver coin fashioned onto thin black rope around his neck, and the small ring pierced through his lower lip. He had a dangerous bad-boy quality, and suddenly Caia understood why Ryder didn't like his involvement in Jaeden's life.

The vampyre looked around the room at them all and then his gaze fell on Caia. Despite his clean-shaven, wrinkle-free face, when Caia met those eyes, she felt as if she was looking into depths that had seen the world in all its forms many times over. The youthfulness combated a confident control she'd never before come across.

"This must be the famous Caia," he said, approaching slowly.

Lucien didn't tense beside her, making her question whether she'd really seen the eerie fascination in his gaze, or if she was just being paranoid.

Jaeden stood between them and smiled anxiously as she introduced him.

"Lucien."

He greeted Reuben amiably enough, holding out a hand. Reuben shook it with a friendly languor and turned back to Vil and Laila. "I don't know if you've been formally introduced, but guys, this is Lucien, Caia's mate."

"How did you know they're mates?" Ryder asked defensively.

Reuben gestured to their clasped hands. "Body language." He turned to Lucien. "I overheard your question to Laila. You should know that *Callan* means *flowing water*. Laila's people consider it rude to call anyone of importance or wisdom by their first name, so she's calling Caia *Callan*, by her element, a sign of deep respect."

Laila smiled at him, nodding in agreement.

Caia blushed.

Ryder sputtered, "How the hell do you know that?"

The vampyre gave Ryder a taunting smile. Caia was with Ryder on this one. Something was off about the guy. "I did a little research after I met Vil and Laila. Found out a bit about their customs and such."

"Why?"

Jaeden sighed. "Ryder ..."

"It's fine, Jae." Reuben waved her off. "I just like to know who we're dealing with."

"We?" Ryder said. "Since when does this involve you?"

"Since he was made aware of Laila's existence," Lucien's voice rumbled with authority and a hint of annoyance.

Caia's head ached with the thought of involving another outsider in her plans. And this particular outsider, she wasn't so keen on. She tugged on Lucien's hand. "Reuben should stick around for now."

The vampyre played with his lip ring, his fangs prominent. "Is that a request or a demand?"

"A demand," she said with quiet dominion, surprising everyone, including herself. But Lucien was right. If she was to pull this off, she had to act like a leader. Unfortunately, part of that meant laying down the law. "We can't take the chance of you leaving and telling anyone about Laila."

"He wouldn't," Jaeden assured her, "believe me."

Reuben straightened, his face free of amusement now. "Trust Jaeden. I'm her friend, which makes you all my friends. I don't betray my friends."

We'll see.

Caia managed a nod, feeling exhausted. "Okay." She smiled at Laila and Vil. "I think I really need some sleep, but I will come by tomorrow to see you both. We have a lot to discuss."

"Wait." Ryder clapped a hand on Lucien's shoulder as they made to leave. "What about me and Jae? Our mating ceremony?"

In a perfect world, Jaeden and Ryder should've had plenty of time to plan a ceremony, but it would be best if they were mated before things went to Hades. Somehow Caia managed to convey this message to Lucien, and he promised Ryder they would talk about it in the morning.

"Good night, Callan," Laila called sweetly as Caia and Lucien left. Caia's face flooded with color again as she thought of what Reuben said.

Lucien chuckled. "Looks like you've got a devoted follower for life."

"She's just grateful."

He shook his head as they climbed into his truck. "You were right. I can't believe that girl is a Midnight. She's as threatening as a butterfly."

"Yeah, well, Marita had her locked up as if she were Ethan reincarnated."

He made a sound of disgust. "I knew I didn't like that witch."

The house was dark when they returned, Ella and Magnus having retired for the night. The thought of bed sounded amazing to Caia as she dragged her body upstairs. Lucien's hand was steady on her back as she shuffled down the hall to her bedroom. When she stopped at her door, Lucien grunted in amusement and took her by the elbow, leading her farther down the hall.

"What are you doing?" she whispered.

He looked back at her as if she were crazy. "You're my mate now, Caia. That means my room is your room." He drew her into the master bedroom. Her pulse accelerated as they entered the largest room in the house, his king-size, four-poster bed positioned in the center. She'd never been in Lucien's bedroom. It was comfortable yet masculine, with a sturdy desk positioned at the back near his walk-in closet and master bath. Near the window sat a chocolate leather corner sofa, some of his clothes draped haphazardly over it.

"Get undressed, get in bed, and go to sleep." He brushed a reassuring hand down her cheek. "You must be exhausted."

Aware only of nodding in agreement and shuffling around to the other side of his bed, Caia's mind whirred. It had never occurred to her that when they returned, they would be living ... well ... like mates.

The bed looked so good, though.

Her hands fluttered to the hem of her shirt, and a burst of nervousness knocked the exhaustion out of her. Glancing up to see if Lucien was watching, the sight of him was enough to make her mouth go dry. He was crossing the room toward the bed, his shirt discarded on the floor, his hair mussed, his cheeks unshaven. The moonlight spilled across the room, highlighting his hard, taut abdomen and the thick ropes of muscles in his arms. She was reminded of the night she lost her virginity to him.

Her libido kicked into gear.

I can sleep later.

With a flick of her hand, the bedroom door swung closed and the key turned in the lock. Lucien looked up from unbuttoning his jeans with questioning surprise.

She smiled at him. "Suddenly not so tired."

His answering grin was so wicked, her heart felt like it was going to burst out of her chest.

* * *

"She's back with the pack." He stared across the table at Nikolai. The magik looked worn out, his usually distinguished demeanor lessened by the dark circles under his eyes.

"Good. We have everything we need, then?"

He shook his head. "There may be a complication."

Nikolai shifted in his seat, and Kirios could tell he was trying not to roll his eyes. His expression read "not again."

"Da?"

He leaned across the Septum they'd been staring at with anticipation. "It has come to my attention that Caia is intending to go to the Council and ask to be put forward as a candidate for the Head of the Daylights."

Nikolai snapped to attention, his black eyes darkening impossibly. "Kirios, you can't be serious? My coven will hear of this ... it could jeopardize our plans."

"You worry too much, Nikolai. My source tells me that the Council doesn't convene for another few weeks. By then it will be too late."

"Why mention it at all?" Nikolai grumbled.

He relaxed back in his chair. "I wanted to keep you apprised of the situation. Anyway, even if she had gone ahead before we could stop it, it would have been a mere hindrance, nothing more."

The magik snorted. "I am tired of hindrances. My Council is eating away at my nerves. I can't wait to begin." His eyes dropped to the Septum.

"So close."

"Da."

CHAPTER 23

The Council

*J*aeden sat anxiously waiting for Caia in Ella's kitchen, her cold hands wrapped around a hot mug of coffee the Elder had planted before her as soon as she arrived.

"I'm sure she won't be much longer," Ella assured her, two flags of color on her cheeks.

Magnus snorted and mumbled under his breath, "Yeah, right."

Jae tried not to laugh. Lykans were a pretty open bunch, but it was still uncomfortable for a mother to think about her kids having sexual relations of any kind, no matter their age. A pang of jealousy hit as Jae heard a giggle from upstairs and the sounds of something clattering to the ground. At least Caia and Lucien were free to be with one another. She had to wait another frigging ten days because her honorable mate-to-be was old-fashioned.

"What do you think of these?" Ella slid a bunch of fabric swatches toward her.

She frowned. "What are they?"

"They're swatches for the chair coverings, for your ceremony. Julia put me in charge of decorations."

Jaeden nodded at the plain cream swatch. "That's nice."

Ever since Lucien had gathered her and Ryder together with both their families yesterday to announce the ceremony could go forward, and preferably soon, her mother had been driving her crazy with recipes and talk of dress shopping. Everyone had burst into discussion, Yvana and Julia arguing over who would take care of the cooking and baking, Lucia asking if Cera would be wearing the same color as Jaeden along with the rest of the women in the family.

Only her father had quieted everyone with a direct question to Lucien. "Why does the mating have to be so soon?"

Lucien glanced at her and Ryder before telling the others solemnly that he had something extremely important to discuss with them at the pack meeting on Sunday. The answer to that question would be answered then.

"Will the fact that my daughter was nearly kidnapped again be brought up as well, because it doesn't seem as if anyone is as bothered by that as I am?"

Of course, she was bothered by it. The thought of going through that all over again … unimaginable. But she had Ryder now, and he had stopped it. And yesterday Cy promised to keep looking into it for her.

"Caia and I are dealing with that," Lucien said in such a way as not to be disputed.

Her father hadn't looked too happy, used to being brought into Lucien's confidence in all matters, and had quizzed Jae all last night about it. As usual, he somehow knew that she knew what was going on. She still couldn't believe that Caia intended to put herself forward for the

Head of the Coven, but she'd watched her yesterday with Laila when she visited with the young couple again, how kind and gentle she was with the girl, how easy it was to believe she could and would take care of everything.

At first Jaeden really believed Caia and Lucien had gone mad, that Caia's ego had inflated since she'd been gone. However, when Lucien explained what Caia had found, that Marita was experimenting on lykan children, Jaeden had become enraged. She felt personally betrayed by the witch.

Still, taking her down was a huge deal.

Yet when Lucien told her what Caia did to the Midnights who planned the attack on the MacLachlan pack, she was blown away. Never had she heard of any magik doing such a thing. Caia was a weapon. The most powerful weapon in their world. She guessed they should feel lucky she was one of the good guys, one of their own.

And that was why she found herself at Lucien's house, waiting for Caia to climb out of her love nest so they could talk. Ryder thought they should clear the air, and she agreed. They needed to trust one another if this was going to work.

"Jaeden!" Caia bounced into the room, her cheeks flushed, her green eyes brighter than jade. "Sorry to have kept you."

Jaeden regarded her knowingly, somehow comforted by the blush that blossomed across Caia's cheeks. It made her seem more approachable. She made a face and sat next to her, glancing idly at the swatches Ella was looking over. Caia grimaced.

"Ah, mating ceremony plans. Don't envy you that."

Relaxing a little, Jaeden shook her head. "My mother is taking care of everything and slowly driving me nuts. It's been one day. It feels like years."

"Tut-tut," Ella admonished. "Your mother loves you. She wants you to have the best."

Jaeden harrumphed.

"Morning." Lucien strolled into the kitchen, his hair more mussed than usual. He threw a scorching look at Caia before noticing Jae. "Hey, Jae." He made his way to the coffee machine. "What's up?"

"I just wondered if Caia had a moment to talk."

Caia nodded at her. "Of course."

"In private?"

"Backyard?"

Prying ears could still find them there. She looked around at Magnus, Ella, and Lucien. Magnus was the only one who noticed. He folded his paper and tapped Ella on the shoulder. "Sitting room."

"Huh, what?" She didn't look up from the folder she was going through.

"Ella, you can do that in the sitting room. You, too, Lucien."

Jaeden smiled gratefully at Magnus and smirked when Lucien couldn't resist pulling Caia in for a kiss as he passed her.

"Ready?" Jae asked, unable to keep the amusement out of her voice.

Caia smoothed her hair, looking a little flustered, but she nodded in the direction of the back door. "Sure. Let's go."

They stood in the middle of the yard, their backs to the house, their eyes drawn to the forest like magnets. A wind whistled gently through the trees, and Jae watched as Caia tilted her face into it, pulling the rubber band from her hair so that it fell down and into the wind.

"Reminds me of the wind in my pelt," she explained, and Jaeden smiled. Somehow it made it better knowing Caia loved her lykan side even though her powers as a magik were phenomenal. "So what's going on?" she asked, lowering herself onto the grass.

Jaeden stretched out beside her. "I thought we should talk … about things."

"Such as?"

"Our friendship. What happened? Other stuff I have yet to explain."

"Friendship-wise, you still have mine. Always will." Caia turned her face away so Jae couldn't read her expression. "When I found out the truth, that *you* weren't you, that you were gone … I was devastated."

Memories of those first two weeks together swallowed her momentarily. They'd hit it off instantly, bonded from the moment they met. A lot of those memories included laughter, lots of laughter.

"You know I haven't asked anyone about that faerie." Jaeden shuddered at the thought of her. "No one seems to want to bring it up. What was it like, Cy?"

Caia turned back to her with tears shimmering in eyes that blazed with hatred and anger. "It was shocking and heinous. She was you, Jaeden. She must have watched you for weeks, memorizing your mannerisms, the way you laugh …"

Jaeden gulped at the thought of that *ghoul* pretending to be her, sleeping in her bed, wearing her clothes, laughing with her friends. "No one had any clue?"

"None whatsoever. It was only when Saffron, Marion's faerie, felt her in the house and knew she wasn't …"

"Me."

"Yes," Caia answered hollowly. "Then I started getting the visions of you through Ethan's eyes."

That someone had paid witness to the scars on her soul was difficult to deal with, but looking at Caia's pained expression—the fury in her eyes because she genuinely cared about Jaeden—made it a little easier to cope. "Ryder told me you saw everything."

Caia nodded, blinking back tears. "I am so sorry I didn't get to you sooner."

"Don't be," Jaeden bit out. "You didn't give up. That's what matters."

"I couldn't save Sebastian."

Like always, his name set off a fire of grief in Jaeden's chest, her breathing labored, her throat burning with unshed tears. He'd been her best friend, and he died trying to protect her.

"Sebastian would've found a way to be there with or without you bringing him along. I was his best friend, and he did what either of us would have done for him."

Caia choked on a broken sob. "I miss him."

Jae swiped at her own tears. "I miss him too. But I'm glad you had each other through it all."

After a moment of silence, one that now felt a little easier between them, Caia reached across and squeezed Jaeden's hand. "Thank you for believing in me. For being willing to fight for me. It means more than you can know." She choked, letting go of her hand. "I thought I was going to be doing this all alone. You've all surprised me."

Jaeden chuckled humorlessly. "There are more surprises to come."

"Meaning?"

She braced herself. "Something happened to me because of Ethan's ... torture."

Caia went on alert. "What?"

Just get it over with. If anyone is going to understand feeling like a freak, Cy will be that person.

"I have telekinetic abilities." She concentrated on a plant pot Ella had placed by the porch stairs and willed it to fly past them and smash against the nearest tree.

She took a little satisfaction in surprising Caia, her jaw

dropping as the ceramic lay in pieces, the plant pulp on the ground.

Then Caia's face tightened with worry, and she turned back to Jaeden with growing panic in her eyes. "I think I know who tried to kidnap you."

* * *

"I CAN'T BELIEVE THIS." Lucien ran his hand through his hair, tugging at the ends viciously. "This is insane."

Caia couldn't believe it either. She'd called Lucien out from the house and had refused to tell Jaeden anything until they were gathered at Ryder's apartment. Caia insisted Laila and Vil be present as well. The six of them sat staring at each other, the atmosphere thick with tension and a terrible foreboding.

"Caia, are you sure?"

She shook her head frantically. "No, I'm not sure. But Mordecai was very interested in Jaeden, and then I overheard him and Marita discussing Jaeden's 'abilities' before they bugged my room. They kept mentioning your abilities in relation to the fact that the 'children weren't reacting in any way.'"

"It's true," Lucien added in a defeated voice.

"And you think it's because she knows about my telekinetic abilities?" Jaeden asked angrily.

"She has trace," Lucien replied.

She has trace, yes, but not like mine. She tapped into Jaeden's trace to find out what she was up to—the illegal rogue hunting. When there, she must've discovered that Jaeden developed telekinetic abilities as a result of Ethan's torture.

The mention of her trace, however, made Caia's heart pump rapidly. "Guys, Marita is keeping tabs on everyone close to me."

Ryder frowned. "What do you mean?"

"She told me her trace isn't like mine. It's not as advanced."

"There's a surprise," Jaeden muttered teasingly.

"No, this is bad, people, very bad. To find someone in Daylight, Marita has to tap into that person specifically. She'll be watching me, through you. I had Lucien on alert, and he's blocking himself from her, but I didn't think about you guys."

Laila's delicate eyebrows puckered into a frown. "What does this mean?"

"No!" Lucien shot out of his chair, his eyes filled with worry. "She knows!"

Caia had to fight to not cry in frustration as she nodded.

"What?" Ryder and Jaeden panicked. "What does she know?"

"We have to believe that Marita knows, through you two, about my plans to go to the Council," Caia explained. "I can't wait around for their next meeting." She turned to Vil, who suddenly looked flustered by the attention. "Vil, you have to take me to Alfred Doukas now."

"What, Caia? Wait—" Lucien crossed the room, taking her by the arm. She felt his grip tighten, his eyes boring into her, full of fear. "That could be a trap. I won't let you risk it."

"Who is Alfred Doukas when he's at home?" Jaeden asked.

Caia peered around Lucien to answer her. "He's a Council member I met at the Center. We hit it off."

"Caia." Lucien shook her. "Please, don't do this."

She reached up to wrap a hand around his neck, drawing him down to place a soft kiss on his lips. "I have to," she whispered as she pulled away.

"What if I say no?"

"Lucien. You know this is our only plan now. Think of the

pack. If Marita knows, she could hold the whole pack as traitors to the coven."

"Then I'm going with you."

"You can't. Vil hasn't even tried traveling with *one* other person before."

"All the more reason for you not to do this."

"Stop thinking like my mate and start thinking like this pack's Alpha."

He growled in frustration and jerked away from her to make his way over to Ryder, who placed a comforting hand on his friend's shoulder.

"Vil, are you ready to do this?" she asked, trying to appear as calm as possible. Inside, she felt as if all her nerves had snapped and her body was barely holding itself together. This was it. This was really happening. She was really going to do this.

The Traveler had gone as pale as she felt, but he nodded determinedly. He turned to Laila, cupping her face in his hands. "I'll be right back for you, I promise."

Laila smiled sweetly at him and reached up to press a kiss on his lips. "I'm proud of you," she whispered back.

Caia held her hand out to him. He reluctantly let go of his girlfriend and strode toward Caia, enfolding his cool hand in hers.

"Good luck, Cy," Jaeden offered.

She nodded and squeezed Vil's hand. "Ready, partner."

"Alfred Doukas?"

"The very one."

Vil blew out his breath between his lips, readying himself. "Okay—"

"Wait!" Lucien called. He looked ready to bust someone apart. "You better get back here pronto or I will kill you."

She grinned at him, trying to appear confident. "I love you too."

His face, along with the rest of the room, suddenly streamed past her in a blur of color and movement. Her stomach plummeted, and she felt as if she had no control over her body. The only thing she could feel was the tight grip of Vil's hand. And then it stopped just as abruptly as it had begun, and she found herself losing balance and falling into Vil's arms.

"Are you okay?" he asked frantically.

She shook her head, trying to clear it, and clambered to straighten herself. When she did, she heard gasps and spluttering from behind them. Vil tensed, and Caia turned in his arms to face Alfred Doukas and who she imagined must be his family. He sat at the head of a grand dining table, men, women, and children sitting around it with him, eating dinner.

She barely registered the room's expensive but old-fashioned décor because Alfred Doukas was gaping at her like a fish out of water.

"What ... who ..." A plump woman at the opposite end of the table threw down her napkin, glaring at Caia and Vil as if they were vagabonds.

"Mr. Doukas." Caia rushed forward, and he pushed away from the table, his face creased with concern.

"Miss Ribeiro ... what on Gaia's earth ...?"

"Please, Mr. Doukas, I must speak with you alone."

Seeming to understand the urgency, he assured his family everything was all right, and led Caia out of the dining room and down a dark wood-paneled hallway to his study. He turned on her as Vil shut the door behind them.

"What is going on?"

Here goes nothing.

"Mr. Doukas, I need you to call an emergency meeting of the Council. Now."

He paled. "Why?"

"Because I mean to ask them for the right to run against Marita for Head of the Coven."

He stumbled back, his hand going to his forehead, his eyes disbelieving. "You can't be serious."

Please believe me, please.

"I am quite serious. I believe that Marita is no longer the right person for the job. Please, I'll explain everything ... to all of you."

"Her family have been coven Heads for four generations. They are the Heads because her great-grandmother uncovered the treacherousness of the previous Head. You will have a hard time convincing the Council that someone of her illustrious family name isn't cut out for the job."

"This is extremely important. I have evidence to prove Marita has betrayed her duty to protect Daylights. Please, I will explain ..."

He stared at her sternly for what seemed like forever and then nodded. "Fine. It best be now before Marita catches wind of it."

Shrugging up the sleeve of his jacket, Alfred pressed one of the tiny buttons on his watch, and it made a beeping noise. He looked up to find Caia and Vil gazing at him quizzically. "The watch was made in magik. All the Council members have one. When one of us wishes to meet, we press this button and the others' watches beep to signal the request."

Caia was impressed. "The CIA would love that."

Alfred chuckled nervously. "Yes, well, they have their own gadgets."

Before Caia could reply, the room began to fill with magiks she'd never met before. Penelope appeared beside Alfred, and she smiled at Caia in acknowledgment. The others glared and frowned at her and Vil.

"What is the meaning of this?" One tall, elegant male magik strode past her to Alfred.

"Is this everyone?" Alfred searched the room. There were nine of them, including Alfred and Penelope. "Very well, ladies and gentlemen. I've called you here per the request of this young lady." He gestured to Caia. She felt their attention on her like burning coals under her feet. She hopped back to distance herself from them. The power emanating from them all together was unlike anything she'd ever encountered. These people were strong and old. And they meant business. The nine of them filed into a line in front of Alfred's desk.

"Is this who I think it is?" a waifish female asked, her sharp gaze drinking Caia in with fascination.

"This is Caia Ribeiro, yes."

A murmur rippled through them like one. It was quite disconcerting.

"And why do you wish to see us, Miss Ribeiro?" Penelope asked her warmly.

Be cool, be confident ... be persuasive.

"I'm here to ask for the right to campaign against Marita for Head of the Coven."

The murmuring turned into heated exclamations, and Caia shifted closer to Vil. He placed a supportive hand on her shoulder.

"Why?" Penelope asked, seeming hurt by Caia's request.

"Because I believe I can end this war, but not using Marita's methods. I'm not asking you to kill her and give me the trace. I'm just asking that you give me the authority to make the decisions in this war. Marita would still continue using the trace, but working *for* me."

A few of them looked disdainful, but Albert's gaze had softened. "That's quite merciful of you, Caia."

"I have no wish to harm anyone. But I don't believe this war will ever find closure under Marita's leadership."

The tall magik who'd spoken first scoffed. "And how do

you think you can do any better? You're barely out of childhood. Marita has led this coven for decades and recently has garnered great victories for us."

"Because of Caia," Penelope inserted. "Marita was doing just as well as any other Head of the Coven until Caia came along. Those victories you speak of have had Caia's hand in them somewhere."

More murmuring as this sunk in.

Caia rubbed her sweaty palms against her trouser legs and stepped forward a little more confidently. She wouldn't tell them her suspicion that Marita had tried to kidnap Jaeden for her own nefarious means; without proof, she would appear a spiteful little girl, thereby undermining her position with the Council. But she would tell them about the children. For that, there was proof.

"While I was at the Center, I followed Marita one day. She disappeared under a trapdoor in the Altar of Gaia. The second marble slab to the right of the statue of Gaia has a gold button attached to it. If you press it, it opens to reveal a basement. Inside the basement, you will find at least one laboratory where Marita is conducting illegal experiments on lykan children who are caged down there."

A flurry of outrage erupted in the room, some admonishing her for such nonsense, others, like Alfred and Penelope, paling in fear.

"All you need to do is send in a spy. Someone who can mask their thoughts well in their trace."

"You really expect us to believe this?" the elegant magik sneered.

"I expect you to go in and find the proof for yourselves."

"Alfred," a surprisingly young-looking magik intoned in a bored voice, "I'll go."

Alfred nodded, never taking his sad eyes off Caia. "We'll get to the bottom of this, Caia, I promise."

She refused to let go of the bigger picture, however. "And when you do?"

Penelope sighed wearily. "If you're proved correct, then Marita will be sentenced and the Council will vote on a new Head."

Be strong. Be powerful. Be confident.

"I will be proved correct. And your decision should be easy. With me as the Head of both covens, I promise I will bring this war to a conclusion. There are Midnights who have an outright aversion to war—believe me, it's the truth. And no one else in our world can do what I can do. Only days ago, I destroyed four magiks in four different locations simultaneously. In my short career as a magik, as one who has had a few battles in the last few months, I've proved the victor."

She portrayed a deliberate iciness, emanating a balanced impression of power mixed with threat. She softened somewhat at their apprehensive expressions. After all, she didn't want them so afraid of her they would take her out.

"We've lost too many people we love to this war already. Make me the Head of both covens and I promise you I will bring it to an end. If you remember ... it has been prophesied."

Her reminder of that small detail drained all color from their faces. After a few moments of thick, shocked silence, they began to speak among themselves, their words so rushed and confused, she couldn't make out what they were saying to one another. Finally, Alfred raised his hands to quiet them and directed his next words at Caia. "We will have to discuss this at length, Miss Ribeiro. For now, we will send Derren in to uncover this laboratory. We will visit you when we know more."

"When can I expect to hear from you?"

Doukas replied, "These things can take days."

She nodded. "I understand. I want to thank you for taking the time to meet with me."

Penelope gave her a bracing smile. "You're welcome. You may go now."

They rushed by her at lightning speed and she realized Vil, with his hand on her shoulder, had taken Penelope's words literally, getting them out of there as fast as he could.

She stumbled away from him, feeling nauseated as they landed back in Ryder's living room.

Strong, warm arms encircled her, and she found herself snuggled against Lucien's chest, his familiar scent soothing her rattled nerves.

"You're okay," he whispered hoarsely.

She wouldn't go that far. They had a long wait ahead of them. If the Council failed, Marita would probably pin them as traitors and have the entire pack imprisoned indefinitely.

CHAPTER 24

Pack Woes

The following days changed over as if it were the passing of a season rather than a week. Arrangements continued for Jaeden and Ryder's ceremony, a commotion that rotated around Caia in a blur as she waited anxiously for the Council to come to their decision. Marion did not appear to question why Caia had yet to arrive at the Center, leading her to believe that the Council had yet to make their discoveries or at least had not made Marita aware of them. The thought of losing Marion's friendship was a sharp ache—another sacrifice she knew would not be the last on this journey.

It was difficult to remember when her life had been anything but this one of power and conflict. Caia wondered if she would ever feel normal again, if *life* would ever *be* normal again.

And the pack was just one more struggle to manage. The

announcement at the pack run on Sunday had been met with shock and anger. Most felt it should've been something they discussed before Caia had gone and spoken to the Council. Lucien faced their resentment like a shield, taking the bullets Caia knew were for her. Trying to explain to them the feelings she'd felt through her trace about the Midnights was met with a mix of confusion and disbelief. The news of Marita's experiments was met with betrayal and a fearful unwillingness to believe it.

Ella and Dimitri in particular were furious they'd kept the information from them, and although fond of Caia, they could not believe she could think Midnights, beings who had tried to destroy their pack, could be anything other than villains. Magnus, as always, was quiet and watchful, his only words a reinforcement in his faith in Caia and his promise to Rafe that he would be there for her, no matter what.

The other older members of Pack Errante were as incredulous as Ella and Dimitri. Jaeden's brother Christian, as well as Alexa and Malek's father, Morgan, and his wife, Dana and Daniel's mother and father—all were hugely against backing Caia in her coup. Their eyes followed her warily, unspoken words thickening the tension between them. *We trusted your father, and look what he brought upon us.* Only Sebastian's parents, Isaac and Imogen, seemed unsure, speaking of their son and his love for Caia, how he would've wanted them to be loyal to her.

And, as both she and Lucien had been expecting, the younger generation—Aidan and the twins, Malek and Finlay, even Lucia and Cera—were willing to consider that Caia could be right. The biggest surprise was Alexa. Having never hidden her dislike of Caia, even more so since she and Lucien were officially mates, she actually stood up for Caia.

"I believe her." She had shrugged, bored. "I mean, come on! These people can't be so stupid that they still see us as a threat to humans when we are so obviously not. Hey, and if Caia does become, like, the Head of Daylights, then the pack becomes royalty. Uh, *hello.*"

So it hadn't been the most eloquent rationale, but it was support, and Caia would take it no matter the source.

In the end, Lucien had come to a fair but disheartening agreement with the pack. If Caia was wrong and the Council didn't find the proof against Marita, Lucien would make sure it was clear those pack members who didn't support Caia's claims were not punished. He told them they could walk away now, but that had only served to anger the pack more. What they really wanted was for him to disown Caia—it was easy to read on their faces as they glared resentfully at her. And no matter how selfish she knew it was, she was thankful he loved her too much to walk away.

That night, Caia was exhausted and wanted nothing more than to sink into bed with Lucien and close her eyes to their problems. Their household was now strained with the tension of Ella's anger, not only at her son and daughter-in-law but at Magnus because of his refusal to agree with her.

As they said good night to Ryder and Jaeden, the last to leave, they were stopped at the foot of the stairs by an unexpected visitor.

"Saffron!" Caia yelped in surprise as the faerie appeared inches before her. The faerie, though somber, managed a wave of hello.

"Good evening, Caia. Lucien." She twisted her mouth as she said his name. Caia wondered what that was about.

Lucien returned the look and nodded a welcome. "Saffron. What brings you here?"

Her beautiful face was pinched with anxiety as she glided past them and into the sitting room. Feeling a little apprehensive at her appearance, Caia followed numbly, waiting for the ax to fall.

"I'm here because I found out that Caia has asked the Council to give her the right to run for Head of the Coven."

"Marion told you?"

Saffron gave her a somewhat patronizing look. "No. That's why I'm here. Marion doesn't know."

Caia blinked, sure she hadn't heard correctly. "How can she not know if you know?"

"Because Marita hasn't told her. Or Vanne."

"How does Marita know? I take it the Council found the proof?"

Saffron shook her head, her face angry. "Derren has been imprisoned by Marita."

Lucien stopped pacing at the window. "What? What the hell is going on?"

"Marita is crafty, Caia. I've never really … well, liked her. She's a different kettle of fish from Marion. I came here tonight to warn you that she won't play fair in this. With Derren in prison, the Council are going to be suspicious of his whereabouts, and they will probably demand a search of the Center. She won't let that happen. I hope you are ready for a bloody and relentless battle with this woman."

Caia gulped just thinking about it. "I kind of have to be."

"I'm afraid Marion will not take this news well when she finds out. She is very fond of you, Caia, but Marita has a way of manipulating the people close to her."

"I won't hold anything against Marion. Marita is her sister. She loves her. She'll believe her."

The faerie nodded thoughtfully. "I, on the other hand, have been around a lot longer. I've felt this change coming. I will try to keep my eyes and ears open at the Center for you, but Marita has tightened her security since the Council sent in Derren."

Caia didn't know what to say. She didn't understand such an offer.

Saffron smirked at her expression. "You might not have my mistress's support, but you have mine."

"That is extremely generous of you," Caia said.

The faerie chuckled, but the laughter didn't reach her eyes, which were hard with determination. "There is nothing generous about my offer, Caia. I have survived this long in this war because I've always chosen the right people to fight for ... the winning side. Quite simply, *you* are the winning side."

Lucien grunted. "Thanks for the support, no matter the lack of sensitivity behind it."

Saffron rolled her eyes at him. "Lykans ... you're so sentimental."

"Seriously, Saffron, thank you. For the heads-up, as well."

"Hmm, sure. I will be in touch."

And then she was gone.

Caia whirled to gawk at Lucien. "Can you believe that?"

He wrapped an arm around her waist, drawing her close. "At least we know you have some powerful support. You might actually win this thing."

"Did you ever doubt it?" she teased.

"Yes."

She smacked him and tried to pull out of his embrace, but he held tight, laughing at her efforts.

"Just for that, no sex tonight."

"Oh, come, *querida*, you know I'm your biggest supporter."

"No, it's too late. Damage done." She sauntered away, heading up the staircase. Teasing him kept the pain of reality at bay for a while. She tried not to smile at the sound of him jogging to keep up, at the same time trying to be as quiet as possible.

As he followed her down the hall to their bedroom, he whispered, "You were joking about the no-sex thing, right?"

She snorted as they entered the room, shutting the door

behind them. "We're balanced on a precipice of potential disaster here, and *that's* what you're worried about?"

He looked at her blankly. "Well … yeah."

* * *

FOR JAEDEN AND RYDER, Caia imagined their big day arrived just as slowly. At least that was the impression Jaeden gave her every time she complained about Ryder's excessive gentlemanliness.

"I'm telling you, I'm losing my mind," she grumbled to Caia as she practiced her telekinesis. Laila and Vil sat on the back porch, glad to be free of Ryder's apartment and taking in the fresh air. Caia liked them nearby, still afraid that Marita would suddenly grab hold of Vil's trace and appear out of nowhere to take them away from her.

Caia chuckled. "You have one more night and then he's yours."

"Yeah, he's going to pay big time for this." She grunted, throwing all her energy into spinning Lucien's weights into the forest. Caia had been impressed by Jaeden's accuracy, but remembering how she'd had to telekinetically throw a car once, she wanted to build Jaeden's strength. And Lucien pretended to be more than happy to donate his training weights for their purposes.

"Nicely done." Caia nodded.

"It's therapeutic," Jae decided, her hair sticking to her forehead with the exertion. "I can't wait to move into Ryder's. My parents are driving me insane."

Caia winced. "I'm sorry about that."

"Don't be. I'm a grown woman with the right to make my own decisions. If I choose to support you, that is none of their business. Personally, I'm disappointed in *them.*"

"They're entitled to their opinion."

"Come on!" Jaeden hissed, throwing a meaningful glance toward Laila. "They've met her. They've met you. You both have Midnight blood. That isn't telling them something?"

"You can't just wipe out centuries of hate, Jae."

She snorted. "Yeah, well, better you than me running this show because I would just lose my crap with the lot of them. How are you so calm, so patient?"

Caia laughed humorlessly. "I'm not. I'm just good at pretending otherwise."

And it was the truth.

Now, as she sat with Lucien in his backyard, watching happily as Magnus asked Artemis to bless the mating between Jae and Ryder, she was uncomfortably aware of the discontent among the pack. Loyally, they had shown up for the mating, but many were avoiding Caia. She felt a little teary when the moon-colored glow lit up between her friends' bound hands. They kissed each other passionately, and she felt herself leaning into Lucien. The pack cheered, and everyone stood to congratulate them.

Caia quickly got out of their way, edging closer and closer to the woods. As they dispersed, walking in little groups into the house where the festivities awaited—weird, strained ones, she was guessing—Caia looked longingly into the dark velvet of the forest.

"You want to run?" a hot breath whispered in her ear.

She grinned. "You have no idea how much."

Lucien took her hand and pulled her into the trees. "Come on, then."

* * *

A LITTLE WHILE LATER, they lay tangled in one another's arms, their clothes abandoned around them. Caia shivered as he stroked her hair, loving the sound of his heartbeat beneath her ear.

Why couldn't this be her life? Why couldn't it be this simple?

"You wish we had a proper ceremony?" Lucien asked her softly.

"No."

He chuckled. "That was certainly adamant."

"Can you imagine all that attention?" She shuddered. "No thank you."

He shook with amusement. "You do realize that running a campaign for Head of the Daylights and actually being the Head of Daylights requires quite a bit of limelight?"

"That's different. That's necessary. I don't need a ceremony with lots of people watching on to know that I belong with you."

He squeezed her closer and pressed a loving kiss to her forehead. "Ah, *querida*. I feel the same."

"Why do you call me that?" she whispered lazily, knowing this moment was a brief slice of sunshine in their murky little underworld. She swore she could feel him smiling into her forehead.

"My dad. That's what he called my mom, and I remember how happy it made her."

"I'm such an idiot," she groaned.

He laughed. "Explain."

"You called me that after the daemon attacked me. If I'd just opened my eyes a little, I would've known how you felt way back then."

"You know now, that's what matters."

They lay there for a while longer, snuggled in the darkness.

"We should get back," Lucien said reluctantly.

"I'm afraid to."

"Why?"

"In case we never have a moment like this again."

"Caia." He pulled her up so he could kiss her tenderly. "I promise you that after the storm passes, there will be plenty of moments like this for us."

Although averse to shimmying back into her strappy dress, Caia did so. Hand in hand, they walked back through the woods to their home.

Where another surprise awaited them.

Jaeden was waiting with Ryder in the backyard, their faces a perfect mirror of anxiety.

"What's wrong?" Lucien picked up his pace.

Jaeden shook her head. "We're not sure. Marion's here."

Caia's heart leapt, and she rushed past them and into the house. She found Marion talking with Magnus, and Caia could tell immediately from her body language that something was wrong.

She must know.

"Caia!" Marion's eyes lit up when she saw her. "Thank Gaia."

Or not.

"What's going on?" she asked in trepidation.

The magik took her by the wrist and led her all the way upstairs and into her old bedroom.

"Marion?"

"Caia, everything is a mess." Marion pushed her hair back frantically. Caia had never seen her so uncollected before. "My sister found out that certain members of our Council have been feeding information to the Midnights! She can't get a handle on all who were involved—they've combined their power to manipulate the trace … so she has dissolved them. The entire Council. The coven is in chaos. There were actual riots inside the Center!"

Marita had dissolved the Council because of her. Caia

couldn't believe it. How could this be happening? This couldn't be happening.

She felt breathless and faint, all of her plans crumbling around her. Saffron had been right. She hadn't been prepared for the lengths Marita would go, to remain in power and annihilate the Midnights.

"How ..."

Marion shook her head. "She has witnesses from within the Council members' households. This level of treachery is unthinkable. Nothing like this has ever happened before."

"How come she's only finding out now? Her trace?"

Marion shrugged but the move was more violent than vague. "She had no reason to suspect them before, so she didn't go looking." But Caia could see the uncertainty in her eyes. This was insane. Irrational. And Marion knew it. She was just ... afraid.

"Why are you here?" Caia asked softly.

The witch scoffed at her question. "I would've thought that was obvious."

Oh crap. She does know about me.

"Caia, we need you at the Center. We held off because of Jaeden and Ryder's ceremony, but it's done now, and we need you there to help control this situation. Half of them admire you and the other half *fear* you. It's perfect."

"Did Marita request this?"

"Who else?"

Did Marita really think she would be stupid enough to return to the Center, to a trap? *She must think I won't be able to come up with a reason not to return with Marion.*

"Okay," she improvised, hoping she looked sufficiently agreeable. "You go back. I have to settle things with the pack. I'll get Lucien to drive me to the portal tonight."

"Caia, just say goodbye now." Marion shook her head.

"I can't. I might not be coming back. This is important."

"Magic Fitness won't even be open by the time you get there."

"Like that will stop me."

Marion heaved an exasperated sigh. "Marita specifically told me to bring you back now. Arrggh. Fine," she snapped. "I'll see you in a few hours."

She disappeared, leaving Caia trembling with relief. She found Lucien waiting for her at the bottom of the staircase and quietly related what had happened.

"What the Hades are we going to do now?" he hissed.

"I don't know." She shook, her heart feeling like it was going to explode, she could feel it in her throat. "I don't know."

She dodged quizzical looks from Magnus and Dimitri who stood in the doorway of the sitting room drinking scotch.

Brushing fingertips absently down Lucien's cheek from her higher position on the stairs. "Six heads are better than two. I know it's unfair, but this is kind of an emergency."

"You want me to get Jae and Ryder."

"Yes. Get them, meet me at the car. We're going to Ryder's apartment to talk this over with Laila and Vil."

He nodded, planting a quick kiss on her lips before he turned to Dimitri and Magnus. Cleverly, he managed to draw them away from Caia while searching for Jaeden and her mate.

Caia blew out a shaky breath and headed outside, taking the porch steps two at a time. Thankfully, the pack had parked their cars around the edges of the circular driveway, so Lucien's truck wasn't jammed in.

She was just about to open the passenger door when she heard a crunch of gravel behind her, and a burst of pain slammed from the back of her head like a speeding train, knocking her into darkness.

CHAPTER 25

Taken

*L*ucien could feel the panic building in his chest, threatening to cut off his airway.

Ryder flew in from the backyard, his breathing heavy. His eyes were bleak as they fell on Lucien, surrounded by most of a very silent pack. He shook his head. "She's not there."

"Lucien!" Malek hurtled in from the front door. "We checked the whole driveway over again. You might want to see this."

He jerked away from his mother's comforting touch, following the boy outside at a frenzied pace. He refused to listen to the whispers among the pack, that maybe she hadn't been taken, maybe she had deserted them. Caia wouldn't leave him willingly. His chest constricted with fear.

Malek led him down to his truck, where Daniel stood by the passenger side, his face pale.

"What is it?" he snapped.

Daniel just pointed and Lucien felt his whole world tilt as his eyes found the splash of blood across the passenger door. Caia's blood.

No.

"CAIA!" He turned and bellowed into the night. "CAIA!"

He would've yelled himself hoarse if Jaeden hadn't broken through the surrounding crowd. Distantly, he saw his mother crying, Magnus close to tears. What were they crying for? She wasn't gone! He couldn't breathe.

"Lucien!" Jaeden stumbled toward him, her face flushed with fury.

He looked at her, dazed.

"Do you think it was Marita?"

"She wouldn't have dared hurt her." Ryder shook his head in denial.

A darkening beast was uncurling in Lucien's chest, growing stronger and more furious every minute he stared at the blood on his truck door. Caia had been missing for an hour. She'd gone missing after Marion had turned up. The beast roared with bloodlust.

"We better hope she hasn't," he ripped out in a voice he didn't recognize, "or my muzzle will be the last thing she ever sees."

EPILOGUE

The Deception

Caia's head throbbed with impossible pain, a pain that shot from the bloody lump on the back of her head down her arms and into her back. She blinked, her eyes adjusting in the darkness of the cold, damp room she now found herself in. She hit up against something hard. As the light filtered into her eyes, she realized she was in a metal cage.

Bile burned in her throat, her terror building. What had happened? Where was she? Oh goddess, had Marita kidnapped her?

A door opened with a burst of artificial light, revealing the face of the distinguished man who stepped quietly into the room.

"Who are you?" she asked, wrapping her hand around the bars. It was then she realized that a glow surrounded the cage. Magik. A shield to stop her attacking with her own.

He winced as he looked her over. "He hit you harder than he should have."

"Who are you? How did I get here?"

"Take a moment, Caia."

At those words, her trace tingled with its familiar icy vapor, and Caia slumped back in disbelief. "Nikolai?" she gasped.

"Well done." He smiled gently at her, and she pushed, trying to feel his intent. Pain exploded in her head. She was too weak from the knock she had taken.

"How?" she managed.

He stepped aside from the doorway and another figure strode in, a smug smile on his face. "I'd like to introduce you to someone. This is Kirios, Caia."

Kirios's dark hair flopped over his forehead in familiar disarray, his pale handsomeness a punch to the gut ...

She snarled in impotent fury.

"Reuben."

ABOUT THE AUTHOR

S. Young is the pen name for Samantha Young, a *New York Times*, *USA Today* and *Wall Street Journal* bestselling author from Scotland. She's been nominated for the Goodreads Choice Award for Best Author and Best Romance for her international bestseller *On Dublin Street*. *On Dublin Street* was Samantha's first adult contemporary romance series and has sold in thirty-one countries.

Visit Samantha Young online at
www.authorsamanthayoung.com
Instagram @AuthorSamanthaYoung
Facebook @AuthorSamanthaYoung
https://bingebooks.com/author/samantha-young